SAVAGE stalker

Savage Angels MC Series Book One

Kathleen Kelly

Savage Stalker
Savage Angels MC Series Book One

Kathleen Kelly

This book is a work of fiction. Any references to real events, real people, and real places are used fictitiously. Other names, characters, places and incidents are products of the Author's imagination and any resemblance to persons, living or dead, actual events, organizations or places is entirely coincidental.

All rights are reserved. This book is intended for the purchaser of this book ONLY. No part of this book may be reproduced or transmitted in any form or by any means, graphic, electronic, or mechanical, including photocopying, recording, taping, or by any information storage retrieval system, without the express written permission of the Author. All songs, song titles and lyrics contained in this book are the property of the respective songwriters and copyright holders.

All efforts have been made to ensure the correct grammar and punctuation in the book. If you do find any errors, please e-mail Kathleen Kelly: kathleenkellyauthor@gmail.com
Thank you.

Disclaimer: The material in this book contains graphic language and sexual content and is intended for mature audiences, ages 18 and older.

ISBN: 979-8401994752

Re-editing by Swish Design & Editing
Proofreading by Swish Design & Editing
Book design by Swish Design & Editing
Cover design by Clarise Tan at CT Cover Creations
Cover Image Copyright
First Edition 2014
Second Edition 2021
Copyright © 2021 Kathleen Kelly
All Rights Reserved

DEDICATION

To my wonderful husband, without you, this book would not have been written. Without you, I am nothing. I love you more than I can say.

Mum and Dad, I thank you for supporting me in this. You are, of course, *not* allowed to read this book. Trust me, you won't want to read the sex scenes. I know I never say it, but I love you and miss you. I know we're seeing more of each other now, but some days, it doesn't feel like enough.

To you, the reader, I am humbled you would even consider buying this when there are so many books out there. Wow! Thank you! I hope you enjoy it, and if you do, please seek me out on Facebook and tell me. I would love to hear from you.

SAVAGE
stalker

CHAPTER 1

KAT

I'm backstage, and my manager, Dave, has cleared out my dressing room. The rest of my band, The Grinders, are in their dressing rooms getting ready for the last song of the night. I can hear the crowd and feel the throb of the people in the stadium. I stare at myself in the mirror. I look freaking terrible—makeup streaks down my face—and I smell terrible. I'm twenty-eight and in good shape. I am a little underweight, but it's normal after being on tour for sixteen months.

This is our last show.

We're at the MetLife Stadium in East Rutherford, New Jersey. There are ninety thousand people screaming my name—Katarina Saunders—Kat to the world. I need a minute to regroup. Being on stage can really take it out of you, mentally and emotionally, not to mention physically. I grab a cold water and drink it down in practically one go. I need to freshen up and get back. One last song, it's the one they're all waiting for—Heaven. Twelve years ago, it became our first number one hit. We've had countless platinum and double-platinum albums, but Heaven was the first, and it's always been my favorite.

As I try to fix my makeup, I realize I have a grin on my face. Fuck, I love this shit. Suddenly, my dressing room door flies open, and I turn, startled.

"Babe, you going back on or what?" It's my boyfriend, Gareth Goodman. He's ten years older than me and is Hollywood's latest action superhero. He is a tool. He's not a bad lay, just not great, and he is fucking one of the backup singers. He thinks I don't know about her. As soon as I figured it out, I stopped fucking him. I've let him go down on me a few times since, but I haven't reciprocated. I've told him after tonight's show I have something important to talk to him about. He's excited because he thinks he is going to get laid and that I want to settle down. Not fucking likely. I see no reason to limit myself to one person forever. "Babe!" he yells.

For Christ's sake.

I only move my eyes to him in the mirror. The fake grin is still on my face, but now it looks kind of creepy.

"Kat?" My manager walks in. He puts one hand on Gareth's chest, and the other grabs the door handle. "Sorry, Kat." Dave pushes Gareth backward. "Three minutes, yeah? Then it's booze, parties, and a well-fucking-deserved vacation for everyone."

I love Dave. He's seen me at my worst and my best, and he loves me right back. Pity he's gay. He knows I need time to think and knows I need to be alone. Dave makes a shit-load of money out of me because he knows how to keep me happy. Pushing Gareth out into the hall is a smart move.

I strip and put on my favorite jeans, a t-shirt with 'Heaven' written across my boobs, and head for the stage.

Truth, my lead guitarist, has started the riff for 'Heaven.' I haven't walked into the spotlight yet, and as I sing, the crowd goes wild. I strut up to Truth and sing the lyrics to him, and he smiles. Turning, I sashay to the edge of the stage as the crowd surges forward. This is what I live for—to perform for an audience, to hear them sing my words back to me, to know I've connected with them.

As the song comes to an end and the lights go down, I'm reminded that this is what God put me on this earth to do.

Two hours later, we're at the Trump Hotel in New York, and I'm in a screaming match with Gareth. I'm so over it. It's still early, I haven't nearly had enough to drink, and I'm more than done with this jerk. He wants to draw it out and make it a very public breakup as his new movie is about to come out, and you know the old saying, 'there's no such thing as bad publicity.' But I don't need the headache. Reporters are already snapping pictures and screaming out questions, and I want out.

"Fuck you, Kat! What do you mean, you need some alone time?" Gareth roars at me in front of the eager and ever-waiting press.

"I think we're going in two completely different directions, Gareth. Could we please do this inside and somewhere a little more private?" He glares at me as I try to keep my cool.

"How much have you had to drink, babe? Is that what this is? A temper tantrum? Fuck, Kat, when you said you wanted to talk, I assumed you were talking about our future, not our ending!" Gareth yells again.

I have had enough.

"No, Gareth," my voice drips with sarcasm. "This isn't a temper tantrum. Yes, I've had a bit to drink, but, baby, not nearly enough for this." I make a sweeping gesture with my arm to take in the press. "You're about to go on a worldwide publicity junket with your movie, and, Gareth, I want to stop. I've been on tour for over a year. I want to get back into the studio, and I want to spend time with my mother. I want this to be over," I whisper now as I don't want the world in on my private life. They can have me on the stage, they can have me when I'm promoting my band and albums, but I don't want my private life on the cover of every sordid magazine across the country.

"You want this to be over? Why do you get to make that fucking choice? I've traveled all over this fucking world to be with you, and what do I get? What the fuck is in it for me, Kat? Tell me!" Gareth's eyes bulge out of his head, and I look away.

My band and manager are looking at us, and it's obvious they're uncomfortable. If I don't stop this soon, one of them will intervene, and then it's going to get very ugly.

"Okay, Gareth, baby, calm down." He doesn't get it, so I guess I need to be blunt to end this quickly. "Let's go upstairs and talk this out, okay? I'm sure we can work something out." He visibly calms down, and some of the tension leaves his body. Gareth looks at the press, smiles, and sort of shrugs.

Asshole is playing to the audience

"You love me, don't you, Kat?" Gareth smiles and

looks like a lost little boy.

Moving right up to him, I smile, lick my lips, and put my hands to his chest. My right hand travels down his torso. With this gesture, Gareth thinks I've changed my mind, and he smiles back at me. Both his hands are on my ass, and the fucking paparazzi are flashing away. It's like being on stage. I grab the keys to his Ferrari Enzo dangling from his belt, and he doesn't even notice. I don't even know why he has a car like this. He can't even drive a stick-shift properly. It's a crime this tool has such a gorgeous car, and it never really gets used to its full potential.

"Gareth?" I say in my best sexy voice. "Did you enjoy going down on me the last few times, baby?" He nods his head vigorously. "Good, baby, 'cause I'm curious about something. Did you go down on Vivian, my backup singer, too, or did you just fuck her and go?"

Gareth completely stills, his smile frozen in time. From his reaction, I've caught him completely off-guard. I push him away and walk backward while I shake my head from side to side. His smile is still fixed on his pretty face. When he glances at the paparazzi, I turn and run. His car is out front, and I'm in the driver's seat with the doors locked before he can even move. I look at him, flip him the bird, and start the car. Quickly, I put the car in first and peel out of the Trump Hotel's driveway in a cloud of blue smoke. The paparazzi are eating it up, but all I can think is, *I'm finally free.*

I have no idea where I'm going. There's enough alcohol in my system that I feel like I'm flying. I shouldn't be driving, and I'm going way too fast. My favorite thing to do, besides sing, is speed. Whether it be on a bike or behind the wheel of a car or speedboat, I love it all.

Suddenly, there's a man in the middle of the road, and everything slows down. He's old, looks homeless by the dirty clothes he's wearing, and his eyes are wide open. And I'm heading straight at him. With only a split second to decide what to do, my hand pulls on the handbrake. I turn the wheel, downshift, and finally, brake.

Thankfully, I miss him. Smirking to myself, I turn the wheel, change gears, floor it and drive straight into a fucking pole. The windows and windshield explode, sending glass slivers everywhere. The airbags go off, hitting me in the face. Instantly, I can taste blood and there's a hot, burning pain in my neck. The front of my shirt feels wet. Just as quickly as the airbags engaged, they deflate, leaving my face feeling hot and stiff, and I can't move. *I can't move!* I try to speak, but nothing comes out. My chest feels heavy, and it's hard to breathe. I feel like I'm drowning, but I'm not in water.

My shirt's wet.

I can't breathe.

I can't move.

"Lady, I need you to look at me," someone says. His voice is so calm, and he looks straight into my eyes. He's black, wears glasses, and he seems about twenty-five. "You have a neck injury. Are you finding it hard to breathe?" I nod. "You have blood going back down your throat. I need to do an emergency tracheotomy, or you're going to drown." My eyes widen, and I try to shake my head. "Calm down, please. I work at Flushing Hospital Medical Centre, and I'm a third-year resident. My name is Jacob Snow. I called an ambulance, and they're on their way, but you have to trust me."

He's perfectly calm, and I know I'm fucked. I try to move my head to let him know it's okay.

"Lady, I need you to keep still. This is going to hurt." He pulls out a small Swiss Army knife and releases the blade. He holds it to my neck, and it's the last thing I remember.

I hear voices and something like a radio being turned up. I hear them perfectly. My eyes twitch behind closed eyelids, and when I finally open them, a blinding light makes me shut them just as quickly. My left leg feels really heavy, and my neck is weird, but there's no pain. The sensation feels like floating.

"Do we tell her?" someone asks.

"No." It's Dave, I would know his voice anywhere, and he sounds sad. I try to open my eyes again, but they're so heavy. "She has enough on her plate right now."

"Dave, man, she's not going to like it, and what the fuck do we do about that fucker, Gareth?" I think it's my lead guitarist, Truth, talking.

"Double security and keep him away from her. Buy him a new fucking car. Hell, give the cocksucker anything he wants, but he's not getting anywhere near her." Dave sounds tired. I try to open my eyes again, but sleep claims me.

When I wake again, a week has passed. My world has completely crumbled, and my life will never be the same. Everything that once was, is gone.

For the first time in my life, I'm lost.

CHAPTER 2

KAT

It's been eight weeks since my accident. I broke my left leg, a piece of metal went through my neck, and the emergency tracheotomy damaged my vocal cords. I'll never sing again. Jacob Snow may have saved my life, but he finished my career. Actually, I finished my career. If Jacob Snow hadn't been there, I'd have died. My band and manager wanted to sue him, but I said no. I owe him my life.

They charged me with driving under the influence. Well, aggravated driving under the influence, and the city charged me for the pole I hit. I know it's wrong, but it's amazing what money can do. Also, the fact it wasn't an election year, and no one wanted to make an example of me, I got off with a fine and twelve months suspended license. I got lucky. Of course, the press had a field day. There was also a huge donation to the 'Citizens Caring for Our Homeless.' It was an idea I came up with, and again, the press loved it.

I'm known as a wild child, but everyone also knows I donate my time and money to a variety of charities. I always have. As soon as I could support myself with my voice, I began donating to a series of charities. I pick a different one every year, and five percent of my cut after taxes goes to that charity, then another five percent goes into a fund to help underprivileged teenagers get into college or simply find their own way. Not everyone is smart with books. I certainly wasn't, but I had a gift. Lots of teenagers are like that. There are more measures of intelligence than books and learning or parroting what those people in charge tell us we need to learn. Some of these kids need the most help.

The night of my accident, my mother died. They didn't tell me for three weeks. I missed her funeral, as I was still in the hospital. I loved her, but I hadn't seen her in three years. We spoke on the phone often, and I always meant to go visit her, but my life got crazier and crazier. I thought I had more time. I thought she'd be around forever. She was a tough old bird, vain as hell, and always laughing.

For the most part, I look like my mom. My light brown hair with blonde and caramel highlights hangs to my waist. My eyes, though, are a very vivid green. Ma used to say it's the only thing I inherited from my father. Thank the Lord for that because he was an asshole.

What I'll always remember about her were her hands. They were always rough from yard work because she loved to garden. As a kid, and even as an adult, if I were sick or upset, she'd sweep the hair from my face and stroke it. I'd feel her rough hands catch on my face and pull the hair out of my eyes. I'll never feel that again or hear her laugh.

The press reported she died of a heart attack when news of my accident reached her, that she died alone, we were estranged, and it was the reason I didn't send flowers or attend the funeral. Truth is, we weren't estranged, I didn't send flowers because my mom didn't like cut flowers. She always said once they were cut, they died, and she didn't like that. The press loves a good story, though, so they ran with the lies, and I'm front-page news across the country.

Dave has kept the wolves from my door—the press, Gareth, the police, and even my band members. He's sorted everything out and has kept me safe, but he's pissed off. They have moved me to the Trump Hotel and have a full-time nurse, a doctor on call twenty-four-seven, and the best security money can buy.

Currently, Dave's looking at me, trying to gauge my mood.

I'm twenty-eight and all alone in the world now my ma has died. She was my only family. My career is over, and I have effectively ended the careers of my band members—Jasmin, Curtis, Blair, Jamie, and Truth. Dave will be fine, though, as he manages a lot of people. They aren't all as successful as us, but he'll be all right. The royalties alone will see all of us into the next millennium, but we won't be a working band, and they are pissed off that I could throw it all away. I don't blame them, I blame myself. I haven't had the courage to see them, and I know I'm making it much worse by avoiding them.

Dave sighs, sits forward, and in a quiet tone says, "You need to do an interview. You need to get a handle on all of this mess before our nation's wild child becomes our nation's favorite prison pin-up. I know you hate interviews, especially after the disaster with leading journalist, Nevada Smith, but suck it up, princess. You owe The Grinders that much."

I wince at hearing my band's name. "Dave, I'm so sorry. I know I've let everyone down. I know I've fucked up. I know I—"

"Shut the fuck up, Kat. Just shut up and listen to me." He stares at me with such an intensity I close my gaping mouth and nod. "You get the cast-off next week, yeah?"

Nodding again, I drag a hand through my hair, pulling it off my face. "Doc says next Tuesday, and

I'll need to use crutches for a while, but then I'm good to go."

"Vocal cords?"

I hang my head, my hair falling back across my face as tears well up in my eyes. "I'm lucky I can speak, but I'll never sing again," I whisper as a single tear escapes and runs down my cheek.

Dave gets up, lifts my chin with his thumb and forefinger, and pushes my hair out of my eyes. Using the pad of his thumb, he sweeps my tear away.

"You're going to be all right, Kat. You have more money than you know what to do with. God has put you on this path for a reason. And you know what they say, 'when one door closes, another one opens.' You need to find your door. The truth is, I'd planned to talk to you about the band and *you* slowing down. You've been in this industry since you were twelve years old, and you've been working nonstop. Your last album sold well, but not as good as the one before it. Although sales have gone ballistic on all your albums since your accident, I thought it was time for you all to scale things back. Do a greatest hits album and focus more on your charities?"

Sitting on my bed, he stares at me. I'm fucking astounded.

A greatest hits album?

"Jasmin has wanted to get more involved with

her musicals. Truth wants to spend more time with his family. Curtis is getting married for the fourth, or is it the fifth time? Blair and Jamie have been eager to do that television show which finds new rock bands and helps them get a recording contract. All of them have wanted to pursue other interests, but they knew you weren't ready. Well, princess, you're ready now. You don't have a choice." I can see the sadness as he nods at me. He's forty-nine, but he looks thirty, he has gorgeous brown eyes which are looking at me with so much compassion that I cry.

"Slow down? At twenty-eight?" I'm shaking my head. Dave cups my cheeks and dips his head in affirmation.

"Princess, you've been on top of the charts more times than I can count. Go out with a bang. Do a kick-ass interview, let people into your life, tell them about your mother, your band, your accident, your charities. Then go get yourself another life away from the spotlight, away from all the madness, and be happy." Dave smiles, though tears fill his eyes. "I've been proud to manage you over the years, but, princess, it's time. And for fuck's sake, if you ever take up with Gareth or any more wannabes, I'll bitch-slap you into your next life."

I laugh. Dave won't tell me what it cost, whatever he did, to make Gareth go away forever. He hasn't even done an interview about me since the accident, apart from saying he hopes I recover and wishes me the best for the future.

Reluctantly, I nod because what else am I going to do? I can't sing, and I had no idea the band wanted to pursue other interests.

God, I really am self-absorbed.

"Who am I doing the interview with? Please don't tell me it's Nevada Smith? She doesn't like me very much."

Laughter rumbles out of Dave's chest as he shakes his head. "No, no, no! It's not Nevada. I've organized an interview with an Australian journalist we met a few years ago. Her name is Liz Hayes. I've told her nothing is off-limits and you'll be as open as a book. The Grinders are going to be there for the last part of the interview. It will boost album sales, and it will put to rest all the wrong information out there about you."

"Okay, Dave. I'll do it, but not until after my cast comes off, and I've talked to my band."

"I know you think they're mad at you, and they were, but not anymore. They're worried about you, princess. They thought they'd lost you. They love you and want what's best for you *and* the band, and no one knew how to approach you with the idea of slowing down."

Looking out the window, I think about everything he's said.

What the hell am I going to do now?

CHAPTER 3

KAT

Sitting in an overstuffed chair in a hotel room with a camera pointed directly at me, I try not to look nervous as my band members all wander into the room and get themselves comfortable on couches. Liz shakes their hands as they settle in for the interview. I'm so nervous I could vomit. We had a sit-down before this interview, and they were all upset with me, but, overall, they were just happy I wasn't dead.

Liz sits down in her chair, crosses her legs at the ankles, and asks, "So, The Grinders are now officially retired, or are you thinking of replacing your lead singer now Kat can't perform?"

Replace me?

That hadn't even entered my mind. Of course

they can. When Mick died of an overdose, we replaced him with Jamie. Jamie is a better drummer, anyway, and he doesn't do drugs, but it wasn't an easy path for us to follow. We had to find someone who fit in with us, and luckily, we found him.

Jasmin answers, "No, we'll not be replacing Kat at this time. We all have outside interests we want to pursue. This band has been in a studio or on tour for sixteen years, and we need a break. We need to heal, and we need to begin living our lives."

Christ, they aren't replacing me at this time?

They've obviously talked about it. Truth pins me with his stare, and he can tell I'm not happy. The others are avoiding eye contact with me.

Truth leans forward, and his shoulder-length black hair falls around his face. "Kat, you had to know we talked about this. We're a working band, and it's all we've ever known. You know we'd want you involved if we decided to replace you. You'd have the last say, yes or no. It would be up to you. Hell, you wrote almost all of our songs. I'd hope you'd continue to write for us." Truth's eyes convey such compassion and sadness. His black t-shirt and leather jacket stretch across his hard muscles, the tattoos which decorate his arms play peek-a-boo every time he moves. He's thirty, good-looking, and screams rock star.

"It hadn't crossed my mind." My voice is husky,

my throat constricts and burns while my eyes well up with tears. "I guess I thought the band was history. I'm so sorry I did this to us... I'm so sorry."

"Kat, do you need a minute?" Liz asks as she hands me tissues. From the look in her eyes, she knows she got one hell of an interview.

"No, she doesn't need a fucking minute," Curtis' voice is hard as he glares at Liz.

Curtis is the only band member who hates the press. He rarely does interviews or goes out into the public eye. He's so far at the other end of the scale from Truth. His blond hair hangs to his waist, but it's always in a ponytail or plait. Sometimes, when he's on stage playing the bass guitar, he lets it out. It amazes me he's always getting married. He never gets them to sign a prenup, so they take him to the cleaners. The last one used him from the beginning, and you could tell she only wanted what she could get. Such a queen bitch. I'm not looking forward to meeting wife-to-be number five. I hope he's picked a good one this time, but I'm not holding my breath.

"Kat," Curtis says. "This is something we'll discuss in private, but not for a long time. The six of us are The Grinders, and for now, that's the way it's going to stay." Curtis looks at me, and one by one, I look each of them in the eye. They all nod and smile at me.

"Thank you, you're the best band members and

friends anyone could ask for." The tears fall down my cheeks, then Blair gets up and walks over to me.

"Get up, honey, and give me a hug."

Blair is thirty-two, six foot four, and built like a linebacker. He plays the saxophone or any wind instrument, and he even taught himself to play the fiddle. I always think of him as a musical genius.

Rising from the chair, he engulfs me in a bear hug and whispers, "Can this shit be done now? Do we have to continue with this fucking interview?"

I laugh, and he leans back from me. Smiling up at him, I nod. "Soon, honey, answer a few more questions, and then we can go and have a drink. Or thirty."

He nods and lets me go, smiling big as he looks at Liz and says, "Yo, Liz, have you heard about the fantastic new show, *Rock Star*, Jamie and I are doing? We're gonna find the best singer this country has ever seen, but they'll never hold a candle to Kat." He looks at me, winks, and goes back to his seat.

I love my band.

Liz Hayes looks at all of us, and like the good reporter she is, she can tell the moment has passed. We aren't going to air any more dirty laundry, so she asks them all how they feel about me and what they're going to do with their lives. I listen and answer every now and then as my band talks.

It's then I realize I may have lost my voice, but I'll never lose them.

CHAPTER 4

KAT

My interview with Liz Hayes was twelve months ago, and considering everything, it went well. Or, rather, as well as it could go. I hate interviews. Don't get me wrong, she was good at her job, but having your life dissected in front of the world isn't fun. They ran the piece over three weeks, and the media hasn't left me alone since.

The accident, my ma dying, my inability to sing, the band and I retiring to pursue other interests—the media can't get enough. The Grinders had all been thinking of doing other things for a while. They all had answers. But me? Nada, zip, bupkis, and the media seemed intent on following me until I had decided, so that's exactly what I did. I made a decision and left it all behind.

Now, I'm hiding out in the house my mother left me. It has a plaque above the front door that says 'Heaven'. She was always proud of me, and I love she named her home after my first hit. Her house, now my house, is on fifty acres in the mountains with fantastic views, and it's very private. In the beginning, I hired a team of bodyguards to keep everyone out. Since then, I've made it even more secure and hidden from the public eye, with twelve-foot fences and a security system to keep everyone out. No one can get in to see me unless I want them to. My groceries are ordered and paid for online, the delivery guy leaves them at my front gate. I don't even have to come out and see him.

The bodyguards were let go three months ago, and I haven't seen anyone since that day. I don't open my front door for any reason. My ma's house has been completely remodeled, and I added a deck at the back. Of course, Dave handled everything for me. He had all of my ma's belongings boxed up and put into a storage facility in Tourmaline, which is the town I live on the outskirts of.

It hasn't been easy for me. The bottle became my best friend for a while. I'd stay in my room and drink until I passed out. One day, I woke up and looked in the mirror and realized I looked like my father. He was an abusive alcoholic. That's not who I am.

I've always loved my alcohol, but had kept it

under control until my downfall. Not wanting to be a washed-up lush, I threw out all the bottles and replaced one habit with another—exercise. It was hard at first as my body is still healing from the accident, and my leg, which was broken, gets really sore if I push myself too hard.

I've been a singer in a band my entire life. Without those two things, I feel completely lost. I need to find a new path, but I often catch myself writing new songs or lyrics down as they come to me. The accident made me take stock of my life and really think about who and what is important to me. I'm trying to do what Dave said and find my door. Music is in my blood, and I have to consider other outlets for it. Somehow, I need to find my place in the industry and regain my confidence and sense of self again.

Even with the months of drinking, I'm in good shape. You can't play to stadiums and not be. Apart from the booze, I lived clean, no drugs. It's too easy in the music industry to get addicted. I'm lucky I got Dave as my manager. He's been more of a father to me than my real one and made it clear, drugs could fuck with my voice. It scared the crap out of me, and I never touched them. In hindsight, he should've said the same about alcohol.

I'm about to go for a run. I am five foot four, so if I don't exercise, my curvaceous butt needs a zip code all of its own. Yes, I have curves, my ma used to say I had the perfect hourglass figure. I like to run, it blows out all the cobwebs in my brain. Since my accident, I need to be careful and not push myself too hard or I feel it for days.

My property shares a creek with the one next door. Someone has built a bridge over it, connecting the two. It's beautiful. It's made of wood and stone and from the workmanship it would have taken a long time to build, and I often wonder why they linked the two parcels of land. The bridge is my rest spot. I take in the landscape and either walk or jog back up the hill, depending on how hard I'm hurting.

I've never encountered anyone on my run in the nine months I've been doing this.

Never wanted to either.

I began this run the day after all the bodyguards left, the day I threw out all of my bottles. The day my real healing began.

CHAPTER 5

KAT

I'm on the bridge looking down at the creek, absently feeling the wood of the handrail. The sound of birds chirping relaxes me, but I feel like I'm being watched. Turning around, I see a man approach from the other side. He's huge, easily six foot six, and has muscles straining against his black t-shirt. He reminds me of Blair. He's ruggedly handsome, with dark hair brushing his collar and some stubble on his face. His eyes are an amazing blue, and he has tattoos going down his arms.

Before I can run for my life, he says, "You must be Ms. Saunders' girl."

I'm speechless. His voice hits me, it's gravelly with an authoritative edge to it, and I like it.

"I'm Dane Reynolds. You're Ms. Saunders' girl,

aren't you? 'Cause if you're not, you're on private land, and neither I nor the owner of the next property will appreciate you being here, darlin'."

"What?" My brain doesn't appear to be functioning properly.

"Darlin', you're on private land," he repeats, and now looks annoyed. Advancing toward me, I feel like a deer caught in headlights. How can such a large man have so much grace?

"I'm Kat," I say, and my voice sounds all breathy, and it's not because of my run.

He stops and says, "Are you Ms. Saunders' girl?" He looks amused, as though I've said or done something funny.

"Yes, she was my ma. Is this your land?" I can't believe I've let a complete stranger affect me so much. I've had fans grovel at my feet, men offering to leave their wives. Hell, wives offer to leave their husbands! What the hell is wrong with me?

"I'm sorry for your loss. She was a good woman. I found her when she passed, and I know it doesn't help, but it was quick. I called the ambulance, but she was gone. Paramedics said it was a heart attack."

"Sorry... you found her? It was quick? Paramedics?" My voice gets louder with every question, and I can feel my throat closing while tears form in my eyes.

"Christ, darlin', you didn't know..." His voice is

soft and tender, slightly above a whisper.

I shake my head with my hands held out in front of me as though I can stop the pain or him from saying anything else. Dane moves closer to me, and I take in his jeans and kick-ass black boots. Not exactly hiking or jogging gear.

"She was super proud of you, talked about you all the time," Dane says. And at that, I completely lose it and find myself wrapped in his hulking frame. I vaguely notice he smells like spice and musk, and he feels good—all muscle and man. "Shh, darlin', I didn't mean to upset you. I wanted you to know she went quickly, peacefully and didn't suffer."

Again, I unravel. I'd have fallen to my knees, except his arms are like bands of steel. My knees give out, and he picks me up and walks me up the hill, all the while whispering to me and holding me tight. We stop a short distance up on his side of the creek, where there's what looks to be a handmade wooden bench made for two. He sits down with me on his lap, and continues to hold me, stroking my hair and whispering words of comfort.

After what feels like an eternity, I calm down. Slowly realizing I'm sitting on a complete stranger's lap, and if I didn't already look like a mess from running, I sure as hell do now. I'm mortified and try to move.

"Darlin', you under control?"

"I'm so sorry, I am not sure what just happened." *I feel like such a dork!* "If you'll let me up, I'll get out of your way." As I try to get up, his grip tightens, and he pins me with his gaze. I'm sure I am about to implode from embarrassment.

"They didn't tell you how she passed? The sheriff didn't tell you?" Dane asks me, looking pissed.

"I, umm… don't get visitors. I mean, I do, but I don't speak to them. If the sheriff has been by, I probably just didn't open the door."

"You didn't open the door?" Now he looks at me with a strange expression, one I can't read.

"No, I don't open the door. Fans…"

Realization dawns on his face. "Fans, darlin'? That happens often?"

I get lost in his eyes. They're the most amazing blue I have ever seen with flecks of black in them, and he hasn't broken eye contact with me since I've managed to get myself under control. I feel foolish sitting on a grown man's lap.

"At first, yes, but now, not so much. Could you, umm… you know… let me up?"

Before Dane withdraws his arms, he asks again, "You under control?"

I nod, and he releases me, causing me almost to fall flat on my ass. Dane steadies me, and we both stand. He towers over me, and I look down at the bench to hide my embarrassment. Then I notice my ma's name carved into the wood at the top.

"Christina?" My eyes are back to his, and I notice he stares at me intently. Something flashes across his face, and then he smiles. Oh my God, it's a glorious smile.

"Yeah, I made it for your ma. Kind of halfway between her house and mine. A resting point before she climbed up the hill. This is where I found her. She was sitting here, and, at first, I thought she was resting, but as I got closer and called out her name, I realized she was gone." His eyes haven't left mine as he says all this, and I feel mine well up with tears again.

"She died here? Not in front of a television? She didn't know about me?" Again, my questions get louder, my throat constricts as tears fall down my cheeks, but this time, I clutch the front of his t-shirt instead of falling at his feet.

"Television? No, darlin', didn't even know Ms. Saunders had a TV. She was on her way to see me and the boys, but she was running late. She was always on time, so that's why I came looking for her." His gaze pierces mine as he asks, "What didn't she know about you?" He almost whispers this last question.

Letting go of his t-shirt, my hand goes to the scar at my neck. It's not as noticeable now, but it's still there. You'd have to be blind not to see it.

"I was in an accident. It's why I didn't come to the funeral. I was in the hospital. They told me she'd had a heart attack when news about me reached her."

Searching his face, I look for the truth.

Dane surprises me when he says, "No, darlin', she was here every Sunday. It was kind of like a tradition. She'd cook up her muffins, then head over to my place and fix me and the boys some bacon and eggs. Then, we'd take her to do her weekly shopping. It became a sort of payment for driving her into town, but we'd have done it no matter what. Your ma was good people."

I'm dumbfounded. I struggle to believe what he's saying.

She cooked for him and his boys?
He took her shopping?

Stepping away from Dane, I run my hand through my hair. As I scramble to process what he's said, I realize I'm staring at him. I can't drag my eyes away from his. Hell, I can hardly breathe, let alone move. This is almost too much for me to deal with today. I haven't had contact with anyone for three months, and now I stand in front of this gorgeous man who says he was the one who found my ma.

I thought her death was my fault.

I fall silent for what feels like an eternity, unable to speak.

Dane breaks through my thoughts. "Ms. Saunders liked to walk to my home. She said it was her weekly exercise. Only time she didn't come was when she was sick, and then she'd phone, and we'd go pick her up. She didn't like it, though. Ms. Saunders was too proud for her own good." Dane looks me up and down and continues, "It took her about an hour and a quarter to get there. She didn't rush, she took her time and rested. Me and the boys made her benches along the way. This one was her favorite. I think because it was the first, and I made it for her," Dane pauses and stares at me intently. Then he reaches out and wipes away a tear which has escaped and fallen down my cheek. "My boys are the Savage Angels, and although we're a tough bunch, we liked your ma. We took turns taking her into town. Our clubhouse is there, so it was never any trouble. Everyone liked and respected Ms. Saunders, especially when she employed us and some of the townsfolk at her transportation business."

"Savage Angels? Clubhouse? Transportation business?" My mind is racing, "What has my ma been up to?"

What the fuck?

I babble like an idiot and pace back and forth in front of Dane, and it occurs to me I don't know this man at all. I'm alone in the woods, and I've had enough freaky fans to last me a lifetime to know better.

So, I back away from him, turning toward the bridge when he says, "Savage Angels Motorcycle

Club, and yeah, darlin', we have a clubhouse in town at the end of Main Street near your ma's company. We have hundreds of members, as we recently patched in a couple of other clubs. Of course, not everyone lives here in Tourmaline. We're spread out across five states."

I'm rooted to the spot, in shock.

Oh.

My.

God!

"Darlin', are you okay?" Dane asks with an amused look on his face.

And out of my mouth, it pours, "I spoke to her every week, and she never mentioned any of this! Why would she keep this from me? She had a whole other life I knew nothing about. I know my life was hectic, and I was always on the road, but she was my ma, she should've told me. Or am I so self-absorbed that I'm oblivious to what those I love want to do?" I stop and look at him. "A motorcycle club? Really?"

And I'm not nearly far enough away from him when he throws his head back and laughs. Wait, he's laughing at me? My God, but he's beautiful, and I suddenly realize I've taken two steps toward him when he looks at me and stops.

"Yes, Kat, I'm in a motorcycle club. Some of the boys are at my home. Do you want to come meet them?" Dane asks.

Then, without another word, he closes the gap between us, grabs my hand, and walks me toward the path.

CHAPTER 6

DANE

I finally make myself known to the one and only Katarina Saunders or Kat. This woman is a fucking legend. Her ma was supremely proud of her, but she missed her more than she'd let on. She always said her Kat would come see her when she finally got sick of the world, or the world got sick of her, and here she is, but it's too late. Her ma was more than good people. She was the sort of person who couldn't stand by if a wrong was being done, even if it meant putting herself in harm's way.

"Son, if a good person stands by and does nothing, then they ain't a good person."

I can still hear her voice in my head like it was yesterday. That's how we met.

A young girl thought playing with a brother

would be fun, but she didn't realize a lamb can't play with a lion and not get attacked. Silly girl thought it was like high school and she could lead him on. Dirt's bike clearly said 'NFNF,' and he even pointed it out to her before she got on it. I looked at him and shook my head, but the chick laughed and jumped on. So, I shrugged and went to my room in the clubhouse with another little thing to relieve myself of some tension. Being the president of a motorcycle club, one I'm trying to clean up, isn't easy. But I'd be fucked if I handed over the title to anyone else. I've been in and around the club my entire life, and it's my family.

As I'm about to mount my plaything for the second time, I hear a scream, and then I hear Dirt yell. I get up, pull on my jeans, grab a baseball bat, and head for the encampment outside.

Once there, I see Dirt on his knees with Ms. Saunders twisting his ear, and the young girl he had on his bike earlier cowering behind her. She's crying, holding up her torn tank top. No one is moving. Everyone's looking at Ms. Saunders before turning their heads to look at me. This is a serious situation. No one bothers a brother on his home turf, but how old is this lady? She looks to be seventy, and she has a brother on his knees? I laugh, then everyone, except Dirt and the female he was with, laugh too. The lady looks at me and sort of smiles, but it's tight, and there's fear in her eyes. Even from across the lot, I can tell she's bitten off more than she can handle.

Putting down the bat, I walk toward her. She looks nervous, but she straightens her spine and squares her shoulders and says, "He was trying to force himself on that young girl, Mary. I've seen her at the local diner, and she can't be more than seventeen."

"Ma'am, it was pointed out to her that getting on the back of Dirt's bike meant a payment was expected. She made the call."

"No, I didn't, I didn't!" Mary shrieks and clutches onto Ms. Saunders.

"Sweetheart, you did. He pointed to his motto 'NFNF' right on his tank."

She looks confused. "NFNF? I thought he was pointing to his bike. I only wanted a ride!" Then she bursts into tears and huddles behind Ms. Saunders.

"Christ, fucking dumb bitch," I mumble to my feet, then I raise my eyes to Ms. Saunders. "You'd best let him go, ma'am. You're on Savage Angel land, and we don't take kindly to strangers beating up on our members." This gets me a few chuckles around the camp, but everyone knows she's crossed the line. "Sweetheart," I say as I look at the girl behind Ms. Saunders, "NFNF means No Fuck, No Fun. He warned you, and you got on his bike, but I can see how you may not have known what it meant. How old are you, anyway?" I ask her, looking at her more closely.

She peeks around Ms. Saunders and says, "Fourteen."

Jesus-fucking-Christ!

I growl and then ask, "You got any friends here, sweetheart?" She nods, and five girls step forward. "You stupid little cunts have got one minute to get off Angel territory. Don't come back until you're of legal fucking age and consent. Do you get me?" I roar.

They all but sprint out of our camp, including Mary. I then turn to look at Ms. Saunders. She immediately lets go of Dirt, who slowly stands right in her space, staring at her with venom in his eyes.

Fuck!

"Dirt! As I see it, this lady saved you from a nickel for sex with a minor. Guess you owe her," I joke, trying to appease him. I laugh, and everyone joins in, except for Dirt. He's staring at her, and she's staring straight back. Hard as fucking nails. I walk up and clap him on the back and say, "How'd this little old lady get you to your knees? Seriously, man, how?" Then I chuckle, and so does he.

Finally.

Crisis averted.

Dirt walks away, pride damaged, but not forever. He's thirty-five, but he looks fifty, and he's not one to be messed with. The boys won't tease him for long, especially if they like their teeth and don't want to spit them in the dirt.

Ms. Saunders moves her gaze to me, and I grab her elbow, moving her away from the brothers. I ask in a quiet tone, "What were you thinking?"

"Son, if a good person stands by and does nothing,

then they ain't a good person. I saw her ride back into your compound on the back of his bike. I know she's only a child, but I didn't realize she is as young as she is. We all know what goes on in here, and she's only a child!" she says the last part in a whisper.

I nod in understanding. Yeah, the town of Tourmaline knows what we are. As much as I'm trying to better the club's image and keep us on the straight and narrow, folks have been around us for over forty years. They think they know us, and maybe they do, but I'm trying to clean us up. For fuck's sake, we even bought the uniforms for the basketball team at the local high school. We're really trying here, but I can see her point.

"I'll walk you to the gate."

She holds my stare for a minute, then nods and heads toward the exit. As she's moving, I can see she's having trouble walking.

How did she get Dirt? She's fucking feeble.

"Hurt my ankle a little while ago, fell over in my garden. It hurt so bad I had to crawl into my house and call an ambulance. I've never been so embarrassed in my whole life!" She stops and looks up at me, wincing at the pain in her ankle, and says, "That guy didn't expect anyone to do anything, but when he yanked her top down, and she screamed. I knew I had to do something. So, I came up behind him and grabbed his ear, kicked his knee, and he went down like a sack of potatoes. But I hurt my ankle

again doing it." Her mouth is in a grim line, then she smiles. "Thank you for saving me." She continues limping.

"Why were you embarrassed about calling an ambulance?" I ask, curious about this old lady.

"I hadn't done my house duties yet, so the paramedics saw my dirty dishes still on the kitchen table. No one comes to visit my home unless it's spotless." She puffs up at the last word, and I laugh.

"Lady, you're fucking tough as nails. You're worried about a few dirty dishes, yet you have no issue going into an MC and fucking with one of its members in front of his brothers because if a good person stands by and does nothing, then she ain't a good person?" I roar with laughter.

She's standing there staring at me, and then she says, "I don't want any trouble. Do you think if I baked him some of my apple muffins, Dirt might calm down?" Again, I laugh, and she's looking at me with her head tilted to the side as though she's trying to figure me out.

"Muffins? I'm sure he'd love some," I say with a chuckle, and with my hand on her elbow, I move her toward the gate again. When we get there, I see something flash behind her eyes, and she's staring behind me. Ms. Saunders smiles and moves away. I look in the same direction and see she's staring at the bus in the distance. Damn, she's missed it. There isn't another one today, and I know the local taxi service

is out of action as their cars are being serviced on my lot. Fuck!

I watch her as she sits at the bus stop bench, though she must know there isn't another one passing by today, and as she isn't heading to the payphones, she must be aware the local taxi service isn't operating. Fuck. I go back into the compound and enter the clubhouse.

Entering my room where my plaything is, I say, "You have to leave, I'm headed out. Don't be here when I come back." I don't even look at her. I grab my keys and make my way to my black Dodge Ram 3500. I get in and pull up alongside the curb in front of the bus stop.

"Hop in, ma'am, I'll give you a lift." She stands, limps toward the truck, and stares at it. At first, I think she's admiring my baby, but this goes on for a little too long. "Ma'am?" I ask her.

As she opens the door and climbs in, she says, "Just checking you don't have NFNF printed on the door somewhere."

I laugh, really laugh, and that's how it all began five years ago.

Dirt loved her apple muffins.

CHAPTER 7

DANE

Now, I'm holding the hand of Ms. Saunders' girl and leading her toward my home. I bought the place next door to Ms. Saunders after I saw it was for sale the day we met when I drove her home. Ms. Saunders had fifty acres, but mine is bigger than hers. My land goes around Ms. Saunders' property. I offered to buy it from her more than once, but she always said it was a place her girl could come and feel safe from the world.

To my knowledge, she never visited her ma here, but I guess the house is hers now. I thought she'd have contacted me when Ms. Saunders left me the transportation business. I admit, I've been watching Kat for a while now. She punishes herself with her jogging, but she's got a fine figure and a great ass. Bet she does weights at home too. Her hair is past her waist, just the way I like it on a woman. It's been a year, and I think it's time she met the boys and me. I kept hoping she'd drop by, but after our conversation, I can tell she didn't even know we exist, so that explains it, I guess.

My home is a big investment for me, and it's only mine, not the club's. Some of the boys are always out here, but I don't mind. My home is big enough that if I want solitude, I know where to find it. I have a few cabins built around the place, but not too close to the main house. They are decked out real nice with kitchenettes, spas, fireplaces for winter, and air-conditioning for summer. I have managed to scrape and build five of them, each angled so they are private and well away from my home. I rent them out from time to time to tourists who want some peace and quiet or those who want to get close, but not too close to the Savage Angels. It always amazes me the number of women who want to tangle with us. The cabins are for the day I retire and hand over my presidency. I'll always be a Savage, but you have to look out for your future. Ms. Saunders liked I felt that way.

I realize I'm not talking, and it's my experience, women seem to like that shit, but not Kat. It's evident she's okay with my silence, as she hasn't tried to make small talk.

The silence stretches another thirty minutes,

before she tentatively asks, "Umm... do we... have... much... farther... to... go?" The last word is a whisper, more like a gasp. I suddenly realize she's not enjoying my silence. She's been trying to keep up with my strides, and I haven't slowed down the whole time we've been walking. Compared to me, she's tiny, and inwardly, I curse myself for not paying more attention to her. Stopping to look down at Kat, her face is bright red, she's sweaty, and she's gulping in air like she can't get enough.

Dammit.

"Let's take a breather here, yeah? It's not far now, only another fifteen minutes or so." She nods, trying to smile, but eventually, she puts her hands to her knees, taking deep breaths. It's pretty much all uphill from where we met. I should've been paying attention. She probably jogged to the bridge, and although I haven't been jogging, one of my strides is probably two of hers.

Shit.

Kat looks at me after a few minutes, and I'm captivated by her eyes. They're beautiful, and I've never seen anything quite like them. They are vivid green. My eyes move to her come-suck-my-cock mouth and then down to the hollow of her neck.

She suddenly straightens and places her hand on her scar. "Yes, it's awful, but you don't have to stare," Kat replies, sounding annoyed.

I cock my head to the side. "Woman, I wasn't

looking at your scar. I was looking at the hollow of your neck and wonderin' if you taste as good as you look."

Kat gasps and stands there. I'm wondering if she's going to bolt when she says, "Right, oookay… then, umm… should I go back, or should we keep going?"

Fuck me. Should I go back, or should we keep going? Is she seriously asking me that? She's been around lunatic fans, and she's followed me into the wilderness. I bet no one even knows where she is.

"Does anyone know where you are? Do you even have a cell phone on you?" I ask, in a pissed-off tone.

Panic races across her features. "No."

"No?"

"No." And now Kat looks around, taking in our surroundings. She looks scared.

"Calm down, Kat, I'm not going to hurt you, but these woods are filled with people and things that could. Did you even bring a cell phone? Been watching you for months, and I thought you had at least some kind of private security, but you don't, do you?" I say with more than a sliver of irritation.

How could she be so stupid?

"I have a security system built into the house and around the front of the property as well, but the back is hard to get to. I guess I thought I was… safe…" Her voice trails off.

I grab her hand and walk at a slower pace toward home.

CHAPTER 8

KAT

OMG... OMG... OMG!

I'm walking through the wilderness with a complete stranger, and he's just let me know

I.

Am.

Alone.

How could I be so completely stupid? I've had fans break into my hotel room, I know how fanatical some of them can be, and I willingly walked through the woods with, yes, a very good-looking guy, but Jesus Christ, what am I thinking? Clearly, I'm not. He's obviously put me under his spell, talking about my ma. Shit, he probably made it all up! He's holding my hand, and I know if I try to run, I've got no hope of getting away.

Do I keep walking? Do I fake an ankle injury? Do I run?

I decide to fake a fall, and as I land, I grab my ankle and whimper. Suddenly, Dane's down on his knees, staring at me with those gorgeous blue eyes.

"Kat? You hurt?" His hands are running over my ankle. I stare at him stupidly. "Kat?" More forcefully, "Are you hurt?"

"My ankle." Dane looks at me for a beat, then he puts one arm under my legs, the other around my back, and lifts me. He continues walking up the mountain. This isn't a good plan. Dane feels like all muscle, and he smells so good.

Fuck me.

Then a thought hits me. I probably smell like my sneakers. That's not good, and I'm all sweaty. I probably also have terrible breath from breathing in through my mouth. Christ, what is wrong with me? I'm in the wild with a total stranger. Who cares if I stink! Focus!

Then Dane says, "Almost there. I'll call Doc Jordan as soon as we get home."

Almost there? Now what? Dane stares straight ahead, breathing a little heavier now. Not surprising, I do weigh one hundred and twenty-two pounds.

When I'm nervous, I ramble. "You know, it's not necessary. If you'll just put me down, I'm sure I can make it back to my place and see…"

Dane stares at me right in the eyes. They are so beautiful, I forget to breathe.

Then he says, "No need, darlin', we're here."

I look up and see the most gorgeous country home I've ever laid eyes on. It's huge, has wraparound verandas, and it's painted a light gray with white trim. It's a three-story home with bay windows, and the second and third stories have wraparound verandas too. This does not look like a home for a biker, but more like a businessman's country getaway. Then I hear whistles and yells, and I see five men working in a four-car garage with very nice motorcycles inside. They approach us with big grins on their faces. Panic fills me. Dane gives me a squeeze, which makes me turn to look at him.

He looks me deep in the eyes and says, "No one here will hurt you. You're Kat, and we all love to hear you sing, but here you'll only be Ms. Saunders' girl. Now, can I put you down, or can you not put weight on your ankle?"

"Ms. Saunders' girl, not Kat? Really?" I ask, dazed.

"Yes, Kat. Ms. Saunders' girl." It's a statement, a promise, and suddenly I know he's a man of worth and can be trusted.

"You can put me down now. My, umm... ankle feels better." I avoid his eyes as I say this, and he chuckles.

It goes straight through me, and Dane says, "Right." He lowers me to the ground as the five men surround us.

Dane tucks me into his side and says, "Boys, this is Ms. Saunders' girl, Kat. Kat, this is Dirt."

A man steps forward. He looks really rough, but he has the most gorgeous smile, and he extends his hand and does a chin lift. "Kat."

The next is Fith, who doesn't shake my hand but smiles at me, giving me a nod. He has tattoos on his neck, and at the base, his name is written in beautiful script and he has really long hair.

Next is Bear, who's huge. He engulfs my hand in his and tries to pull me toward him, but Dane doesn't release me. Bear's eyes move to Dane, and he stops pulling while his smile on his big beardy face gets bigger.

Then there's Rebel, who's the youngest of them all. He kind of smiles and looks embarrassed.

Finally, there's Keg, who says, "You look just like your mamma." At which point, my eyes fill with tears.

Dane looks down at me with concern, and I feel like a complete idiot. "My ankle hurts pretty bad."

Releasing me, he hoists me up in his arms, and then carries me into his home.

CHAPTER 9

BEAR
Road Captain

I'm the Road Captain for the Savage Angels. Been in the club since I was seventeen, and I'm forty-nine now. I've seen some shit in my day, but the Angels have never been in better hands. Dane is tough but fair. You fuck with him, you'd better bring it because that boy doesn't know how to back down.

In all my years, I've never seen Dane look at any woman the way he's looking at Kat Saunders. He's fucked every piece of ass from Tourmaline to the coast, and not once has he ever failed to share them with us.

Never.

But as I tried to pull Kat out of his grasp, he held on, and when I look into his eyes, I finally see it. He's taken possession. Not an easy road ahead of him, though, because she's famous, and she's family because of Ms. Saunders. President or not, he fucks this up, he'll have more than a few of us to answer to. Ms. Saunders helped many in the MC with everything from a job to a hot meal and a willing ear. She was one hell of a woman. If Kat is anything like her ma, she's good people. Ms. Saunders was a nice old lady, but she had a long memory and was hard as nails.

Standing next to Dane, I'm a good four inches shorter, and where he has a washboard stomach, I'm shaped more like a barrel. I have long, curly red hair with a beard which goes down to my belly. My beard is lighter than my hair, it looks odd, but you know what? Fuck it. I hate to shave, and I like it. My nose is broken, and it's always red. People think it's because I drink, but I've been sober for over ten years, so fuck 'em.

CHAPTER 10

DIRT
Sergeant-at-Arms

It's interesting to watch Dane with this one. He's different. Maybe he's finally found a princess for his fucking house. It's too big for one man—it needs a family or at least a woman.

I'm thirty-five. I look older, but you spend enough time on the back of a bike, living hard like I do, you'd look the same. I have hazel eyes, I'm five foot nine, and I have dirty-blond hair. There's a scar running from my temple into my hair. Got it in a knife fight. I don't like knives, I prefer fists.

Ms. Saunders was a tough old bird, but she took a shine to us, and without her, I'd be doing a stretch in the joint right now. Not just over that stupid little cunt who was only fourteen. Ms. Saunders got me out of some serious shit, and I never got to pay her back. Guess the debt I owed her goes to her daughter now.

Dane had better watch him-fucking-self. I'm sure the boys in the MC wouldn't appreciate it if he treats Ms. Saunders' girl with anything but respect. We owe the old broad that much.

CHAPTER 11

FITH
Soldier in the Savage Angels MC

I'm surprised Dane is carrying such fine piece of ass into his home. No female has ever come out here. He does them at the compound, but never here. She's Ms. Saunders' girl, yeah, but she's still Kat-fucking-Saunders.

Man, I love her voice! The chick can sing, and from what I've heard about her, she can party with the best of them.

I'm six foot four, built, and I take shit from no one. My name says it all—Fucked in the Head. Club gave me the name when I was nineteen after I jumped onto a speeding car, went through the windshield, and killed the motherfucker driving it. Got away with it, too. I claimed I accidentally killed him when he ran into me and I went through the windshield. It's not how it went down. I timed it well, jumped onto the car when he aimed it at me, let my body smash the windshield, then pounded my way through it. I broke my wrists but got that motherfucker!

Ms. Saunders always made me cinnamon muffins because I don't like apple. Haven't had a lot of good in my life, but she always made a point of being nice to me. She also kept me out of prison. Owed her for that, and I never got to repay the debt. Without her, I wouldn't have had a job, either. She made me her foreman at her depot. She was a crafty old bird, had big plans for the club. Don't think she ever got around to telling Dane what she had planned. She wasn't as nice as everyone thought, but she liked me, so we were solid. I think I'm the only one she trusted with her extra business.

CHAPTER 12

REBEL
Soldier in the Savage Angels MC

Fuck me, Kat Saunders!

I have all of her albums, and I don't have any favorites. They're all cool. I've been to see her in concert, I don't know how many times. She looked at me. At me! I'm exactly her type. Twenty-eight years old, six foot four, a shaved head, and I keep in shape.

I met her once in a bar, and I'll never forget it. She was drunk off her ass. Kat was there with some guy, then suddenly, she walked up to me, grabbed my face, and kissed me! The guy pulled her off, but she smiled at me, and said, "See you around, baby." Then the guy dragged her out of the bar, but I knew she and I were meant to be.

Ms. Saunders talked about her a lot. I know her favorite color is yellow and her favorite flowers are gerberas. I listened carefully when she talked about Kat. I wanted to know everything, and now, here she is.

But the way Dane is looking at her makes the hair on the back of my neck stand up. And he's taking her into his home. He's never done that before. I love and respect my president, but this is Kat Saunders, she's famous, beautiful, and I saw her first.

CHAPTER 13

KEG
Soldier in the Savage Angels MC

Christ! I think I made her cry, and I can't fucking handle women crying. I've been on this earth for thirty-seven years, and the only woman I make cry is my old lady, Jenny. Fucking bitch rides me hard. She's the only woman I've ever had more than a one-night-stand with. Jenny didn't grow up with the club, so she doesn't understand what happens on a ride stays on the ride. A man's got needs.

I'm five foot ten, and my body's in pretty good shape apart from a bit of a beer belly, but if I hit the gym, that shit would be gone. I have dark brown hair that's going gray at the temples and the best fucking mustache you've ever seen.

It was Ms. Saunders who sorted the shit out with

the sheriff and kept more than a few of us out of prison. She never spoke to me directly about it, but without her, I'd have done a stretch for sure. That fucking prick, Justice Leaverton, has a lot to fucking answer for. Fucker thinks he owns this town because it was his great-great-great-fucking-granddaddy who founded Tourmaline. But the truth is, without the Savage Angels, this town would've disappeared forty years ago, and we all know it.

CHAPTER 14

KAT

I have been placed in the living room on a black leather couch, which is huge. In the middle of the room, against one wall, is the biggest fireplace I've ever seen, with a humongous television mounted above it. The entire house, from what I've seen so far, is very masculine, with lots of dark colors, leather, and wood.

It really needs a woman's touch, I think to myself. A few lighter, softer colors here and there, or even a few vases of flowers around the room, would make it a little homier. I love flowers. My ma's garden is full of color, even in winter. I pick them and put them all throughout my home.

Dane walks back in with tissues and an icepack. He places the icepack on my ankle, which is on top of a pillow. I'm on my back with my legs and feet on his luxurious leather couch. The ice feels cold, but there's really nothing wrong with my ankle. I try desperately to figure out how to get the hell out of here when he says, "Phoned Doc Jordan. Sorry, darlin', but he's not in town today. He's at the other end of the county looking to some of the hill folk who don't come into town. Give me your keys, and I'll get Rebel to go to your house to get you some clothes. You can stay here the night, and if you can walk on it in the morning, I'll take you home or to the Doc's."

"What?"

"Kat, give me your keys and security code." Dane looks annoyed and even a little frustrated with me. He probably feels responsible.

How the hell do I get out of this?

"Umm… it's so not necessary. If you could give me a lift home, I'll be fine from there." Then, I give him my best smile, but he doesn't return it. In fact, now he looks angry, but then he sighs and runs his hand through his hair as he holds my gaze. His voice is tight, clipped, and not to be fucked with.

"Darlin', I can see you aren't getting this. Give me your fucking keys and security code, and I'll get Rebel to get some of your things, 'cause baby, you're staying here tonight."

I really don't like the way he called me baby or the way his eyes seem to penetrate my soul. I unclip my keys from my waistband, put them in his hand, and say, "It's really not necessary, you know. I've been looking after myself for a long time now." As I utter the last, something flashes behind his eyes.

"Code, Kat."

He looks furious now. I stare into his eyes and say, "15770."

"15770?" He repeats, disbelief evident in his tone. I nod, and he repeats in a stronger, louder tone, "15770? Jesus, Kat! That's the number on your house!"

"Yeah, I know, it's so I remember it," I say it in a whisper.

Dane gets up and leaves the room, anger flushing his gorgeous features.

Fuck. Fuck. Fuckity fuck. Fuck!

Now, what am I going to do?

CHAPTER 15

DANE

I can't believe a woman whose entire life has been in the limelight would use the number on her house as her security code. Jesus-fucking-Christ!

I find Rebel in the kitchen talking with Dirt about Kat. He's always been a fan. Even told Ms. Saunders he went to her concerts.

"Rebel, I need you to go to Ms. Saunders' place and get Kat some clothes for today, tonight, and tomorrow."

He looks up, and he's got this huge grin on his face.

"Really? Did Kat ask you to ask me to do that?"

"What?" Now, I look at him, and he's pumped. "You on something?" The kid looks juiced.

"No, I'm not on anything, but we have Kat

Saunders in your house, sitting in your chair, and she's asked me… me… to get her some clothes." I look more closely at him, and I've never seen him look so happy. He's been with us a little over five years, and he sticks to himself. He's good in fights, keeps his head in negotiations, but I've never seen him with a girl. Always thought he swung the other way. Never bothered me. But looking at how excited he is right now, maybe I'm wrong.

I grin at him.

"Here are her keys, code to the house is 15770. Now, clothes for today, tonight, and tomorrow. Got it?"

"Yeah, sure, Dane. Tell Kat I've got it covered." Rebel leaves with more bounce in his step, grinning like a fool.

I look up at Dirt, grin, and shake my head.

Dirt looks at me, amused. "How's her ankle?"

"Nothing wrong with her ankle," I answer, smirking.

"What? Then why do you have her flat out on your couch with an ice pack on it if there's nothin' wrong with her ankle?"

Dirt is my Sergeant-at-Arms, and there's no one I trust more. It hasn't always been this way, but over the years, he's proven himself on more than one occasion, and he was the natural replacement after Ray got killed by the Road Hellions. We'd never had any problems with them before, so we were unprepared for the attack. We lost Ray, they lost thirty. Ray was worth a lot more than thirty.

I look at him and smile. "She's faking it, but it's my fault for spooking her when I didn't mean to. I questioned her about being out and about alone, without a cell or letting anyone know where she is. Saw the panic in her eyes, but it was too late, 'cause next thing I know, she goes down with a twisted ankle."

"She didn't let anyone know where she was or what she was doing? Christ, a fall down this mountain and her neck would snap like a twig, especially with the way she jogs down it! And what's this about she doesn't even have a cell phone? What if she'd tripped? If something happened during the winter, she could've died from exposure."

Now Dirt's mad. We've all seen her jogging for the past many months, but none of us have made a move. We were giving her time, but I got tired of waiting. She's single, female, and has a fucking great ass. What more do I need?

"I know, man, yeah? Anyway, thought I'd bring her here, let her calm down, then take her home. But, fuck me, she's better in person than on TV. Those eyes, man... I thought it warranted further exploration."

Dirt looks at me and grunts. "She's Ms. Saunders' kid, you remember that."

"Dirt, my man, I don't need you to fucking remind me who she is. I miss Ms. Saunders, too, and I wouldn't disrespect her daughter even if she turned out to be a tricked-out whore with a nasty habit. She'd still be Ms. Saunders' kid. I thought she'd come to us before now to discuss her mother's will and the transportation business, but I got tired of waiting."

At that, he nods and walks to my fridge and pulls out a beer. I walk back to the living room to see Kat.

CHAPTER 16

KAT

Oh my God.

Oh my God.

Oh my God.

How had I gotten myself into this? How? For twelve months, I've stayed away from everyone, but now, here I am, on a strange man's couch, and I'm staying the night with a fake injury! Deep breaths, deep breaths.

"Darlin', are you all right?" It's Dane, and the concern on his face is obvious.

"I'm fine, really, but I need to get home." Now, he looks at me with his head tilted to the side. He's freaking huge, and I think he's looking at me like I'm a medical experiment.

"Darlin', you've twisted your ankle, you live

alone, and, as luck would have it, none of the boys are staying out here tonight, so we'll have the whole place to ourselves. Which is good because then I can tell you a little more about your ma and her business."

Great, I'm staying here with him alone! It's obviously been too long since I've gotten laid, and, may I repeat, how did I get myself into this? Now I realize I haven't said anything, and he's staring at me again.

"Dane, I really appreciate you taking care of me, but—" I say, but he interrupts me.

"Darlin', it's no trouble. Now, how do you like your steak cooked? And do you want a beer or something stronger for the pain?" There he goes again. His smile looks like he knows something I don't.

"Scotch is good, and do you happen to have any ice?" This all comes out in one great big hurry, so it almost sounds like one word instead of a sentence.

He looks at me, then throws his head back and laughs. It's a fucking glorious sight. His neck is divine, something you could run your tongue along. Wait, what am I thinking?

"Yes, Kat, I have scotch and ice. Your ma liked it with her scotch, too." His eyes are smiling at me, and he has great laugh lines.

"You made drinks for my ma?" I stare at him intently now. Clearly, I didn't know my mother as well as I thought I did.

"Yeah, darlin', she didn't like beer, and she liked her steaks bloody."

"Yuck! Bloody? I'd forgotten she liked her meat cooked that way. I don't want it overdone, but it has to be far from bleeding on a plate or trying to crawl away from me."

This gets me another laugh, and it is such a great sound. It seems to rumble up from his chest, and I like it.

CHAPTER 17

KAT

Dane comes back into the room and says, "Steaks are defrosting for dinner tonight, but what would you like for lunch? I make a mean grilled cheese sandwich."

"I haven't had a grilled cheese in ages. Thank you, sounds good."

He smiles at me, and I can't help but smile back.

He walks over to me and puts the ice on my ankle. "Darlin', it doesn't work unless it's on your ankle."

I feel my face flush. My deception feels utterly foolish now, but I can't reveal I don't really have an injury.

I mutter, "Thank you." I look around the room, unable to meet his eyes.

He turns on the television and hands me the remote. "Here, darlin', something for you to look at and take your mind off the pain while I make us lunch." Then he winks at me and leaves the room.

I play with the remote, channel surfing, but not really watching anything. When he returns a short while later, he finds me sitting up on the couch.

"You really need to keep it elevated so it doesn't swell. The ice helps, too," he says as he puts my grilled cheese sandwich in front of me.

"I can't eat lying down." I can't get myself to admit the truth. "I'll eat, then lie back down and ice it after."

He grins at me and says, "Good idea. Did you find anything on the TV you want to watch?"

"No, I don't really watch TV," I admit.

He grabs the remote from me and switches it off. Then he sits next to me on the couch, and I feel a spark as his leg brushes against mine.

"Are you planning on settling in Tourmaline?" he asks before he bites into his lunch.

"That's a hard question. To be honest, I haven't really explored the town. I've spent a year in my house." I take a bite of my sandwich, and the only sounds are of us eating. "You're the first person I've spoken to in three months. I guess I need to get out more," I say with a smile on my face.

He grins back at me and says, "Really? I'm the first person you have spoken to in three months?

You really need to get out more."

I chuckle. "It's not that easy. There are reporters to worry about and the odd way-too-friendly fan. It's just me now, no security, so I have to be a little careful. You never know who you can run into, especially in the woods."

He smiles at me and nods. "Yeah, darlin', you've got that right."

We finish our lunch in silence, then he grabs our plates and heads for the kitchen. I feel every little movement he makes. His arm brushes against mine, and my stomach flutters, he moves his leg against mine, and my core clenches. He sits so close to me that my body is overloading with sensations.

I lie back down on the couch, feeling foolish. He returns a short time later and asks, "Do you want a scotch neat or would you like a soda?"

"Soda, please. Don't care what, so long as it's cold."

He does a chin lift and disappears again. He returns and sits on the coffee table directly in front of me and holds out my drink.

"Thank you. You know my ankle doesn't feel as bad, I could just go home."

"It's all good, darlin'. I wouldn't feel right about letting you leave. What if something happened to you? And it must be giving you some grief, or you wouldn't have laid back down." He smirks at me.

I go up on one elbow to take a sip out of my soda

bottle and say, "Thank you. It's not true what they say, chivalry isn't dead."

His laughter fills the room, and I'm mesmerized by this man. I shake my head and lay back down.

"I don't think I've ever been described as chivalrous! That's a new one." He chuckles and questions, "Would you like me to take you on a tour of Tourmaline? It's a pretty little town. Pity you didn't get out and see it when it was snowing. Do you ski? Cause the snow's always good in winter."

"You know, I've never tried. I've water skied but never snow skied. I'd like to see more of Tourmaline. A tour would be nice."

He grins, "Good. I'll make some time for you this week. Have you ever ridden on the back of a bike? It's the best way to see it."

I nod. "I love to ride. I have a couple of bikes at my home in LA, but it's been a while."

He raises his eyebrows and says, "Really? That's cool. I don't have any spare rides at the moment, so you'll go on the back of mine."

"Sounds like fun." The idea of being pressed up against him appeals to me in so many ways.

"Your ma didn't like bikes. Too dangerous, she said. I was always offering to take her for a ride, but she'd scowl at me and say no!" He laughs to himself as he reminisces.

"I can't believe you even had the courage to ask! I never told her I even owned a bike! She'd have chewed me out over it!" I giggle at the thought of it.

"You know, you look better in person. Your ma showed me photos of you, but they don't do you justice." Dane has completely thrown me with his declaration.

To cover up my shock, I say, "Ma showed you photos of me? Which ones?"

"Most of them looked like tour photos. You were either on a stage or at a recording studio."

I smile. "Now, I understand. Most of them were taken by Truth. He likes to take a photo as you're about to say or do something, so you look like a dork, then he posts it for the world to see. I didn't even know he sent them home to Ma." I chuckle to myself.

"You still look better in person, but she also had professional photos, too." Dane stares at me.

I look away. "Your home is amazing. Have you lived here long?" He doesn't answer, so I look at him. "Dane?"

Dane smiles. "I got an architect in, and she helped me design it. I told her what I wanted, and together we came up with this." He raises both eyebrows. "Of course, it wasn't that easy, but we got there in the end."

I nod. "I only ever built one home, the one in LA. I also had to have a recording studio built inside, but it took forever to come up with a design."

The sounds of a bike filters through the room,

and Dane stands. "Must be Rebel with your clothes. I'll put them upstairs. I won't be long."

Dane leaves me lying on the couch, and I ponder my predicament. I obviously can't leave, and I have to admit, he's easy to talk to and not bad to look at either. I just hope the rest of the day is as easy as it's been so far.

The afternoon turned into evening, and dinner went well. Dane could definitely cook, and he told me stories about my ma and how they met. I still can't believe she walked straight into a biker compound and grabbed Dirt by the ear! From the little I've seen of him, he isn't someone you'd fuck with. My ma had a very black and white view of what was right and wrong. At least I thought she did, so how the hell did she become friends with bikers? I listened to the stories and laughed a lot. Ma didn't judge a book by its cover, even so, bikers?

The more Dane talks, the more I like him. I could see why my ma gravitated toward him. Dane is very good-looking but not in a pretty-boy-way, and he commands your attention when he enters a room. I like he has made plans for his future and how he has a beautiful piece of land and is sharing it with the public, even if it's for a price. It shows he's thinking about his future, but he's the president of the Savage Angels, and they aren't to be fucked with.

During dinner, Dane asked me very little about myself. He seemed content to talk about himself, his club, and my ma.

"The accident that gave you that scar, did it take your voice, too?" Dane suddenly asks me, breaking through my thoughts.

His question has taken me by surprise. Fuck me, I'm dumbfounded, and I know I have to say something.

"Yes. I can sing but not like I used to. I've lost the higher range, can't sing most of my fucking songs anymore. Do you know 'Heaven'?" Dane looks at me and nods. Fuck, everyone knows 'Heaven.' "I can't sing it anymore. After the accident, they told me my vocal register might be different. My manager wanted to do a greatest hits album, but after I'd recovered, we went into the studio to re-record some of the older stuff. We wanted to put a bit of a new spin on some of them. 'Heaven' had a whole verse taken out of it, and we were going to put it back in. But after one recording, hell, it wasn't even the entire song, I could tell my voice was gone, and the look on the guys faces just confirmed it. I got into my car, drove three days straight, and came here. They've all gone on to do other things, and they seem happy." I don't tell him the accident was my fault, that I'm an idiot. I lost my voice, and I lost the one person who truly knew me, my mother.

"Fuck, darlin', that's awful." Dane looks at me with empathy. "Can't imagine how hard it has been on you."

Suddenly, I'm so tired. In fact, I'm exhausted and an emotional wreck. I've been fed and have had way too much scotch, and now I want to sleep, but where am I sleeping?

Dane studies me for a moment, then suddenly he knifes up, puts an arm under my knees and one around my back, and lifts me as if I weigh nothing.

"Dane!" He's given me such a fright. "What are you doing?"

"Darlin', you look wasted. Time for bed."

Oh. My. God!

He carries me down a hallway, a very attractive one at that. Two people could walk side by side down it, and there'd still be plenty of room. I try to look around and take in my surroundings when he moves up the stairs.

"Dane, put me down before you hurt yourself!" He laughs, and I can feel it go all the way through me. His eyes look more beautiful when I'm this close and he's laughing.

"Darlin', I've carried heavier loads than you. Besides, I don't want you to hurt your ankle any more than you already have."

Dane looks at me and smiles like he knows something. I'm not sure if I want to be part of his private joke. Then I realize he's stopped walking, and he gently puts me to my feet. I look around, and I'm in an amazing bedroom decorated in blues and whites. It's gorgeous and very feminine, not like the rest of the house at all.

"Darlin'." Dane points to a closed door off to one side. "Bathroom's through there. Rebel put your clothes at the end of the bed, and I'm right next door if you need anything. Just yell, and I'll hear you. Now, will you be all right to shower and get yourself changed, or do you need some help?"

Oh, my Lord, I so need some help, but out of my mouth comes, "I'll be fine, thank you."

I reach up and squeeze his arm and smile. He looks down at my hand and growls, then he looks at me and nods, turns on his heel, and leaves the room.

Interesting.

His demeanor took a sudden one-eighty turn.

What's up with that?

Perhaps my touch affected him as much as he affects me?

CHAPTER 18

DANE

I can't believe the effect this woman is having on me. I could easily have picked her back up, thrown her on the bed, and helped myself to her. Is it because she's famous? The connection I had with her ma? Or is it she's the first woman I've ever had in my home? Whatever the reason, if I hadn't left her when I did, I'd be making her scream my name by now. I can hear her in the shower, so it's time to hit the gym.

An hour later, I walk back down the hall, and as I get to her room, she opens the door. She's wearing a pale pink silk nightie which barely covers her ass, and I can tell she's not wearing any underwear. It also rounds her ample breasts, so they are up and out there. I'm having a serious conversation with

Rebel in the morning about the clothes he chose.

"You okay?" I ask as I stare at her chest. I want to taste her. Christ, I need to get myself under control.

"Dane?" It sounds like a question, and I realize my gaze hasn't left her chest. I force my eyes to meet hers, and her breath catches.

"I was in the gym in the basement. Everything okay?" As I say this, I move closer to her and lean against the door frame, completely invading her space.

Kat's breath catches again, and liking the sound, I smile down at her.

"Y-yes." Her eyes drop to the floor. "You have a basement?"

Laughing, I nod. "Yeah. It's full of gym equipment. When your ankle is better, check it out. Do you have one at your house?"

She hasn't moved away from me, and slowly her gaze comes back to mine. "One what?"

"A gym." Reaching up, I tuck a few strands of hair behind her ear, and as if she can't help herself, Kat leans into my hand.

"Yes, I do and a recording studio."

My hand goes to the scar on her neck. Lightly, I trace the edge with my fingertips.

"I didn't think you could sing anymore?"

Kat moves away from me, her eyes back on the floor. She nods and wraps her arms around herself.

"I play guitar. I'm not as good as Truth." A small

smile plays on her lips, and she looks up at me. "Don't you ever tell him I said that."

"He's the lead guitarist, yeah?"

Kat nods. "With an ego the size of Texas." Her smile grows bigger.

"You miss him?"

"Yes, but not like that. He's like this annoying brother I flirt with, but we both know it means nothing. We've been through a lot together." Her hand comes up and touches the scar.

I enjoy hearing her talk, and I'm pleased Truth isn't a love interest, even though he has a reputation as a man-whore. A very public one. He's left a long list of broken hearts and sordid love stories in the tabloids.

"So, you play guitar in your studio?"

Kat nods. "And I thought maybe one day I could produce or manage a band." The smile comes back. "Kind of a way to keep myself in the business, even if I'm not part of it anymore."

"That's good. But Kat Saunders will always be a part of the music business. Your songs will be around for a long time to come."

Kat smiles, but this time it doesn't reach her eyes. Leaning further into the room, I look around and then stare straight at her. She takes a moment as she's looking around too, and when she finally looks back at me, I'm an inch away from her face.

Kat looks at me like a deer caught in headlights,

a little scared but unable to look away. Unable to resist anymore, I reach out and touch her face. Her skin is soft. I trace her jaw with my thumb, then plunge my fingers into the hair at the base of her neck, and as I move into her, my mouth smashes down on top of hers. She smells and tastes so fucking good. Her hands have gone up and under my tee. I walk Kat backward toward the bed. If I don't get inside her soon, I'll explode.

Wrenching my mouth away from hers, we lock eyes. "Now's the time to tell me to go. If you don't want this, you need to tell me."

Kat's response is to pull me in closer, her hands cupping my face. She takes a step back, pulling me with her, then her knees hit the bed, and we fall. In no time, I've got a hand between her legs, and she's so wet. Kat whimpers, and I'm desperate to be in there. I plunge two fingers into her pussy, and she moans into my mouth. She's slick, tight, and I need to taste her. I slip my fingers into my mouth, and fuck me, she tastes sweet. Moving down her body, Kat grabs a fistful of my hair and pushes my head between her legs. I like a woman who knows what she wants and isn't afraid to say it. Kat's completely hairless. Fuck me—a dream come true. Nothing's worse than a mouth full of fucking pubic hair. I lick her slit, and as I do, I stick a finger inside her, and she almost arches off the bed. I use my other hand to push her back down. Then I throw her legs over my shoulders, grip her ass, and enjoy my feast.

"Dane, don't stop, please don't stop…" It comes out soft but ends on a high note, and she watches me eat her. I look into her eyes as I drive two fingers into her, and she comes right then, screaming my name. I finish her until she can't take any more.

Getting up, I move into my room, open my bedside table, and pull out a condom. While I roll it on, I try to get naked at the same time, before returning to her room.

I stumble through her doorway, and she's up off the bed and heading for the bathroom when she sees me and stops. But before she can turn all the way around, I grab her and kiss her neck.

Fuck me, she tastes amazing!

"Dane?" It comes out as a whisper, and again, it sounds like a question.

"Yes, Kat?" I growl into her neck, all the while pushing her toward the bed.

"I thought you'd left…"

Stopping what I'm doing, I turn her around. "No, Kat, I went to get protection. You can never be too careful." I have both of my hands framing her face, and she looks surprised.

"I thought you didn't want me…" she continues to whisper. Is this fucking woman serious?

"Darlin', why the fuck wouldn't I want you?" I smirk a bit arrogantly. "You taste as good as you look, and you just screamed my name. It's my turn for some fun." Christ, she looks embarrassed. Maybe all the stories about her aren't true?

I rub my chin up her neck and suck on her ear, making her whimper, then I kiss her. She sounds so fucking good.

My hand grips her breast, and I run my thumb over her nipple. Kat moans, so I push her onto the bed, spread her legs, and drive straight into her. She's so fucking tight. I pull out slowly and go back in just as slow and watch her as I do. Her head moves from side to side.

"Faster, baby, faster." Kat's voice is filled with desire.

"Soon," I ground out. Her eyes pop open and hold my gaze—she looks glorious.

"I need you to move faster, baby, I'm so close…"

"Soon, wanna watch you for a bit, Kat," I growl at her.

She plants a foot in the bed, shoves, and I find myself on my back as she rides me. Impatient, I like it. I grip her hips, controlling the pace, and I help her move faster. Suddenly, she screams, and her sex is convulsing around my shaft. I can't believe I am so close to coming. I'm not a teenager anymore. Usually, I can go for hours. Kat keeps moving, and she moans as she comes again. Fucking spectacular. Her neck is arched back, and her hair is hanging down in long tendrils. I've never seen a more beautiful sight.

My turn now.

I knife up, take a quick suck on her nipple, and flip us, so she's flat on the bed, and I'm still inside her. I move, pumping in and out of her, when I hear, "Dane, look at me."

I didn't know I'd closed my eyes. I'm driving into her, and her sex envelops my cock perfectly. Slowly, I open them, and she stares at me and smiles.

"You feel so fucking good," I say this as I push back inside her. She smiles wider, and I drive into her one last time, completely planted inside this woman who has me spellbound. The power she has over me is astounding. I'm spent. Kissing her thoroughly, I slowly pull out, and push myself up the bed. I slip an arm under her head, drag her closer to me, and throw a leg over hers, feeling very satisfied.

CHAPTER 19

KAT

"Darlin, that was worth waiting for."

"I'm sorry?" I ask, a bit confused.

"That was worth waiting for," Dane repeats himself.

"But we only met today. We've only known each other for a few hours."

"I knew your ma, so it's like I already know you a bit. And I've been watching you for a while."

My whole body tightens. I think I've even stopped breathing.

"Darlin', relax, it's a small town, and I live next door to you. I just meant I've seen you going up and down the mountain plenty of times, but you really should do it with a cell phone or one of your bodyguards."

"I let them go a little while ago. There didn't seem much point in having them around anymore."

"Still, you should be more careful. You never know who or what could be in the woods."

"You've been watching me?" I ask carefully.

"Yeah, darlin', I've been waiting for you to come to us. I got impatient, so I came to you instead. Your ma meant something to us, to this town. I'm surprised she never mentioned us or the problems with the town."

"There are problems in Tourmaline? It's in the middle of nowhere." Now I'm even more confused.

"Yeah, darlin', it's true, but most of the truck routes go through Tourmaline on their way to the rest of the country, and the train rail runs right through as well. We have a huge distribution business operating out of here. Your ma owned one of the largest trucking and distribution networks in the country. The Savage Angels helped keep the routes free and clear, and your ma paid us a fee. Been looking after it ever since she passed, but she should've left it to you, not me."

"My mother must have had a good reason to leave it to you. Until today, I didn't even know it existed." I sit up and look down at Dane, confusion clouding my features.

"Christ, Kat, how do you not know any of this?"

Dane stares at me with such a look of disappointment. He's right, I should've tried harder. I should've made the effort, but how do I tell him I'm really a self-absorbed has-been, who should've been closer to her mother but thought I'd have more time?

"We spoke almost every week, but I've been recording or on tour since I was twelve years old. I was either in a recording studio or in another country. Ma never told me about the things she did here, and I guess I just assumed she came here to retire. I know I should've tried harder, but my life was crazy."

"She secured the distribution rights to deliver Carnivale cigarettes across the nation about three years ago. In her first year, she ran into trouble with her trucks being hijacked, so she asked if the Savage Angels could act as security, and she gave us a cut of her earnings. Good money, darlin', and we've been doing it ever since."

"I didn't know. Ma used to own a small trucking company, but that was years ago when I first hit the stage. She sold it when I was twenty. I thought she wanted to retire, even though she was only in her fifties then, but she'd been working since she was nine. What is the name of the business?" I'm snuggled up to him, and he feels warm and smells amazing. It's been way too long since I've been in the arms of a man.

Dane laughs and rubs his nose with mine. Then, he looks me in the eyes and says,

"Grinders Transport."

My band's name, and I didn't even know.

Dane smiles at me. "She loved you, Kat. You were all she ever talked about."

CHAPTER 20

KAT

I'm awake, and I know it's early. I look over, and my bed is empty. I hate that, the walk of shame. I sit up and look around, but Dane's nowhere to be seen. Now, I feel like a fool. Don't get me wrong, I've had my fair share of one-night-stands, but I felt a connection with Dane. Maybe it's because of the relationship he had with my ma.

I drag my tired butt into the shower and do what I have to do. Then, I go through the bag that Rebel got for me. Thank the Lord, he packed some of my jeans and a t-shirt. He even put in some of my sandals, but the underwear is a little risqué for everyday wear. Well, whatever.

I'm showered, dressed, and carrying my bag out the front door when I run into Bear. This guy is enormous, and he walks toward me with a big grin on his face.

"Mornin', Kat, sleep well?" He looks so amused. I'm sure Dane has told him all about it, about me. Fuck it, I'm a big girl and far from a virgin. Two can play at this game.

"Haven't slept that well in forever, Bear. How about you?" I purr this out and lick my lips, then I stare him straight in the eye.

Bear looks taken aback and does a slow blink. Then he looks me up and down, and somehow, he looks disappointed in me. Christ, have I read this situation completely wrong? I woke up in an empty bed, and Dane is nowhere to be found. Isn't it the universal sign for leave and don't come back?

"Well, that's good… umm… Dane had to leave early on club business, but he told me to tell you he'd meet you back here for lunch."

Christ, could I be a bigger idiot? This guy now thinks I've made a pass at him.

"Bear, I'm so sorry. I thought when I woke up this morning, and Dane wasn't here, that he wanted me gone. I feel like such an idiot."

I'm not looking at him as I say this. Instead, I stare at his chest, and I can feel my face burn. Bear laughs, and it rumbles up out of his chest.

"He said he left you a note near the coffee machine in the kitchen, didn't you see it?" Bear smiles at me and pushes me back through the door, herding me toward the kitchen at the back of the house.

The kitchen is freaking huge. It's all black and white with granite countertops and stainless-steel appliances. Over in the corner is a coffee machine, and right next to it is a folded piece of paper. Bear walks up to it, picks it up, smiles, and hands it to me.

> *Kat,*
> *Had to go into town to look after club business. Be back later. Wait for me, I won't be long.*
> *Dane.*

"Umm... thanks, Bear. I really need to get home, though, so do you think you could drive me?"

"Sorry, babe, no can do. Dane said you were to stay here until he gets back. He'd have my nuts in a vice if I didn't do as he said."

"I really need to get home." I stare at him, he smiles at me, and shakes his head.

"Few of the boys are outside, and some of them really want to meet you. Guess you'd call 'em fans of yours. You'd make their day if you came out and said hello. They also knew your ma and liked her. I'm sure they'd like you, too. Anyway, Dane won't be long."

Fans. Great. And I slept with their boss. Fantastic. I walk over to the coffeemaker, open the cupboard directly above it, find the mugs, and pour myself a cup. I look back up at Bear, put on my best fake smile, and say, "Excellent, I'd love to meet them. Do you want a cup?"

"That'd be good, haven't had my caffeine quota for today." Bear grins at me.

What else can a girl do but meet her admirers?

CHAPTER 21

KAT

Bear leads the way back outside. The yard is full of bikes. I count at least twenty and a crowd of men, plus a few women, surrounding the area. The outward appearances of these bikers convey roughness, and they represent their loyalty to the MC with the Savage Angels colors they wear. All eyes come to me. Seeing as it's early in the morning, I can't believe I didn't hear all these bikes pull up. Everyone has stopped talking. It feels like this when you play a small venue—they're all waiting for me to say something.

"Morning! Does anyone want a coffee?" I've tried to project my voice to sound bubbly, but these are bikers, and I don't know anyone here. Not really, anyway.

"Fuck me! Did Kat Saunders offer to make us coffee?" This comes from a guy who's sitting on his bike. He has a big grin on his face, and everyone laughs and talks amongst themselves, but they are all still looking at me.

I shake my head and say, "Fuck, no! Kitchen is through there, and he who gets there first will get coffee, the rest will have to refill the machine and wait."

The guy on the bike bursts out with spontaneous laughter, causing every person around him to laugh as well. He gets off his bike and stalks toward me. His gaze rakes over my body, looking me up and down, and it's openly carnal. This man is good-looking, but he's so cocky. You can tell as he stalks toward me, he thinks a lot of himself.

"Well, hello, Kat. Name's Judge, and I could do with a cup of joe." He holds out his hand, and I move toward him when I realize Bear has moved up and is standing right beside me.

"Don't mind him, Kat. Judge thinks he's a ladies' man, but he'd best remember whose house he's standin' in." Bear looks him right in the eye, and it's not a friendly look. I can feel the animosity between these two, and I don't want an altercation because of me.

"It's okay, Bear. Judge is just saying hello, right? Dane should be here soon, and it'd be nice to get to know some of his men." I smile at both of them, and then another guy walks up.

"Pleased to meet you, Kat. I'll be going in to get my coffee before it runs out." He smiles, and I laugh as he pushes his way inside.

The others slowly follow suit, and I make friendly conversation with some of them. All the women wait outside, which is kind of weird. There're only about six of them. They're standing in a huddle near the garage, looking at me and talking.

Making my way down the stairs, I walk toward them. I smile, but they don't appear too friendly.

"Hey, ladies, coffee's inside if you want a cup."

The one nearest me moves to the front of the pack. She's got her hair pulled back in a ponytail, and her face has way too much makeup on for this time of the morning. She's wearing a skirt so short, it really leaves nothing to the imagination.

"We're good. Dane don't like bitches in his home."

"Dane doesn't like bitches in his home?" I say this with my mouth hanging open and my voice kind of high-pitched. "You've never been inside his house? Any of you?"

"No, obviously we're not rich and famous, only good for the clubhouse, and, honey, we've all been in his room there," she says with a smile and nods.

Some of the girls behind her are doing the same, but one of them looks shocked. Their spokesperson made her point perfectly clear—they've all fucked the president of the Savage Angels.

"Well, you should go in and get coffee. His home is gorgeous, and the coffee's not bad, either." I smile at them, trying to make it appear as though she hasn't gotten under my skin, even though she has.

The one who looked shocked steps forward with a smile. "Don't mind us, Kat, we're just jealous you've been inside Dane's home. Do you really think he won't mind if I get a coffee?"

"Guarantee it. Come on, I need a refill." I smile at her, grab her arm, and we walk toward the house. The others all stay behind, and I can hear them muttering behind my back.

"I'm Jess," the girl tells me as we move toward the house. "I've only been around the club for a few months. Thanks for the offer of coffee."

"All good, Jess. How come no one's been out here?"

"The guys come out here all the time. It's only the females who aren't allowed. I think it's 'cause Dane doesn't want the headache of dealing with..." she makes quotation marks in the air, "... 'bitches' at his home. The clubhouse is different. There's always a party there. Here, it's more businesslike." She has her hair pulled up in a messy bun, and the more she talks, the more attractive she looks. Jess is friendly, and I like her.

"Is she always like that?" I turn and motion toward the group of women, but I keep walking.

"Yeah, she's hoping to be someone's old lady, but if you want my opinion, she's fucked one too many of them for any to take her seriously. Would you want to marry someone if you asked the question, 'Please stand up if you haven't fucked her,' and no one does? Nah, she's never going to be anything but a plaything."

"How about you, Jess? Are you someone's old lady?" We've made it to the front door, and I herd her down the hallway toward the back of the house and the kitchen.

"Not yet, but Luke and I have been spending time together. He's only a prospect, but I know he'll get patched in." Jess smiles, and she's even prettier. We've hit the kitchen, and all eyes turn to us. Some of them have gone out to the back deck, but the rest of the bikers are all staring at me.

"Any coffee left? Or do I need to make a new pot?" I ask with a smile.

Judge laughs and says, "Told ya, Kat Saunders is going to make us coffee!"

Everyone laughs, and I shake my head, walking toward the coffee machine. I open it, throw out the old grounds, spoon in new coffee, and fill it up with water. All the while continuing to smile and shake my head.

"It's coffee, Judge, not a three-course meal." Jess stands right beside me, and she looks nervous. I look at her and say, "Jess, honey, the mugs are in the cupboard there. Grab yourself one." She looks at me smiling widely and goes to get herself a mug.

CHAPTER 22

DANE

I get home to find twenty bikes at my house. I don't think I've ever had that many of my men out here at the same time. Not since I first built it. I can see a few of the club's 'Angels' huddled together over by the garage. The girls give a wave, and I do a chin lift in response. As I mount the stairs, I can hear laughter coming from the back of the house. I walk out to see Kat sitting on the railing. There's another girl, I think her name's Jess, sitting in a chair right beside her, and she has tears streaming down her face from laughter. All eyes are on Kat as she tells a story about one of her concerts and an overzealous fan. She looks gorgeous. She's sitting in the sun, and her hair is fucking spectacular. I'm leaning on the door frame with my ankles crossed, listening to her while the guys all laugh. Bear looks pissed, though, and he stares at Judge with rage clear in his eyes. I'm struggling to figure out the cause of the angry glare when Judge, who's standing beside Kat, reaches out and touches her on the leg, his hand lingering on her skin. She's gotten to the end of her story, and laughter fills the deck. Before I realize what I'm doing, I'm across the deck, and I've got Judge by his t-shirt, backing him up further down the deck.

"You don't touch what is mine..." I practically snarl this at him, and the guys part to let me through.

Judge has his hands up, and he says, "Be calm, brother, didn't know you'd made a claim. Thought she was there for the taking."

Everyone has gone quiet, and Bear has come up behind me. He always has my back.

I release Judge, straighten his tee, smile, and say, "Now you know." He's still got his hands up, and he lowers one to shake my hand. I grab it and say, "We're good."

Turning, I walk back to Kat. She looks confused. When I reach her, I move between her legs and kiss her on the lips. Keeping my position between her legs, I turn slightly, grabbing one of her hands, and put it on my stomach. She puts the other one on my shoulder, and I say, "Can a guy get a cup of coffee?" The whole lot of them, including Kat, burst into laughter. Jess looks like she's about to pee herself. "What's so fucking funny?" I smile as I'm looking around. Kat squeezes my shoulder and has her face pressed there as she's unable to speak.

Jess gets up and says, "It's all good, Dane. I'll go make it."

Even Bear and Judge are doubled over with laughter.

Who knew coffee could be so funny?

CHAPTER 23

KAT

Dane has kept me tucked to his side or within arm's reach since he got back from town. For a badass biker, he's very affectionate. Judge has kept his distance since the incident on the deck, but he does smile at me and wink when Dane isn't looking.

Everyone is slowly making their way out. I've had more than a few chin lifts and even a few light arm punches. Guess they like me. Jess has found her Luke, and they look great together. He's got her by the hand and is taking her through the house to his bike when, suddenly, she stops, turns around, and runs back to me.

"Thanks, Kat, I had an awesome time. Maybe we can do coffee again?" Jess's smile is infectious, and you can't help but like her.

"Absolutely, honey, looking forward to it. Maybe you could come to my house next time?"

Her smile gets bigger, and she grabs my hand. "Really? To your house?" Jess asks excitedly.

"Yeah, honey, it's just up the road."

She nods and smiles, then we hear, "Yo, babe, time to go."

It's Luke, and he's obviously had enough and wants to get on the road. She looks at me, does an eye roll, looks over at Dane, and says goodbye. Then she rushes away.

Dane comes up behind me and hooks me around the waist, and says right next to my ear, "Think you've won that one over, darlin'. Don't think I've ever seen her look happier, and she's never even said hello to me before. Well done."

I twist my head and look up at him. He's smiling at me. "Jess is really nice, but I can't say I like the other women much."

His face changes, and he asks, "Did something happen?" Now he looks pissed, and I try to twist in his arms to evade him, but he won't let me.

"No, no, no, they made it plain they didn't really like me. It's not a big deal."

"If it weren't a big deal, you wouldn't have brought it up. What did they say?" Annoyance is evident in his tone.

"One of them made it very clear that you've, umm…" I really don't want to say it.

"Very clear that I've what?" Then I can see he gets it, and his mouth looks tight. Dane shakes his head at me. "Darlin, I'm not a monk, and a man's got needs, but you're the first and only woman I have ever had stay here with me. I'm sorry I can't change the past, but we've got something good here… so let's see where it leads. If it's good, we'll keep going, and if not, we'll go our separate ways. No harm, no foul."

Dane stares at me so intently, and I can see he means it.

This causes my insides to flutter, but I say, "You're using a basketball term on me? Really?" My lips turn up in a smile, and I laugh. My reaction takes him by surprise, but then he joins me.

He twists me around and kisses me as I laugh. Dane has me backed up against a wall when I hear someone loudly, clear their voice. Dane sighs, leaves both hands on my face, and twists his head to see Bear with a huge grin on his big face.

"Dane, the rest of us are going for a ride down through the Gorge. You wanna come, or are you busy?" Bear started out looking at Dane but has ended up looking at me, and he's grinning like an idiot.

"I'm good, Bear, have fun." Dane practically growls these words out, and Bear turns on his heel and heads for the door. I stare after Bear when I realize Dane is looking straight at me, "Did you have a good time with my brothers?" he asks me.

"Yes, they're a nice bunch."

"Nice?" He throws his head back and laughs. Wow, he looks fantastic when he laughs. Then his face takes on a more serious expression. "Darlin', one thing, though, don't let the brothers touch you. That's not cool."

"Don't let the brothers touch me?" I'm confused. "When did the brothers touch me?"

I can tell he's not angry, but I'm not sure what it is I've done wrong.

"Judge touched your leg."

I can tell this is a major issue with him, but seriously?

"Okay, but it meant nothing. People touch me all the time. They like to touch their idol. Some people believe they have a relationship with me because, as I sing my songs, they think I'm singing only to them. I have fans, and, sometimes, it comes with the territory. They feel let down if I don't interact with them, and sometimes it's a simple handshake. At other times, it's a hug or a kiss on the cheek, or some go for the grope and a serious kiss. It's part of being me," I try to explain.

"Part of being you? People touch you all the time?" Dane's voice has gone soft, but his eyes are still intense but full of kindness. "There is a time and place for people to meet Kat Saunders, the superstar, but when you're with me, you're just Kat, and the brothers or your fans don't get to touch you. When you're with me, you are only mine." Dane finishes with a smile, and his hands cradle my face.

"It's not that easy. If we take this any further, you're going to find that out."

"Darlin', if we're going to take this further? We are taking this further, and so far, it's been good." This man is so intense. I feel so safe in his arms. But protect me from the world?

His thumbs are rubbing my jaw. "World's a big place, Dane. Not everyone wants to kiss me, some want to do me harm, and I'm not sure you can protect me from everyone."

Dane leans into me and says, "I can, and with my brothers, I will. You'll be safe, Kat, I promise."

Then he kisses me, and his hands are everywhere. Suddenly I don't care about fans or anything else. I only need him to be inside me, driving me over the edge.

CHAPTER 24

DANE

This woman tastes so fucking good. I pick her up and take her into the living room. She straddles me, wrapping her legs around my waist as I walk her toward the couch. She moans as I kiss her, and, fuck me, that alone could send me over the edge.

I throw her on the couch, and she immediately gets up on her knees and undoes my belt. I pull off my shirt, and she suddenly loses interest in my belt and licks and kisses my stomach. My dick strains against my jeans, and I need to be inside her. Bending down, I pull her tank up over her head. She has the sexiest bra on I've ever seen—it's black lace over red satin. It cups her breasts nicely and pushes them up and out, just begging for my mouth. I graze my thumbs over her nipples, and she pushes against me. I push her back, take off my boots and jeans, and, as I do, she kicks off her sandals and shimmies out of her jeans. Fuck me, she's wearing matching underwear.

Kat has curves. There's nothing worse than some of the skanks that hang around the clubhouse who are all skin and bone. You feel like you'll break them, and they don't have boobs unless they're fake, and then it's like a stick with balloons to play with. Not my scene.

She lays down, eyes half-mast as she drinks me in. Slowly, she moves her hands down her body until she reaches her core. My dick comes to attention as she rubs herself. I bend over her, pushing her bra down, and draw one of her nipples into my mouth. Her eyes snap open, and she groans in ecstasy. Grabbing her panties, I rip them down her legs. She spreads for me, and I plunge my rock-hard cock into her. She's so tight and wet, I can't control myself. I thrust in and out, and she feels amazing. I use my fingers and work her clit. Kat's orgasm hits her, and her sex clenches around my shaft as I go in and out of her pussy. She opens her eyes, and they're sexy as hell.

"Fuck me, Dane, fuck me." I roll her nipple with my thumb as she moves with me. My girl likes it rough. I kiss her vigorously, our tongues dueling. I rub my stubble up her neck and grab her breast with my hand, and then suck her nipple, hard. She arches off the couch and moves her hips faster. I can feel she's close again, so I move my hand slowly down her body while she begs me to touch her, "Please, Dane, please, please, please?"

The last word is breathy, and she tries to push my hand between us. I rub her clit, and she's almost there when I stop and demand, "Promise me no one will touch you again."

Her eyes are open. "Dane, please, I'm so close, baby," Kat protests.

"Promise me." I've stopped moving my hips, but I can't hold out for long. She looks incredible—her face is all flushed, and her hair has fanned out behind her. I can see the desire in her eyes.

"You'll keep me safe?" she asks, panting.

"Yes," I growl.

"Then, I promise." I move again without abandon and use my hand between us, bringing us both to orgasm at the same time.

Fucking brilliant.

CHAPTER 25

REBEL

I look through the window of Dane's living room. I've got my hand around my cock as he pounds in and out of her. It should be me. I met her first all those years ago. I tasted her first. She should be mine.

I explode all over his window, but they are so wrapped up in each other they don't even notice me. I can't believe they didn't check to make sure we'd all left before he fucked her. She's beautiful and supposed to be mine.

Zipping up, I back away slowly, so they don't notice me. Everyone else has left. I make my way around the back of the house, go in through the doors to the deck and yell out, "Dane, man, you around?"

I can hear her laughing, as is he. Then I hear a crash, followed by swearing, and the entire time Kat's laughing.

Dane yells out, "Be there in a minute, brother. Wait there, yeah?"

She should be laughing with me, not Dane.

"Sure, Dane, I'm in the kitchen getting a coffee. You want one?" I shout back.

Her laughter gets louder, and then Dane stumbles through the door, only wearing his jeans.

"No, Reb. How come you're still here? Thought everyone had left to do the Gorge."

I look at him, and he smiles. He looks fucking happy. Anger rages through my system, but on the outside, I smile, shake my head, and say, "No, brother, had no interest. Thought I'd work on one of the basket cases in the garage."

Basket cases are bits of Harleys we've collected over the years. We probably have enough bits and pieces to build us a dozen bikes. Usually, we make them, paint, and sell them. Sometimes, if you're really attached to it, Dane will let you keep it.

"Not today, Rebel. Go find yourself something else to do."

As he says this, Kat comes up behind him and puts both her arms around his middle. He lifts an arm, and she slides around him until she's tucked into his side, and he's playing with her hair. Kat's dressed, but I can see her jeans aren't done up.

"Hey, Rebel, thank you for getting me something to wear." She smiles at me, and she looks beautiful. I can feel the vein in my neck pulsate. All I can think about is having my cock buried inside her.

But I smile. "You're welcome, Kat. Anything for you." Dane gives me a funny look, so I smile, move toward the back deck, do a two-finger wave, and say, "Later." As I walk around the back of the house, I can feel my anger about to explode out of me. Getting to my bike, I head to the clubhouse. There's bound to be some little thing there with long brown hair I can take my frustrations out on.

CHAPTER 26

KAT

I'm on the back of Dane's bike. I can feel the wind in my face, and I'm pressed so close to him my private parts are on high alert. I haven't been on a bike for a long time. I'd forgotten how fantastic it feels. Unfortunately, because I live right next door, the ride is cut short.

He pulls up in front of the gates to my home, and I reluctantly get off and go over to punch in the security code. The gates slowly open as I turn back to Dane and look at him—he looks fucking fantastic sitting on his Harley. In fact, I've never seen a more magnificent sight. His bike suits the powerful man he is. It's black and chrome, just as beautiful as the man who rides it.

He smiles at me. "Darlin', you gonna get back on

or stare at me some more?"

"I'm thinking I want to stand here and stare a while."

His smile gets bigger, and I slowly make my way back to him. The driveway to my home isn't all that long. I have a tarred, circular driveway with flowers bordering both sides. In the middle of my garden is an immense oak tree. It looks a lot older than the house, so I'm guessing my ma planned the garden around it. He pulls up at the front, and there's another gate to get through to get into the house.

We both get off the bike, and he walks up to the keypad and punches in the code. "Darlin', you really need to change your code. It's way too easy." Dane stares at me, and I can tell this is one argument I'm not going to win.

"I know, I know, but no one has gotten into the house or the garden for that matter." I have my hands up, trying to placate him.

"Kat, it's not safe. Do you have a guy who can do it? If you don't, I know a guy."

"You know a guy?" I ask as he smiles at me and nods.

"Yep, that's what I said."

I look at him and smile back. "If you could contact your..." I make quotation marks in the air, "... guy, I'd appreciate it. Otherwise, I'll have to call Dave, and I think he's in Bora Bora or somewhere tropical."

His eyebrows draw together, and he questions, "Dave?" and from the way he has said it, it's a question he doesn't look happy about.

"Yes, Dave. He's my manager. Well, he was my manager. I'm not really sure what he is now."

I look at my shoes as I finish talking, and suddenly he's in my space. His hands are at my jaw, tipping my head back. "Sorry, darlin', didn't mean to upset you. I'm guessing Dave did a lot for you?"

"Dave did everything for me. He even did the renovations on this house. He has a great eye and superb taste. You'd like him, and he'd definitely like you."

"No more Dave, darlin'. You need something done and can't do it yourself, you come to me. I know people in all walks of life, and if I don't, one of the brothers will." Dane takes my hand and walks me toward the gate to get to my front door. The gate is wrought iron and has been powder coated black. I love them, they were about the only thing I got to choose for the house. Going through them, we reach the front door. Putting the key into the lock, he opens the door, guiding me just inside before he shuts it. "Wait here." I'm confused as to why I have to stand in the entry of my home, but I do as I'm told and simply wait. He comes back a few minutes later, smiling and shaking his head. "Are you sure you're Ms. Saunders' kid?"

"What do you mean?" I smile at him, but I don't

understand why he'd ask me that.

"Your ma was a neat freak, darlin', and your bedroom isn't neat." Dane keeps smiling at me while he bends down to brush his lips against mine. As he does, his thumbs sweep across my nipples.

Pushing into him, I deepen the kiss. My hands move into his hair, seemingly by themselves. He picks me up and walks me into my living room, where he stops and throws me on the couch. It's a large tan leather corner couch which looks out over the view at the back of the house. It's comfy as all get out. You can sit on it, lay on it, or, as we're about to do, fuck on it.

I take my clothes off, ridding my body of the material that's between us, and I look at him as he does the same. I'm naked, kneeling on the couch, and Dane walks over to me, turns around, showing me his back. He's all muscle and tattoos. He has wings which go out over his shoulders, and in the center of his back is an angel holding a sword. Under the wings, on either side of the angel, are the words 'Savage Angel.' There's so much detail in this tattoo. The angel's head is bowed with the eyes staring straight at you, and the sword is huge. As I study his tattoo, I can't help but trace the delicate lines with my fingers.

His lips are turned up into a half-smirk as he turns back around.

"This is who I am. I'm a Savage Angel. The MC

means everything to me. I'm their president, and I intend to stay that way for a really long time. If you and I keep seeing each other, and I hope we do, do you think you could fit into our world?"

I laugh, and his smirk dies on his handsome face. His mouth is set in a serious but firm line.

"Do I think I could fit into your world? Dane, I'm Kat Saunders. I'm freaking famous, and you're worried about me?" I grab his hands and pull him down onto the couch. In a soft voice, I say, "You're about to become famous, just by being seen with me. Your face is going to be plastered on every magazine around the world, and you're worried about me?"

"Your fame is fleeting. The Savage Angels have been around for over forty years. Eventually, the world will leave you alone. But the Savage Angels will still be here. I'm not going to lie to you, Kat. If you want to see this through, it's not always going to be an easy path." His eyes hold such intensity, but then he smiles and says, "Now kiss me and show me what your pretty mouth can do."

I get close to him and stop about an inch away from his mouth. I capture his eyes and smile, but he's impatient and leans in to kiss me. His tongue immediately darts into my mouth and tangles with mine. Breaking kiss, I lick down his neck to his chest. He grabs my hair and pushes my head down toward his cock, but he doesn't need to be so pushy.

I'm headed that way, anyway. I like a lover who knows what they want. I lick his cock, and I can hear his sudden intake of breath. My mouth closes over the tip, and my tongue gently massages the sensitive nerves underneath.

"Jesus, that feels fucking fantastic. Don't stop, darlin', don't stop." He's got both hands in my hair now, and he's pulled it up in a ponytail, away from my face. He pushes me up and down, but I know what I'm doing. I can feel he's almost there, so I look up at him. He's got his eyes on me, his face a mask of desire.

I have a hand between my legs, and I'm working my clit. I can feel it building when he grabs me under my armpits and lifts me. I straddle him, and I'm so slick, I impale myself on his shaft, gyrating my hips as I do.

Both of his hands are on me, moving me faster. I place my hands on his shoulders and roll my hips.

"Babe, I need your hand between my legs, make me come, honey," I whimper. Dane smiles and does what I ask, and I can tell by his face he's close. I move faster, his fingers are working me, and it hits. It's huge, and I just keep coming. He flips us over, and I wrap my legs around him as he pounds inside of me so hard and fast. His face is buried in my neck, then he arches his back and thrusts in as far as he can go, and he's done. I'm euphoric.

That was the best.

Ever.

This man fits me perfectly—he's good-looking, easy to be around, and has made me come every time we've had sex. No one has done that.

Ever.

He falls to the side of me. His back is to the couch, and he pulls me, so I'm lying halfway under him. His fingers trail down my body as he kisses and sucks my neck. Trailing his fingers down between my legs, he works me up again. His mouth captures my nipple, and his tongue rolls over it as he sucks it in. I arch off the couch, but he pushes me back down.

I grind down on his hand and look at him. He smiles. "You look beautiful like this," he murmurs.

When my orgasm hits me, I scream his name.

CHAPTER 27

DANE

I'm on my bike and headed to the compound. I can still see Kat's face in my mind as I made her come the second time. Fucking glorious. I didn't want to leave her. I don't know what it is about her, but I want to be with her and protect her. Unfortunately, I have shit to do. I need to make sure the depot is running smoothly and there are no problems at the compound. Justice Leaverton, the town's mayor and the unofficial 'King' of Tourmaline, has been making my life harder since Ms. Saunders passed. No one expected her to leave me Grinders Transport. We all expected it to go to Kat. I'm not sure, but I think he wanted to buy it. He's made offers in the past to Ms. Saunders, so I guess he thought Kat wouldn't want it, what with her being a rock star and all. But he got stuck with me instead, and I have no intention of selling. The Carnivale Cigarette Company contract alone is worth major money, and with my help, Ms. Saunders expanded her business into other areas.

The rumor is, Leaverton wants it for the land. He owns the land on both sides, and town gossip is he wants to build an exclusive housing development and already has investors lined up. Tourmaline doesn't need exclusive, high-priced homes. It does need industry to keep the town alive, obviously, and that's what we are. We're on the outskirts of town, so he can't use town planning against us. It's a typical small town, where all the industry is at one end. We don't have any major retailers here. It's all mom-and-pop businesses, and the townspeople support them. The tourist trade picks up in the winter as it's one of the prettiest towns you'll ever come across, and the snow is fantastic.

But without industry, like all small towns, it would die. Leaverton doesn't care about the town, though. He only cares about money. If you build an exclusive housing development here, it would create jobs in the short term, but long term, there wouldn't be anything left here for the people. They would have to travel to one of the major cities for work, and it's about an hour away. Eventually, they would move, and the town would cease to exist.

Ms. Saunders worked damn hard to make her

business thrive, even doing deals with the rail companies. She was a smart woman and had her hand in more than a few people's back pockets. There's no way I'm going to let Leaverton destroy all her hard work to make even more money and become king of this town. Tourmaline is home, and I'm going to do my best to make sure it stays that way.

CHAPTER 28

KAT

I've been lying on the couch since Dane left, gazing out at the view. As he was leaving, he was thoughtful and placed a throw over me.

I contemplate getting my ass off the couch to clean myself up and think about what I'm going to make us for lunch. Mentally, I scan my fridge as I make my way to my bedroom. I stop dead in my tracks just inside the door.

What the fuck?

My bedroom looks like it's been ransacked. My chest of drawers is all open with clothes hanging out of them. I cross the room to my closet, and all the clothes that were once on hangers lie in a mess on the floor. It looks as though my closet has had a bomb go off in it.

Fucking Rebel. It has to be him. He's the only one who's been in my house. I can't believe he did this! I'm going to have to wash everything! A little-known fact about me, I won't wear something after it's been on the floor. No wonder Dane asked if I was my mother's daughter. I'd have thought the same as he did. Don't get me wrong, I like a clean home, but my ma went overboard. A home is for living in, and housework will always be there tomorrow.

I begin the chore of picking up my clothes and am putting them in the clothes hamper when I realize my bed is unmade as well. I always keep it made, it's a habit from my youth. Rebel must be a fan.

Sigh.

Those sheets are getting washed too, just in case. I've had more than one creepy fan leave me a present in the sheets.

A few years ago, I rented a home in Incline Village, Nevada, which was gorgeous, situated on the lake with views to die for. Unfortunately, it also came with a creepy fan. I came home one day to find him naked in my bed with a pair of my panties. Thankfully, I was with Dave, and the guy didn't make a fuss. He stayed in the bedroom until the police came and arrested him.

Back then, I had a team of people looking out for me, but now, it's only me, and it is going to be a really long day. I'm going to wash a set of clothes, put them in the dryer, then have a shower and wash everything else.

In between loads, I'm going to make lunch for Dane. I'd planned to go to the shops and pick up some groceries, but now, I'm going to make do with what I've got, which is good. I haven't gone into Tourmaline yet, and I'm not sure I'm ready to meet the locals.

CHAPTER 29

KAT

It's been three hours since Dane left, and I've got chicken and vegetables in a pot simmering on the stove. My ma was a hell of a cook, but I'm more of a one-pot wonder. Being on the road all the time and without a lot of room in a tour bus, you learn to get creative with your cooking. Otherwise, it's restaurants or takeout, and it loses its appeal after a while.

I've only managed to accomplish three loads of washing with my fourth in the washer. I'm lost in thought while I fold clothes, so when the buzzer at the front gate sounds off, it startles me. It can't be Dane because he knows the code. I make my way toward the speaker when I hear a voice come through the intercom,

"This is Justice Leaverton for Kat Saunders. Hello? Is anyone there?"

He sounds annoyed, and I hit the button and say, "Hello, sorry, Ms. Saunders isn't seeing anyone. Please move along."

There's a pause, then, "Could you please ask Ms. Saunders to come to the intercom or open the gate so I might explain my business with her?" He's said my name as if it's offensive, and I have no idea who this man is.

I walk to my front door, but obviously not quick enough because the man's voice breaks over the speaker again, "For the love of all that's good and mighty, please ask her to come to the gate! I won't take no for an answer!" I'm out my front door and through the gates, headed toward the main one when I hear him yell into the intercom, "I only want a word with her! I've been trying for months! If you could just—"

He's really well dressed in a very nice dark gray suit, and he's driving a black Mercedes, but he looks stupid as he yells at my intercom. I'm on the other side of the wall looking at him through the glass of the door built into the wall, but he hasn't noticed me yet, so I clear my voice.

He stops, and his anger is evident. As he walks toward me, I'm glad he's on the other side of my wall. He must be six foot five, well built, early thirties, good-looking if you like the blond pretty boys.

"Can I help you, Mr.?"

"Justice Leaverton, my name is Justice Leaverton."

"How can I help you, Mr. Leaverton?" He reaches for the handle to the door in the wall, but it won't turn unless I buzz him in, and I have no intention of doing that.

He tries to turn the handle, but it doesn't budge. "May I come in, Ms. Saunders? I have matters of some urgency to discuss." He has brown eyes, and I can't help but think he'd make a great model. Perfect cheekbones, full lips, but there's something in his eyes, I'm just not sure what.

"Ms. Saunders?"

"Sorry, Mr. Leaverton, I don't see anyone. Not yet, anyway." I try to placate him with a smile, but he's looking down at me as though I've lied to him.

His face is a mask of contempt when he says, "I see, so the Savage Angels obviously don't count? They certainly aren't anyone in my books, either."

He smiles as he says this, and it's anything but friendly. I can't hide the look of shock as it goes across my face.

"I'm sorry?" I ask, perplexed.

"I've been trying to get a hold of you for months, and this morning, the whole town is talking about you hanging out with those bikers." He says the last word with a sneer and a look of disgust on his face.

"What, Mr. Leaverton, does that have to do with you?" I have my hands on my hips, my face a mask of anger. "Mr. Leaverton, I don't care what it is you think you need to discuss. Please move along, or I'll have you arrested."

I turn and am headed back to the house when he yells, "Wait! Please, wait! I apologize for my outburst. I'm a little frustrated at not being able to contact you first."

Turning back around, I look at him. He's got his hands on either side of the door, leaning on it, and he looks slightly defeated.

"Contact me first?"

I've stopped walking, and I'm facing him, but I haven't moved back toward the gate.

"Yes, Ms. Saunders, contacted you first. Before they could poison you against me." He stares at me now, and I must have a look of complete confusion on my face as he straightens up and says, "Fuck, they haven't mentioned me, have they?"

He's dropped his arms to his sides, and he looks as though he's made a mistake.

"No, Mr. Leaverton, they haven't mentioned you."

"Justice, please, call me Justice. I thought because of my previous run-ins with them, they might have spoken to you about me. I apologize, if I could come in and talk to you, to explain my—"

The low growl of a Harley sounds in the distance.

The engine gets louder, and Justice turns his attention to Dane as he comes into view. He pulls up in front of the Mercedes, punches in the code, and drives into my yard. He stops at the control panel and hits the button for the gate to close. Dane parks his bike, climbs off, and stalks directly to me.

"Is he bothering you, Kat?" Dane hasn't even looked in Leaverton's direction. His gaze doesn't deviate from me.

"No, Dane, I explained to Mr. Leaverton, I'm not seeing anyone at the moment."

He reaches for me, grabs my hand, and walks us toward the house.

"Reynolds! My business is with her, not you! Let her speak to me!"

At that, I stop and turn back around toward him. I can't believe this guy. Who does he think he is? Let her speak to me?

"Mr. Leaverton, it will be a cold fucking day in hell before I get permission from anyone to do anything. I have no idea who you are, and I really don't want to know. You're no one in my world, and I'd appreciate it if you moved on before I have you arrested." I turn back around and head toward my front door with Dane in tow.

When we get inside, he laughs.

"Dane, what's so funny, and who *was* that?" I ask, exasperated.

"That, darlin', is Justice Leaverton, but he's no one in your world." He laughs again, and I must look completely confused, so he grabs and kisses me then asks, "What smells so fucking good?"

"Lunch, and I know his name, Dane! But who is he?"

"Darlin', you made me lunch?"

He grins and tries to kiss me, but I smack his arm and yell, "Dane!" He grabs me, throws me over his shoulder, and takes me to my bedroom, where he throws me on the bed. "Dane! Will you stop! Who is he?"

He grabs both my ankles, pushes my legs apart, and pulls me down the bed so I straddle his standing frame.

"Dane!" But I laugh, so he knows he's won. "Stop!"

Dane puts his hand over my jean-clad crotch and rubs my sensitive core, then bends over me with one hand holding his weight on the bed. He leans down and rubs his chin along my neck.

I moan, and he stops what he's doing, stands up, and says, "Sorry, darlin', I'll stop."

He's smirking, has both his hands on his hips, and he has such a smug look on his face.

"If you stop now, I won't feed you, and you'll go hungry," I purr, my voice coming out breathy and full of lust.

"There are other things I can feed on," he growls

as he drops to his knees and pulls me toward his body. "And I intend to get fed."

CHAPTER 30

DANE

I sit at Kat's kitchen counter as she moves around the kitchen getting plates, knives, and forks out, and it hits me how easy this is. I've never done easy before—there's always been drama or baggage, but as I sit here and watch her, I understand this woman could fit into my life so easily. She gets along with my brothers, and she put Justice Leaverton in his place without any help from me. Kat is strong, financially independent, has a fucking fantastic body, and she's making me lunch.

"Earth to Dane, babe, you in there?" Kat stands there with the fridge open, holding up a beer with a huge smile on her face.

"Sorry, miles away. A beer would be good, darlin'." She walks toward me with her arm extended, holding it out to me. As soon as she's within reach, I pull her in between my legs and put my arms around her. "So, what did you think of Leaverton?"

She looks annoyed and pulls the side of her bottom lip into her mouth, and I have to kiss her. She looks so fucking cute. I pull an inch away from her, and her eyes are closed with her lips slightly parted.

Damn, she's so fucking hot.

"So, darlin', what did you think of Leaverton?" I repeat my question.

She opens her eyes and looks at me. "Who?"

I laugh and pull her closer, wrapping her snuggly in my arms. "Leaverton, the fuckwit who was at the gate when I got here."

Kat leans back from me and tilts her head to the side. "I'm not sure. He said he's been trying to talk to me for months. He also said something about talking to me before you poisoned me against him?"

"Your ma had dealings with the Leaverton family. I know they wanted to buy her business because of the land as they've just about bought up everyone else's land. She wouldn't sell, though. She employed thirty people on a full-time basis, and in the peak season, like Christmas, she'd get in another dozen or so casuals. To a small town like Tourmaline, it's a lifeline. If she had sold, and thank fuck she didn't, Leaverton would have had the land rezoned as residential and built exclusive homes. Unfortunately, for the people who live here, it would've meant they would have had to travel to the next town for work and eventually, they wouldn't be able to afford to live here, or they would move away to be closer to their work. Now, it's all fine for the folks who have money and will use their new home as a holiday house or for weekends only, but for the ones who have lived here all their lives, it would mean the town wouldn't be able to support them."

She nods her head and then asks, "How many businesses have held out? Please tell me my Ma wasn't the only one."

"No, darlin', there are still a few left, but if your ma had sold, they would have eventually, too. Did you read her will? Do you care she left me the business, 'cause if it's a problem, Kat, we could work something out."

"No, no, no." Kat places her hands on my chest and shakes her head. Fuck, she's cute. "I don't need a transport business. I didn't read her will, Dave handled all of it for me. I was a bit of a mess with my accident, my band, and my ma. All I wanted was this house, and she gave it to me."

"I'm glad you don't want it. Although, I do feel like we should give you something for it," I muse out loud. Again, she shakes her head. "Kat, she was your ma."

"Yes, she was, Dane, but as I said, I don't need a transport business, and I sure as hell don't need more money. I'd like to see it, and I would definitely like to see more of Tourmaline. If you really feel the need to pay me, though, I'm sure we could work something out…"

She smiles mischievously at me and chews her bottom lip. Her hands are working their way down my body.

"Darlin', are you making an indecent-fucking-proposal?" I grab her ass and pull her closer to me. "'Cause if you are, I'm so down for it."

Moving my hands to her face, I kiss her, and she makes the cutest little sound, but I pull away before the kiss becomes too heated. A man's got to eat, and if I'm going to keep up with her, I need sustenance. Her eyes are at half-mast, and desire is exuding out of her.

"Kat, I need food, man can't live on pussy alone. Although with you, I'm willing to try." I grin at her, and she slaps my chest and pushes out of my arms.

"Yes, babe, we need to keep your strength up! You have a lot to pay me for." She winks at me before she moves to the stove. It smells fucking fantastic. I open my beer and swivel around to watch her as she ladles her stew into bowls.

"What do you think Leaverton wants if I don't own the business or the land?" Kat asks me this as she puts a bowl down in front of me and sits next to me.

"I don't know. You really should read her will and make sure you have everything you need."

Kat shakes her head again, making a dismissive noise, and waves her hand around. "Dane, seriously, I know nothing about that kind of business, and I'm not interested."

"Darlin', the land alone is worth a small fortune," I say this as I take my first mouthful of her stew, and it's absolutely fucking delicious.

"Be careful of bones, I'm pretty sure I got them all out, but don't choke on me." She's looking at me, and she looks more than a little annoyed. "I don't need the land, the money, or the business. However, I do need a job. I have no idea what *kind* of job." Kat has drawn her brows together and stares at me.

"You know, I could use a hand in the office. Grinders Transport was left to me, and I pay the club a fee for doing the ride-alongs, but I have to look after the garage at the compound, and it belongs solely to the club. There are days when it all gets a bit too fucking much."

"I know nothing about transport companies or garages or anything. Hand me a guitar and a microphone, and I can rule the world, but without those things, who am I?" Kat appears so lost as she says this.

"You are a fucking amazing cook, and you're

fucking amazing in bed," I tell her. She smiles now and shakes her head, so I continue, "And you can do anything you set your mind to. I really need someone to answer the phones and take orders for pickups. A fucking monkey could do it."

"Well, thank you very-fucking-much." She smiles, so I know she's not pissed, but I tread carefully just the same.

Putting my hands up in a placating manner, I say, "Darlin', I didn't word that very fucking well, and I know you aren't stupid, but you would be doing me a solid if you could help me out until I get an office manager. I haven't put someone in because I was waiting to see what you wanted to do. I guess I thought because you hadn't contacted us, you wanted to take it further. I've been waiting for a lawyer or papers to turn up and for you to take what's yours. It hadn't crossed my mind you didn't know about us."

Kat looks down, chewing on her bottom lip. Anyone could see she's affected by this.

"I feel like I missed out on so much. Ma didn't tell me, but I never asked. We'd talk about where I was, what I was doing, who I was with, how the band was going, but apart from asking her about her garden, I was clueless."

"Your ma was a very proud person. She loved you, and she talked about you a lot. I don't know why she didn't mention us, Grinders Transport or tell you about Tourmaline. Maybe it was because she didn't want to worry you, or because she really wanted to know about you, only you."

She looks at me now with tears in her eyes, and she nods. I reach out to cup the back of her head and kiss her forehead.

I'm holding her close when I hear a beeping noise. "What is that?"

She lets out a big sigh. "My dryer is finished, and I can put another load of laundry in. My clothesline is full, and that's why the dryer is on."

I laugh, "So, you cleaned up your bedroom, and I didn't even notice."

Kat's expression tells me she's pissed now. "Make sure you thank Rebel for getting some clothes for me."

"Darlin', Rebel would do anything for you. He used to ask Ms. Saunders about you all the time."

She gets up to clear the plates away. Then she ladles the leftovers into plastic containers to freeze.

I have no idea why she's pissed. I guess it's because Rebel saw how untidy she can be.

CHAPTER 31

KAT

I'm tidying up the kitchen as Dane makes some business calls. I must admit it's nice to have a man in the house. It's a pity one of his men is a real fan. I didn't say anything to Dane, nor will I, as I don't want to cause any problems. I'm used to freaky fans, so I'll be sure to steer clear of Rebel in the future. Fans come with the fame, and Dane will learn that soon enough.

"Hey, darlin', I'm going to head back to town. Do you want to come with, or are you going to stay here?" he asks with a smile.

"Do you mind if I stay here?" I need some time alone.

"Fuck, no! Darlin', I've got work to do, and you'll only distract me," Dane says with a smirk on his face. He grabs me around the waist and kisses my neck. "Darlin', some of the boys might drop by. I want someone to have a look at your security system."

I frown and say, "Not today, babe, please?" I need to recharge my batteries.

"Okay, darlin', not today. But soon, yeah?" he asks me with a frown. I smile to reassure him.

"Do you want me to come to your home tonight, or are we going to stay here?" I ask as I trail my hand down his muscly torso.

He smiles and kisses me. "How about I come here? That way, I can get to know you in your own environment. See what you like, see what you don't like. Maybe put some of those changes into my home, so you'll be more comfortable there."

I can't believe the generosity of this man and how far he's willing to go to make this relationship work, and we've only just started.

"Dane, I'd like that. I can cook again, and it will just be the two of us." Then I let my hand go up under his shirt, making circles on his skin.

He grabs my hand and chuckles. "The two of us sounds good, darlin'. But I really need to go now. I have a lot of work to do." He moves my hand to his lips and kisses it, all the while, a smile tugs at his lips.

"Okay, okay, off you go. Is there anything you don't like to eat?" I ask as he puts my hand on his chest and holds it there.

"No, darlin'. I'll eat just about anything." He moves away from me and says, "I'll be about two or three hours. Is that cool?"

"Yeah, babe, that's cool. I'll prepare something that'll keep for a while. Spaghetti or a stew, something like that. Is that okay with you?" I ask a bit unsure.

"Darlin', after the chicken dish you made, I'm sure it will be good." He kisses me and heads for the door, but then stops and turns around with a smile on his face. "Looking forward to seeing you later."

Then he closes the door, and I'm left with the dilemma of deciding what to make us for dinner.

CHAPTER 32

JUSTICE

Fucking Dane Reynolds. It's more than obvious he's fucking Kat Saunders. Fuck, fuck, fuck! It has been bad enough having to deal with her mother and those heathens who took to her like fucking puppies, but it's the same story all over again.

The Savage Angels are a disgrace to Tourmaline. We should've run them out of town years ago. Now, they are trying to clean up their act and go on the straight and narrow. They're involved in all kinds of activities in the community. Fuck, they even sponsor the local basketball team, the Tourmaline Tigers. Dane-fucking-Reynolds has managed to pull them out of their illegal activities and set them on the road to redemption in the last five years.

But there are those of us who remember.

We don't forget so easily.

I've been trying to get Mrs. Saunders to sell me her property at the end of town for years. I even offered to move her to another location. Now, the fucking Savage Angels own it. However, all isn't lost. I own some land up on the ridge to the north of the town, and Ms. Saunders also owned a plot up there. I almost had it, all the old bat had to do was sign the papers. If I can get her fucking daughter to sell me that plot of land, I can still get the deal to go through for the housing development.

Tourmaline has been in my family for generations. People believe I want to destroy the town, but it's not true. I want to see Tourmaline change, grow, develop, and become a thriving community. I want to bring a better class of person to my town—a wealthier, better-educated community, where it's still safe to leave your doors open at night.

I've tried on more than one occasion to get the Savage Angels thrown out of town, and no, I haven't always followed the letter of the law. Fucking Ms. Saunders saw to it they didn't get the blame. I don't know how she found out about my plans, but I'm lucky it didn't blow back on me. God knows, if she'd wanted to, the whole town could've been told about what I'd done. I could've been arrested, or, worse, the Savage Angels could have been told, and then I'd find myself in a shallow grave somewhere.

It was the last time I tried to get those savages run out of town. I thought I had everything organized. I thought my plan was flawless.

Ms. Saunders was running more than cigarettes with those savages. I figured out how she was smuggling the guns, but, fuck me, they didn't know. How they could be so stupid and not know is beyond me.

I put two pounds of heroin in the back of one of her trucks, one in her office, and another pound in the compound of the Savage Angels' clubhouse. Wasn't easy getting the pound into the compound. I used one of the females who hangs around with them. I think her name is Stella, she's always with them. I have avoided her since, though. I think she's worried I'll tell them about her part in all this, but if I do it, I'm sealing my own fate as well. We have a mutually beneficial agreement to keep our mouths shut. If she rats me out, she's as good as dead too. They don't take kindly to traitors, especially when it's one of their own.

The sheriff of this town is a good man. He knows those bikers are trouble, always have been. Lately, they've been pumping money back into the town, trying to make themselves 'clean.' The sheriff agreed to run the raid on Ms. Saunders' and the club. Unfortunately, he didn't do it all at once. It might have worked if he had. Somehow, Ms. Saunders found out, so there must be a leak in the department. It's the only explanation as there was no other way they would've known.

I watched from across the street as the police went into Ms. Saunders' office at Grinders Transport. She came back out, looked straight at me and waved. I walked toward her, and she met me on the sidewalk.

"Justice, they aren't going to find what you left them."

"Ms. Saunders, I think you have me confused with someone—"

"Now, now, now, Justice. We both know what you've done, but it's not going to work. Don't worry, no one but me knows it's you." And she leaned closer to me, saying, "Not even the Savage Angels. You try this crap again, and those packages you left will end up in your house, in your car, and at the house of whomever you're fucking at the moment."

She rocked back on her heels, hands behind her back, and she looked so smug. She was five foot one and looked like your grandmother. I had no idea what she was capable of.

"Whomever I'm fucking at the moment?" I had my hands on my hips, and I towered over her. "You listen to me, you stupid, stupid woman, I want your land, and I want those bikers gone—"

She got up on her toes, leaning into me. "And I want there to be peace on earth and good will to all men, but it's not going to happen, so neither of us will get what we want. Tell me, Justice, did you handle any of the packages yourself, without gloves? Because I'm not that stupid." The look of shock and disbelief which went over my face must have made her fucking day. "I thought so. Now, I know you think you know what's best for this town, and I can see the benefit of having more people move here, but you can't have this." She motioned toward the front of her business. "My transport business is staying right where it is." She put her hands on her hips, took a step, and she looked angry. "I'll consider selling you my land on the ridge, but if you try this shit again or go after me or mine, I'll be visiting you in prison!"

I put my hands up in front of me. "All right, all right, maybe I went too far, but—"

"Maybe?! Maybe you went too far?! Who's the stupid one now, bitch?"

"You're a piece of work, you know that? This whole town thinks you're this sweet little old lady. Fuck, even those bikers think you are. Does anyone actually know who you fucking are?" I'd raised my voice, and she laughed.

"Justice, it's all about public perception. I protect what's mine, and the next time you buy smack off a dealer, maybe you should check who his friends are. Yes, Justice, I know a lot of people. I've been on this earth a long, long time. So, a

truce, then? We'll talk about my land, and you'll leave the Savage Angels and me alone. I have plans for them."

She was staring me straight in the eyes, her lips pulled back in a sneer, and, looking at her, I believed she was capable of anything. I had definitely underestimated this woman.

"You have plans for them?" Now it's my turn to laugh. "Lady, these aren't boy scouts you're dealing with, but if you are willing to sell me your land and overlook my... indiscretion, you won't have any further problems with me."

"No, I won't have any further problems from you, will I, Justice? Because if I do, we both know what will happen. I also want you to stop pestering the folks around here to sell their properties to you. You'll get what you want up on the ridge. Besides, you'll get more money for it, it has a great view." I was looking at her with disbelief. She's nothing like I thought she was, and I watched as she re-arranged her features and smiled at someone behind me, "Fith, what are you doing here?"

I turned around as one of those bikers came toward me.

"You okay, Ms. Saunders? Is he bothering you? 'Cause I can move him the fuck along if he is?" He made it a question, looking at me as though I was the scum of the earth.

"Fith! Language! And no, Justice and I were having a quiet conversation about the future of my town."

"Sorry, Ms. Saunders, it's hard to remember my manners with this fucker around. Why are you out here on the sidewalk anyway?"

She smiled at him and grabbed him by the arm. "Can you believe it, someone apparently thinks we're smuggling drugs interstate? The sheriff is doing his job and following up with a warrant and a search. He has one for the clubhouse, too." She turned back around, smiling at me. "Justice was saying that he thinks it's a stupid thing to do, weren't you, Justice?"

"Yes, ma'am, stupid to underestimate you, that's for sure. If you were going to do something like that, you'd have someone in the sheriff's office on your payroll to tip you off."

She laughed while Fith and I stared at her. "Oh, Justice, you make me sound like a criminal mastermind," she said the last words with hardness in her voice. She turned back around, grabbed Fith by the arm, and they walked toward the Grinders Transport office.

"Now, Fith, did the boys tell you I cleaned out the clubhouse yesterday? You wouldn't believe what I found in your room! You really need to keep it clean, it's not sanitary to keep it like that." She looked up at him, and he looked uncomfortable.

He glanced at me. "You didn't have to do that, Ms. Saunders, I can clean my own room."

"Nonsense, that's what friends do for each other." She turned back to look at me. "Until we meet again, Justice, you stay out of trouble." She smiled at me, but it never reached her eyes, and then she looked at Fith, moving him toward the office once more.

He kept looking very uncomfortable, and I got the feeling she'd found something else besides the drugs that I had planted in Reynolds' room. I remember wondering what was in Fith's room.

But all that was a long time ago, and now I'll never know. All I need right now is for Kat Saunders to sign over the land, so I can get construction started. If she's anything like her mother, she's probably going to screw me to the wall too.

CHAPTER 33

KAT

It's been two months of fun with Dane and his boys. They have welcomed me with open arms, and there's been no hero-worship of me at all. They treat me like a normal woman. Today, I've invited Jess for lunch. I'm at the grocery store in town buying coffee as I've had more than a few of the Savage Angels visiting, and they drink a lot of coffee. I stand in front of all the different brands trying to decide if I should buy the largest container when the ringing of my phone gets my attention.

"Hello, this is Kat."

"Hey, Kat! It's Jess, I'm standing at the front of your house. You wanna let me in?"

"Christ! I'm sorry, Jess! I'm at the grocery store in town. I can't very well invite you over for coffee if I don't have any."

"Oh, it's okay. I'll wait."

This girl is so damned sweet. Her personality bubbles up out of her, and you can't help but like her.

"No, no, no, let yourself in. The code is 15770. You'll need it to get through all the gates, and the spare key is under the third stone in the garden bed next to the front door."

"15770?"

"Yes, I know, I have to get it changed. Dane is arranging for a guy to come out." I giggle as I bend down and grab the largest container of coffee I can find. Jess laughs with me.

"It's a good thing you're getting it changed, 'cause, baby, that's way too easy!"

"Enough! Dane has been riding me on this! Anyway, let yourself in, get comfortable, and I'll be home soon."

"Okay. Is it all right if I listen to music until you get back?" Jess asks.

"Babe, listen to music, watch TV, drink hot water as there isn't any coffee, whatever!" I tell her with laughter in my voice.

Jess laughs, and I can hear as she punches in the code. "Okay, okay, thank you! See you soon!"

"Yeah, babe, you will. I need to pick up a few extra things while I'm here, so I might be thirty minutes, maybe an hour away. Is that cool?"

"It's cool, I'll keep myself occupied."

"Thanks, love, feel free to make yourself at home." I hang up and toss my phone into my bag.

I'm juggling coffee, milk, and a few other things and wishing I'd gotten a cart when I hear a voice behind me.

"Ms. Saunders, would you like a hand?" his voice is familiar, and as I turn around, I see it's Justice Leaverton.

"Mr. Mayor, how are you?" I ask him, and his eyes widen.

"Someone told you I'm the mayor?" He smirks, and then he reaches out to take some of my burden from me. "I'm fine, Ms. Saunders. How about we get you a cart?" He motions with his head toward the carts, and we walk toward them.

"Thank you, Justice, I appreciate the help."

"Justice? May I call you Kat?" he says with a smile. I'm reminded of how handsome he is. I bet most of the women in town are lusting after him.

"Kat is fine," I say with a grin.

When we reach the carts, he puts my groceries inside one. "We really got off to a bad start. I wanted to make a good impression on you. If you have the time, I'd like to discuss a business proposal with you. Your mother and I were about to go into business together before she died. I was hoping to continue with you?" He sounds a little desperate, and his eyes plead with me.

"Justice, I'm sorry, but I have someone waiting for me. Perhaps we could make an appointment and sit down and discuss this at a later time?" I really need to get home to Jess.

Justice sighs and says, "How do I arrange an appointment with you? Do I call the Savage Angels?"

I'm annoyed. "Mr. Leaverton, if you need to book an appointment with me, I suggest you ring me."

I push my cart away from him when he says, "I'm sorry, Kat. It's been a long morning, and I'm afraid I've taken it out on you. I need to sit down with you at your earliest convenience and discuss some land you own up on the ridge. Your mother was going to sell it to me, so I could continue on with my housing development project. Unfortunately, as it's taken this long to talk to you, a number of my investors have pulled out. I was hoping to sit down with you and discuss your possible investment in this venture."

His honesty takes me by surprise. "Okay, Justice, how about next week on Monday? We can sit down and go over things. I really do have to rush, I have a girlfriend waiting for me at home. I was supposed to be at home when she got there, and that was about half an hour ago," I explain to him.

Justice's smile gets bigger. "Thank you, Kat. You aren't going to regret listening to my proposal. I look forward to seeing you next week. Come to the

Town Hall, Monday, at say, ten?"

I nod in agreement and move away, but he grabs my elbow and holds out his hand. I immediately grasp his, and he shakes it vigorously.

"Goodbye, Justice. See you Monday."

A huge grin creases his face, he lets go of my hand, and I continue with my grocery shopping. But the longer I stay in the store, the larger my audience becomes. People are openly staring at me as I try to decide between which brand of milk I should choose.

When I finally decide, a woman grabs the same brand and says, "It's my favorite, too."

I smile at her and increase my pace, but now I have an entourage, and I know getting out of the market isn't going to be as easy as I originally thought.

CHAPTER 34

JESS

I can't believe I'm alone in Kat Saunders' house! I can't believe she likes me! The woman is famous, and she has left me alone in her house!

I make my way into her home, and I'm heading for the kitchen when I hear a noise coming from the back of the house. It's probably Dane, so I call out, "Hello, Dane, you here?"

Silence greets me, but I keep walking. Her house is enormous and beautiful. It has lots of windows across the back and exposed beams on the ceiling. The flooring is polished concrete in the bedroom wing with polished wood floors in the living areas. I'm pushing doors open and yell out to Dane when I feel something hard collide with the back of my head. The pain is staggering and brings me to my knees. I'm supporting myself with my hands when a pair of boots appear in my line of sight.

"You shouldn't be here. I'm waiting for her."

When I look up to see who looms over me, he punches me in the face. I scream, and then he grabs me by my hair and drags me into a bedroom.

"I'm waiting for her... but you'll do. You'll do fine."

His voice sounds devoid of emotion but is kind of familiar. I haven't seen his face yet. I kick and scream, and I try to get away when he lets go of my hair, picks me up, and throws me on the bed.

"Please, let me go! I won't tell! Please! Let me go!" I beg as blood and tears run down my face. My head hurts. I scramble up the bed. "Kat is coming home soon, she just called me. She'll be here any minute!"

He makes a noise, and I look at his face. It can't be him, it can't be! He smiles and undoes his belt.

"Sweetheart, I can be quick." I make a desperate dash for the door, but he grabs my head and slams it into the wall. Everything is going black when he says, "Oh, no, you filthy little slut, you need to be awake while we play. I want to hear you scream."

CHAPTER 35

KAT

It's been a long time since I've done any grocery shopping, and although the Savage Angels treat me like a regular person, the rest of the world still treats me like a freak show. It took forever to get out of the supermarket, and then the fucking press turned up. Seriously, who wants pictures of me shopping?

It's been nearly two hours since I spoke to Jess. She must think I've gotten lost. Of course, the press follows me home. I thought I'd be old news, but it would appear it's not the case.

I pull into my driveway, punch in the code, and drive into the garage. As I get out, I can hear the music from inside. Jess has it blaring.

I open my front door and head for the stereo to

turn it down.

"Jess, where the hell are you? Sorry I took so long, reporters and fans showed up, and I really needed to buy some groceries. Wanna help me bring them in? Jess?" I head down the hallway to my bedroom, still calling out for Jess when I see the door to one of the guest bedrooms is open. "Jess, are you in—" There's blood everywhere, and I see someone on the bed. I scream and back out of the room. The body on the bed is naked with a pillow over the face, but the rest of the body has been cut up. "Jess, where are you?" I scream and hurriedly back out of the room when two arms wrap around me.

Frightened, I kick and scream, and I try to twist in his arms when he says, "Darlin', Kat, it's me!" Dane, it's Dane, but I'm still trying to get out of his arms. "Kat, what's wrong? Calm down, what's the fuck—"

I pull out of his arms but fall to my hands and knees. I look up at him, but he doesn't look at me. He's staring at the bed.

"What the fuck? Kat, who's that? Jesus!" He looks down at me in shock and holds out his hand to lift me. "Kat, we need to get you out of here."

"Jess, we have to find Jess." I grab his hand, and he helps me to my feet. Then he grabs me by the shoulders and puts me in the hallway.

"Stay here. You see anyone, you scream as loud

as you can, and I'll be here. But I have to go back into that room and see who it is, okay?" He looks intently at me. "Darlin', nod, so I know you get me."

I do as he says then he turns around and goes back into the room. He's only gone for a few seconds, and when he appears back in the doorway, his face is blanched and his mouth tight. He reaches into his pocket and puts his phone to his ear.

"Dirt, I need you to get a few of the boys together and clear the reporters away from the front of Kat's house. Move them down about one hundred yards. Then I need you to come and stay with Kat outside and do not, I repeat, do not enter the fucking house, and for fuck's sake, keep Luke away from all of this." He staring at me and I realize I'm shaking. He shakes his head and talks again. "No time, brother. I'm going to head to the sheriff's as soon as you get here. I'll need you to take care of Kat. No reporters." He hangs up the phone, grabs me by my bicep, and quickly pulls me toward my bedroom.

"Darlin', I need you to grab a jacket. Don't touch anything you don't need to."

"Is, is, that Jess?" I whisper, and I don't know why.

"Kat, jacket, okay?"

I walk into my closet, and it's been trashed again with clothes thrown everywhere.

"Dane, I didn't leave it like this. It wasn't like this."

I turn around, and my whole room looks like a tornado went through it. He grabs my face in his hands and rubs his thumbs across my cheeks,

"Kat, look me in the eyes. It's okay. Forget the jacket, you can have mine. Let's get you outside."

Dane takes my hand and pulls me through the house when I hear the sound of several bikes. We go through the front door and out into the sunshine, and Dane takes off his jacket and puts it around my shoulders.

"Don't go back inside. Dirt is going to look after you as soon as he clears the reporters away from your gate. I'm going to see the sheriff, make sure this doesn't get blasted all over the radio." He bends down, knees bent, trying to be at my eye level with his hands on the tops of my shoulders. "Everything's going to be all right, but I need you to stay outside. Do you get me, darlin'?"

I must respond because Dane straightens, his posture towering over me, concern and anger written all over his face. Dirt comes through the gate, and Dane pulls me into his side. Dirt gets off his bike and hurries toward us.

"Brother, what the fuck? Got the boys to clear them like you asked, but seriously, what the fuck?" Dirt stares at me and then looks at Dane, runs his hand through his hair, and then folds his arms on his chest. "Jesus, brother, who is it? How bad?" Dirt stares at Dane as he says this, then Judge drives through the gate.

As Judge makes his way toward us, Dane motions Dirt to stay, and he walks me toward Judge.

"Judge, need you to look after Kat for a minute while I talk to Dirt, yeah?"

Judge nods his head in understanding, "Yeah, Prez, of course. Come here, sugar, those colors look good on you." He winks at me and moves me further away from the house.

I can see Dane and Dirt talking, and Judge is trying to get me to speak to him, but I feel overwhelmed. Is that bloody mess in my home really Jess? Sweet Jess, who did her best to make everyone laugh? If only I'd been home earlier, if only I'd gone shopping earlier in the week, she might still be alive.

Dane and Dirt stand in front of me. Dane has my face in his hands and says, "Get out of your head, Kat. You didn't do this. This is some sick fucker who's probably looking for you. This is on him, not you."

I shake my head violently from side to side. Dane pulls me into his crushing embrace. I feel safe, protected, and loved.

"Darlin', this isn't your fault." His voice is rough. "Jess wouldn't have blamed you, either. She'd be mad as fucking hell if you were doing that to yourself." Nothing is said for a few minutes, but then he pushes away from me. "Kat, I'm going to leave you here now with Dirt. Judge and I are headed into town."

I nod.

"Prez, you'll need your cut," Dirt reminds me.

"No, brother, I don't. I want everyone to know she's mine and she's protected by us. I'll get it when I get back."

He says all this while holding my gaze, and I can't help but think something deeper has happened. Dirt grabs me by the shoulders and turns me toward the bench seat in my garden.

CHAPTER 36

DANE

I've seen some fucked-up shit in my day, but what was done to that girl, Jess, is brutal. She had stab wounds, scratches, slices, and parts missing. Whoever did this is one fucked-up motherfucker. I only hope the sheriff doesn't think it's me.

The ride into town doesn't take long. The sheriff, Carlos Morales, doesn't like the Savage Angels. His predecessor was on the payroll, but Morales made it clear from the beginning he wasn't interested. He appears to be a good and fair sheriff, but we'd all breathe a lot easier if he cooperated with us.

There are twelve deputies, and more than a few of them are on our payroll, but Morales has slowly been weeding them out. We've had to get smarter about what we get them to do and how we pay them.

I get off my bike, and Judge approaches me. "Dane, do we need to call Jonas back? Don't you think the VP should be here while all this shit goes down?"

"Brother, he's with some of our southern counterparts trying to sort out a deal. He's needed there, but if they arrest me, we'll need to call him back."

Jonas hasn't been the same since Ray, who was our previous VP, got killed. I sent him to look after the southern chapters to broker a deal to help him get some perspective. He's my closest friend, but he needed the space.

I walk into the sheriff's office and glance around the room. It looks like every other law enforcement office I've ever been in—the same boring color scheme, the same layout with the desk at the front, sheriff's office at the back, and cells to the left and the back of the building.

Officer Barrett is at the desk, and he's on the payroll.

"Barrett, is the sheriff in?" I ask him, and he looks up at me, smiles, and shakes my hand. We've known each other for years.

"Dane, man, how're you doin'? Yeah, the sheriff's in his office, you want me to get him?"

"That'd be good. Tell him it's important."

He steps out from behind his desk and

disappears down a hallway which angles toward the back of the building. A few minutes later, I see Morales emerge and make his way to Judge and me.

"Brother, I don't know why you don't let me get something on this guy. It would make this type of thing go a lot fucking smoother," Judge mutters behind me.

He's right, I know it's the smart thing to do, but if we're trying to clean up our act, having a clean sheriff on our side might prove useful.

"Reynolds, what can I do for you?" Morales is your typical-looking Latino with short, dark hair that's parted on the side, is easily six foot one, and he's lean but built.

"Sheriff, I have a situation. Can we speak privately?"

He opens the gate and gestures me to follow him to his office, and Judge follows me through.

Once inside, he goes around his desk and sits downs. "Pull up a chair, tell me what you need."

"You know Kat Saunders has moved into her ma's house?"

Morales smiles. "Heard she's moved on a few things since she's been here." He has his eyebrows raised and looks at me as though we're both in on a private joke.

I ignore his comment. "There's been a murder at her home. It's one of the girls who hangs with us, Jess... I don't know her last name. She's been cut up real bad. I came here to tell you face to face to minimize the fucking press. My boys have moved those vultures further down the road and are only letting people who live there through."

Morales gets out of his chair, opens his top drawer, and grabs his gun. Then he turns around to get his hat. "Did you or any of your members do this?" Morales growls at us.

"No, I didn't fucking do this! And as far as the Savage Angels go, I don't know, but if they were fucking involved, and it's not fucking likely, I'll find out. I came here for Kat. I came here to try to make this go easier on her."

"Well, aren't you the regular knight in shining armor? What's your angle on this?"

Now I'm mad. "Angle? There isn't a fucking angle. I care about this woman, and I cared about her ma, you know that. I want this to run as fucking smoothly as possible. My boys have been told not to go into the house and to fucking wait for you."

Morales comes right up to me, chest to chest, but I'm taller, so I'm looking down on the fucker.

He leans in and says, "If I find out you've had anything to do with this, I won't hold back, get me? Now, has anyone been in the house?"

"Kat found the body, but I went in to see who it is. I didn't touch anything. That's it, and, Sheriff, I fucking get you." I lean down into him as I say it, practically spitting on him.

"I'll need you and your man..." he gestures to Judge, "... to stay here. My deputies and I will go and get Ms. Saunders' statement and bring her back here. She'll need somewhere else to stay tonight, or at least until we can get the scene processed. Can you see to it for me?" He might not like me very much, but he's good at his job.

"Yes, Sheriff, I can do that. What about my boys guarding the road? What would you like me to do about them?"

"For now, could we please utilize them to keep the press at bay? That's a good idea." He wipes his hand over his face. "This will be my show, Reynolds, are we clear?"

"Wouldn't have it any other way."

"Good. What a fucking mess. This is going to go national. Hell, probably international. I'm going to have to call in the State Troopers to handle the press." He walks toward the front desk. "Barrett, you need to call the coroner and the CSI team from Pearl County and have them meet us at the Saunders' place. Don't make any comments to reporters and advise everyone else to do the same. I'll not have this turning into a circus."

Barrett looks at his boss, then back at me. "Is everything okay?"

"No, Barrett, everything isn't okay. Murder at the Saunders' place." Morales is looking at Barrett as if he's under suspicion.

"Billy and I go way back, Sheriff. We've known each other practically all our lives."

I don't need another deputy getting fired from this station.

He nods. "Good, you'll have plenty to talk about then. Barrett, help your friends here to a desk and take their statements. They're not to leave this building."

Morales stops and looks at me, shakes his head, and makes his way out of the building.

"Dane, man, what the fuck is going on?" Deputy Barrett looks confused, and from the last look the sheriff gave me, I don't think he'll have a job for much longer.

"Fuck, if I know, Billy. Where do you want us to sit?"

CHAPTER 37

KAT

I'm pacing across my lawn when the police get here. There are three cruisers, and I cringe inwardly. This will be a complete media circus. I glance at Dirt, and he lets the officers in through the gates. A lanky man in a uniform gets out of one of the cars and heads toward me.

"Ms. Saunders?"

"Yes." This one word is so hard to choke out, it's only a whisper.

"I'm Sheriff Carlos Morales. Dane Reynolds is at my station giving a statement. We'll take you to him shortly, but before we do, can you tell me what happened here?" He has a kind face and a soothing voice.

"I was supposed to be home to meet Jess for

coffee and girl talk." Tears streak down my cheeks, and I fall to my knees. "But I didn't have any coffee." Hysterical laughter bubbles up out of my throat, and the sheriff drops down into a crouching position in front of me. "Who invites someone over for coffee and doesn't have any?"

"Ma'am, you're in shock. Let's get you into my cruiser, we can talk more there." He helps me to my feet and guides me over to it. "Now, Kat, can I call you Kat?" I nod and look him in the eyes. "Okay, Kat, what time were you supposed to be home?"

"I was meant to meet Jess at twelve for coffee, but I got stuck in town. I don't normally go grocery shopping, and she called me when I wasn't here. I told her to let herself in and I'd only be about thirty minutes, but with all the press and I was messing about... I don't get to do normal stuff very often."

He gets in the back of his cruiser with me. "Normal stuff?"

"Yes, normal stuff like grocery shopping or walking around town without a group of bodyguards." I'm staring at my nails. I can't make eye contact, this is all my fault. "It took me about two hours to get home."

I can feel him stare at me. "Kat, this isn't your fault." I glance at him, but he's not staring at me, so I follow his gaze to see a deputy throwing up in my garden bed. "I have to leave you for a minute, I need to talk to my deputies. Will you be all right?" I nod, and he leaves me alone in the cruiser.

The vehicle bounces slightly as the sheriff climbs out. I watch as he talks to one of his officers. When Dirt enters the conversation, I freeze. There's lots of hand gesturing, and the sheriff disappears into my house. Dirt stands for a moment, then turns on his heel and heads my way.

Dirt opens the door and peers inside. "Kat, I'm going to take you down to the station on my bike. You cool with that? They want to ask you a few more questions."

"Thanks, Dirt, I need to see Dane."

"Yeah, babe, you and me both."

Getting out of the cruiser, I make my way toward Dirt's bike.

"Do you think she went quickly?" I stare at his profile, waiting for an answer. He looks at the ground and shakes his head.

"From what the deputies said, she put up one hell of a fight. They think she got a piece of her attacker in her teeth and under her fingernails. If he's in the system, they'll get this fucker." My eyes brim with tears which threaten to fall. Dirt stares at me with concern in his eyes and says, "Your tears won't bring her back. You need to be strong right now, and we need to get you to Dane."

As we make our way back into town, the reporters follow us, and by the time we make it to the station, there's a frenzy of flashes and clamoring.

Dane comes out of the station and tucks me under one arm, quickly taking me inside, amid the reporters yelling questions.

Once inside, he moves me to a chair and sits on the desk in front of me. "You okay, darlin'?"

"No, not really." I look down at my hands. "Dane, I know you said you'd take care of me, but my manager, Dave, will know how to handle the reporters."

"Darlin', I know you've had a scare. Fuck, everyone is going to be shaken, but what the fuck can Dave do, that I can't?"

I can tell from his tone, he's pissed. Dave has been handling me since I was twelve years old. There's nothing he doesn't know and nothing he can't fix.

"Dave can call an international press conference and get all the reporters out of town. He can get my home cleaned up as if nothing happened. Dave can get things done." I'm staring at his handsome face, and he scowls at me. "Babe, please, let me call Dave and let him handle this mess. Your club is about to be inundated with reporters, and Dave can spin it, so you guys are the good guys instead of reporters making shit up, 'cause babe, that's their business."

I grab both his hands as I say this, and although he doesn't look happy, he relinquishes his control and nods his head in agreement.

"Okay, darlin', call Dave. Until we find this fucker, I want you at my home, under my roof, in my fucking bed. Do you get me?" He pulls me to my feet, and I'm standing between his legs.

"Yes, babe, I get you."

Dane smiles at me, pulls me into his embrace, and kisses the top of my head.

"Good. Have you spoken to Sheriff Morales?" he asks.

"Yes, but only briefly. I was told to come back here and give a statement. It should've been me. I was supposed to be at home, but I'd run out of coffee, then I got caught up in town..." I babble.

"Get out of your head, darlin', no good thinking about what you could've done. Hell, if you'd been home, for all we know, you could be fucking dead now, too."

"I was just getting to know her." I sigh and look around. "Does Luke know?"

"Yes, got a couple of the boys with him. He really cared about Jess. They should leave him alone with the fucker who did this, and vengeance would be paid tenfold."

"Has anything like this ever happened in Tourmaline before?"

As much as I don't want this to be the work of a mad killer, I don't want to believe a young girl lost her life because of me. No, I don't want it to be true. Freaky fans are part and parcel of being famous, but to think one of them is capable of this? Please, God, no.

"No, darlin', we haven't had a murder in Tourmaline for nearly five years. The last one was a domestic dispute which went really fucking wrong."

Suddenly, the doors to the sheriff's office fly open, and a dozen reporters are flashing away with their cameras, yelling out questions.

I move out of Dane's arms and walk toward them, anger bubbling up out of me.

"Enough! A beautiful, wonderful girl has lost her life! Can you please all wait outside!"

"Kat, is it true she was raped and murdered in your bed?"

Fucking bloodsucking leeches.

I straighten my spine at the vile reporter with a look of contempt on my face.

"This is an ongoing police investigation. I haven't even given my formal statement yet. I will say, a body of a young girl was found in the guest bedroom of my home." I pause and look around the room. "I'll not confirm the girl's name until I know her family has been notified, and I'd appreciate it if you all would do the same."

"Kat, is it true you're dating the president of the Savage Angels, and this could be a revenge killing from a rival gang?"

I stare at the leech in disgust and reiterate my point. "As I have already stated, this is an ongoing investigation, and I don't want to speculate about the particulars of the situation. But I will say this, yes, I'm seeing Dane Reynolds, president of the Savage Angels. Now please get out before you get thrown out!"

CHAPTER 38

DANE

I'm so fucking impressed. This woman, who has had her world shaken, has fucking stood up and told the reporters to fuck off. She did it with style and grace. You can tell she's used to being in the spotlight.

The pride I feel at her standing up and speaking out, words can't describe it. She announced to the world she's mine. That word, 'mine,' has been floating around in my head a lot lately. I've never sought out a special female. I've had girlfriends, yeah, but nothing too serious. I have never felt the need to settle for one. But standing here, staring at her as she speaks to the vultures who want to be the first to get the story, I want to protect her, keep her safe and away from prying eyes. I also want to bend her over and fuck her as soon as we're alone. *Mine.*

The reporters all filter out of the room. Kat turns around and sighs before she looks at me.

"That should do it. Dave is so much better at this than me." Her eyes plead with me, and I know if I say no, she'll do it anyway.

"Call him, darlin'. Do it now. Then you can give your statement to Deputy Barrett, and I can get you home, safe." I pull her back into my arms, my hands resting on her waist.

She leans into me, not breaking eye contact. "Thank you, baby."

Then she moves out of my arms and makes her way to another desk with a phone and dials. I look around at the men in the room—Dirt, Judge, and Deputy Billy Barrett—and they all have their eyes on her ass. I stand up, all eyes, except Judge's, come to me.

I clear my throat, and eventually, Judge drags his gaze to mine, and the fucker is smiling.

"She's calling her manager," I tell them. "Hopefully, he can come and make this fucking circus disappear. In the meantime, we need her to give a statement, then move her into my home or here in town at the compound. Fuck, which one is the best place to keep her protected?" I know the compound will be easier, but it's not exactly lush accommodations.

"She'll be more comfortable at your home, Prez,

but the compound would be easier." Dirt stares at Kat as he speaks, then moves his eyes to me. "If we have twenty of the boys in and around your home, and as long as she stays in the fucking house, she'll be safe. It's probably easier with the reporters, too. We can block the road and keep the fuckers out. You can't do it here in town."

I nod, and I raise my eyebrows to Judge. "Thoughts?"

The fucker is still smiling. "Dirt is right, the compound would be easier, but your home is in the fucking wilderness, and if we can block the road, we'll be fine," Judge says the last part, staring at Billy.

"Dane, I can't make that decision, but I'm sure the sheriff will be on board. He won't want a bunch of outsiders in town making his life difficult." Billy stands near the gate to the front of the building. He grabs a pen from one of the desks and a clipboard with some paper on it. "I should get her statement now. I'll need to take Ms. Saunders into one of the interrogation rooms where it's quiet. Will you be okay out here by yourselves?"

"I'll come with, but why an interrogation room?" I stand and walk toward Billy.

"Ahh, sorry, Dane, you can't be in the room. It has to be her account of the events. We talk to everyone in there as the sheriff has had cameras installed, so there's no confusion if the witness changes his mind or a suspect says we manipulated a confession out of him."

"How long have the cameras been in there?" I ask as Kat moves back toward me.

"Sheriff had them installed a while ago but didn't tell anyone until we had a problem with a case that went south. Guess he's checking up on all of us." Billy looks annoyed. He moves toward Kat, grabs her by the elbow, and motions with his clipboard that she should come with him.

"Dane?" She stands next to me and has her hand on my chest.

"It's all right, darlin', Deputy Barrett, Billy, has a few questions for you. I'll be here if you need me." I touch my forehead to hers. "You'll be fine." I kiss her forehead, and she moves away from me, following Billy into the hallway.

"Dirt, can you organize the extra protection at home? Judge, could you set up a blockade on the road? I'll get Rebel to sweep the house, make sure no one has put bugs in it, and make sure there's no fucking intruders." My boys nod in understanding and make their way out of the bullpen.

"Will do, Prez," Dirt says.

Judge stops and looks at me. "The road will be easy. I think we'll only need four guys on it, maybe, for safety's sake, six. Won't be hard to stop traffic going in or out. Hell, we know everyone in town, and something tells me this is an outsider, not one of our own."

I nod, and Dirt stares at Judge. "You're fucking right there, brother, no fucking way this is local." Dirt opens the front door and heads out into the mass of reporters and flashing cameras.

Judge pauses and stares at me. "I'll stop at the compound and send some of the boys to move these fuckers back and to escort you home. Do you want your car?"

"Yeah, man, it'll be easier for Kat. Just in case those fuckers out there get too close," I say in a gruff voice. He nods and heads through the door only to stop again.

"The sheriff?" asks Judge.

"What about him?"

"He told us to stay put."

"Leave him to me. I'll explain to Billy we needed to get Kat out of here. The sheriff should understand."

"He's not known for being *very* understanding where we're concerned."

He's right, but this time the sheriff is going to have to cut us some slack.

CHAPTER 39

KAT

Thankfully, the deputy makes it quick and easy for me to give my statement, and now I'm in Dane's car, and we're headed home. Before we got in the truck, Dane slipped his cut over my shoulders. It's miles too big for me, but I feel a little less stressed wearing it and breathing in his scent.

Calling Dave isn't so easy, however. I only managed to get a hold of one of his personal assistants. He has three, and the one I got is low on his totem pole. I know she'll call him, and I can only hope, wherever he is, he'll decide to come help me.

I have my phone in my hand, and I'm thinking about calling Truth from my band. But I don't want them swept up in another scandal I've created.

"Darlin', unless you have mystical fucking

powers, the phone can't dial itself. What gives?" Dane's voice pulls me out of my musings. He grabs my hand and studies me for a moment before returning his eyes to the road.

"I think I need to call my band. Well, only Truth. I'm worried about them."

"So, call him. It's not your fault someone killed Jess in your home." He runs his thumb over my knuckles.

"Okay, I will, but is it okay if I call when we get to your house? So I can have some privacy?"

He scowls and takes his eyes from the road. "Do you need privacy from me, darlin'? We're in this together. I thought we were on the same page."

"I'm not used to having someone to share the load, Dane. I'm sorry. Yes, we're in this together, and no, I don't need privacy from you." I can't believe I mean what I'm saying. I feel like I've known him forever.

The rest of the drive is done in silence, and as we pull into the courtyard in front of the house, I'm surprised to see at least a dozen bikes out front. We also had an escort from the sheriff's office. The Savage Angels really do protect their own.

Dane opens his door and looks at me. "Stay here, Kat. Need to make sure the boys did a search of the house and it's all clear." Then, he gets out and shuts the door.

Dirt meets him halfway across the courtyard,

and they both stare at me while they speak, but as I'm still inside the truck, I have no idea what they are saying.

Dane moves toward my side of the truck and opens the door.

"Everything's clear, Kat, not one cocksucker to be found." Dane smiles, but it doesn't reach his eyes. He extends his hand, and I grab it, jumping down from the truck.

"I knew you'd keep me safe." I throw myself into his arms. He's not expecting it and rocks back a step.

"Jesus-fucking-Christ, Kat." He laughs.

"What, baby? You'll catch me if I fall." Dane swings me around, and we move toward the house.

"Of course, I will, but a little warning next time would be nice," Dane scolds me.

"What type of warning? A special code?" I tease. "I know, I'll say 'savage' and throw myself at you." I laugh, feeling a little light-hearted despite what's happened.

"Savage, it is, darlin'. Works for me."

"Glad to see you two are laughing. The house has been swept, and we have the road blocked. No one is getting in or fucking out without our knowing about it," says Dirt as he walks toward us.

Dane raises his hand, and Dirt claps it. "Thank you, brother."

They shake, and Dirt looks at me. "Do you cook,

Kat, 'cause I'm fucking starving."

I laugh, "Yes, I do. Let's go see what temptations await us in the culinary delights of Dane's kitchen!"

"The culinary delights of my kitchen, what the fuck, Kat?" Dane laughs as we go inside. Dirt follows on the heels of his president.

Bear appears in the kitchen and barrels past Dane to engulf me in a hug. "Are you all right? Can I get you anything? Have you eaten?" His questions are coming out hard and fast, and he's practically squeezing me to death.

"Bear, stop! You'll crush her," Dane says, but there's humor in his voice.

Bear lets me go and holds me at arm's length. "Sorry, Kat, I'm sorry. You okay?" He's looking at me with concern.

"Yes, Bear, I'm okay. I wasn't the one hurt." Tears well up in my eyes.

"Do we know who did this?" Bear's voice is angry as he looks at Dane and Dirt.

"No, brother. Whoever did it didn't hang around." Dane's tone conveys just how upset he is.

"Do we think they were after Kat? Do we think they're still here? Do we have any idea as to who it could be?" Bear is firing out his questions and getting louder with each one.

"Brother, settle. Kat has had a fright. We've lost a member of our family. Right now, we need to get fed and take stock of our situation. Can you help with that?" Dane asks in an authoritative tone.

Bear nods, pulls me into another embrace, then stalks out of the house.

"I think he likes you," states Dirt, and he laughs.

"Is he normally like that?" I ask.

Dane shakes his head. "No, Kat, I've never seen him behave like that before. He must really like you."

Dane smirks and looks at Dirt. "It's not his normal behavior. He's loyal to the MC, and you, Kat, have become part of that. Wearing the Prez's cut proves it."

I nod and head for the fridge. I'm hungry, and so are they.

As it turned out, Dane didn't have a hell of a lot in his kitchen except for bread and frozen steak, so steak sandwiches it was. He and Dirt didn't seem to mind, though. In fact, they had two each, but it was over an hour ago, and now I sit on Dane's couch with my phone in my hand. He sits next to me as I ring Truth.

Truth picks up on the fifth ring. "If it isn't the Queen of Rock. I knew you'd call me sooner or later,

Kat, but to be honest, I thought it would be sooner. Like before they found a dead body in your bedroom?"

"Fuck me, sorry, Truth. I guess it's news everywhere, yeah?"

"Yes, my Goddess of Rock. It. Is. Everywhere." Truth emphasizes each word as he speaks.

"I'm sorry, I've been..." I begin to say, but he cuts me off.

"What the fuck are you apologizing for? Whatever the fuck happened isn't your fault!" Truth yells now, and I've taken the phone away from my ear because he's so loud.

Dane takes it out of my hands. "Truth? This is Dane. You need to calm the fuck down, yeah? You're freaking my girl out, and I can't have that."

I'm dumbfounded he's taken the phone from me, and I stare at him with my mouth open in shock.

Dane says, "Yeah, she tried to call Dave, she's waiting for him to call back." He nods into the phone, eyes glued to me. "I think it would be best. Kat could use some friends around her right now." He reaches out, touching my face. "No, you'll all stay here, my house is big enough, and it's well-fucking-protected." He lets his hand drop and continues, "Cool, man, see you then." Then, he hangs up.

I stare at him. "Darlin', before you get angry at me, let me tell you something. We're a team. I'll not have you upset, and it's my fucking responsibility to keep you safe in every way." He drags me onto his lap, but I'm still not happy, and he can tell. "Your band and Dave are on their way. They should all be here tomorrow."

I can't help but feel relieved knowing those I love are on their way to me, but Dane needs to know I can take care of myself.

"I wasn't upset, you know. Truth is being overly dramatic. It's his way." I pout at him and fold my arms across my chest. "If I need you, Dane, I'll ask you for help."

"That's right, you'll yell savage, won't you?" He smiles at me, and I can't help but give in and smile back.

"Yeah, that's right, savage. So, no helping until I yell, got it?" He raises his hands as if to give up.

He looks at me for a few seconds, and then leans in and kisses me thoroughly. I feel it to my core. I can feel him get hard beneath me, and I straddle him and grind into him. My sex throbs, and I need him inside of me.

"Darlin', as much as I'd like to fuck you right now, there are too many people in my house, so we'll have to go upstairs to my bedroom unless you want an audience?"

Is this a challenge? Does he think I won't fuck him with people in his house? I grind into him again and remove my top and undo my bra.

"Fuck me, baby, do it now and make it hard and

fast. It'll be good, baby, promise," I purr as I kiss his neck and undo his jeans.

Then Rebel opens a door and walks into the room. "Hey, Prez, do you need me to—"

He stops mid-sentence and doesn't look happy. I laugh, but Dane looks seriously pissed.

"Rebel, man, can you give me a minute and keep everyone out, yeah?" Dane growls out his order and keeps me pressed up against his body.

I laugh, but when Dane puts me to one side, gets up, and throws my top at me, I immediately stop.

"Fucking hell, Kat! If I wanted to treat you like the whores who hang around with some of the MC, I'd fuck you at the compound! Get dressed, and I'll see you upstairs."

I'm completely shocked. He. Is. Pissed. He waits until I've got my bra and top back on before he leaves the room. Now, what am I supposed to do? I can't go home, but after his explosion, I can't stay here.

I open one of the French doors which lead to the front porch and come face to face with Bear.

"You supposed to be out here, Kat?" Bear grins at me and looks around.

"Just needed some fresh air. How are you, Bear?"

"Pretty sure Dirt said you were to stay inside..." He looks at me quizzically, ignoring my question.

"Surely, I'm safe with you out here, and you didn't answer my question. How are you?" I smile and try to get him to talk to me. There's no way I can handle seeing Dane at the moment. I need some time to sort out what happened.

"I'm good, good." Bear's big beardy head bobs up and down. "But I'm dying to take a leak." I burst out laughing.

"Well, go. Don't let me stop you."

Bear shakes his head from side to side. "I'm the only one out here. There are some brothers up on the road, but I'm the only one here at the front of the house."

"Bear, how is anyone going to get me if you lot have the roads blocked, have swept the house, and there are a ton of you inside, huh? Go, I'm not going anywhere."

He looks down at me. "I know you're right, but…" He sighs and is doing the pee-pee dance, but I'm sure he isn't even aware of it.

"For the love of all that's good and wonderful, *go*!" Then I walk behind him and give him a shove.

Bear nods and makes a move to the door. "You stay right here, okay? No wandering about!"

"No, no, I'll be out here for a bit, and then I'm headed upstairs with Dane."

"Good, and thanks, Kat."

He almost runs inside, well, as much as a big guy can run.

Finally, I'm alone, and I go to sit on the stairs leading into the front entrance of the house. My life has been one hell of a rollercoaster. I can't believe someone killed Jess in my home, and I'm not sure what just happened with Dane. Standing up, I walk across the courtyard, past the garages, and see the path which leads back to my home.

"Fuck it, I could use the exercise," I mutter to myself. I look around to see if I'm being guarded. Seeing no one, I walk toward my home.

CHAPTER 40

DANE

There's no way I'm going to have sex with my girl when the guys are just outside the door, able to hear everything. Kat isn't a skank you take to a meet-and-share with everyone. She's mine, no one else's. I'm not going to share her.

I stand in the kitchen and glare at Rebel. Doesn't he know how to knock? Fuck! Not his fault he walked in. I was going to let Kat take it a little further before taking her upstairs. I know I've overreacted with her, but what the fuck was she thinking?

"Reb, man, what the fuck is up?" I growl. I'm taller than him and have more bulk. He's still a big guy, and with his shaved head, he can look mean, but he's no match for me.

"Prez, I was only coming to ask if you wanted me to go and get any of Kat's clothes for her." He's moving from foot to foot, and his hands are clenched into fists. "I didn't mean to walk in on you."

Rebel stares at me, anger blazing in his eyes. He really looks pissed. There are a few brothers on the back deck looking in. I see Fith make a move toward us.

"Sorry, Reb, it's not your fault. I'm annoyed Kat is in this fucking situation." He stops moving from side to side. "I let things go a little too far in there just now, but it's not your fault, brother. That one is on me."

Rebel takes a step back. "You let things go a little too far? You fucking think?" His eyes widen, and his voice rises to a decibel I've never heard come from him.

"What the fuck, man? I don't owe you a fucking explanation for fucking anything." I take a few steps toward him, my voice remaining in a low tone, but I can feel the rumble of a growl deep in my chest.

Fith opens the sliding door to the back deck.

"Prez, everything okay in here?" He quickly glances from me to Rebel. He looks confused, but the man is my soldier and always has my back. He moves closer to me in a defensive manner. If shit goes down, Fith will be quick to act.

Rebel looks between Fith and me. "Yeah, Fith, everything is fucking fine. I guess I'm a little stressed out with what happened to Jess. I'm not thinking straight." He directs his stare at me.

I walk over to him and clap him on the shoulder. "All good, man, all good. Sorry if I took your head off. I'm sure Kat would appreciate it if you went to her house and got her something to wear. Could you get her a jacket, too? In case we go for a ride." I have no idea what has gotten into him.

All the tension seems to seep out of Rebel, and he smiles at me. "Yeah, Prez, I can do it for her." Rebel turns and heads for the front door.

"What the fuck was that all about?" Fith asks, his features contorting in confusion. He watches Rebel intently as he disappears down the hall.

"I fucking overreacted when Rebel walked in on Kat and me in the living room."

Fith stares at me, a knowing smile forming on his lips. "Well, fuck me, if I'd known you were up to something in there, I'd have walked in on you myself!" He chuckles. "I would've loved to get an eyeful of the one and fucking only Kat Saunders. Probably would have creamed myself right there!"

I glare at him, but can't help it, I smile. Fith has never made it a secret that he likes Kat, but he knows she's mine, and he's never done anything too inappropriate to her. He's a dirty bastard, though.

"I don't want to fucking hear you say that again.

Am I fucking clear?" I shake my head in disapproval at him.

The man's tattoos are to be admired, especially the script on his neck. He's a valuable member of the club—loyal, trustworthy, and an excellent fighter. If we need to intimidate someone, Fith is the go-to guy. When he stares at you, you can't help but feel the darkness which lives inside of him, but there are times when he takes it all too far. He'll always be a soldier because he doesn't think far enough ahead.

"Yeah, brother, I fucking hear you," Fith answers, giving me a grin.

Dirt comes into the room, "Hey Prez, I saw Rebel leave. Is everything okay?"

"Yeah, he's off to get Kat some clothes from her house." As I say this, I motion toward the coffee machine. Both he and Fith nod, and I get cups out of the cupboard.

"Dane, how many people have access to Kat's house? Don't you need a code or something?" asks Dirt.

"Yeah, man, the code to her gate is the same as the ones for the house. It's the street number, a fucking moron could figure it out." His eyes widen, and I nod. "Then you need keys to open her front door."

The coffee machine has finished, and I'm pouring the coffees when he asks, "The code is the same?"

Dirt shakes his head in disbelief, and I shrug. "How many people would have access? How many people would know how to get through all of her security?"

Dirt reaches for his coffee, and the scar which runs down his face looks more pronounced today. It usually only looks like that when he's angry.

"Me, you, ahh… Rebel, obviously Jess… but, man, it's fucking simple to figure out. Getting the keys would be the hardest part, but the lock would be easy enough to pick if you knew what you were doing."

I can see where this conversation's headed. It's not something I haven't thought about, but the only ones who know the code are family, the MC, and there's no way any of us would've done that to Jess, especially seeing as she was Luke's girl.

Luke may only be a prospect, but you could tell he cared about her. She wasn't like some of the other skanks which hang around the club. She didn't fuck anyone else. Hell, Jess didn't even look at anyone else. You can tell the ones who are looking for a brother who's higher up in the MC, and she wasn't looking to trade up.

Fith is looking at me. "Is it possible it could be one of us? I don't want to fucking say it, man, but if it's one of us, she's not safe."

Dirt nods, and I have a sick feeling in my gut. "Whoever did this expected her to be home. Everyone knew you were at work. You asked her in front of most of the MC at the compound last night if she wanted to join you, and she said no. So, we all knew she was home alone. When did she invite Jess over?" Dirt is rubbing his scar as he speaks. He's my Sergeant-at-Arms, and I trust him completely.

"Fuck if I know, man. Probably last night or the day before? I have no fucking idea, which means the fucker is after Kat."

The feeling in my gut gets worse as I move toward the door to the living room. I need to make sure she's safe.

As I open the door, Bear walks toward me. "Hey, man, how come you aren't upstairs with Kat?" He chuckles to himself and has a smug look on his face.

"What the fuck does that mean?" I say as he barrels past me and toward the coffee.

"Spoke to her outside, and she said she was headed upstairs to be with you." He points his chubby finger at me and then tries to be sexy by throwing his hair over his shoulder and looking at me with pouty lips.

Everyone erupts in fits of laughter. Bear is my Road Captain, everyone likes him, but damn, he can be a nosy motherfucker!

"Don't ever look at me like that again, you fucking pansy." I laugh. "Did she really go upstairs?"

Everyone is still laughing as he says, "Yeah, man, left her on the front veranda, and she said she's headed up. Why?"

"We kind of had a disagreement earlier. You know how fucking sensitive women can be, thought she'd still be sulking about it." I was too hard on her, and I shouldn't have said what I did. I need to find her and apologize, but I don't want her thinking she can flaunt herself in front of the brothers.

"Kat Saunders doesn't strike me as the kind of woman who sulks, or am I fucking wrong?" Fith puts his cup in the sink.

"No, you aren't wrong, but I was hard on her and overreacted."

I look up, and Fith has a grin on his face. "Fuck me, Dane Reynolds, president of the Savage Angels, is pussy-whipped. Never thought I'd see the fucking day!" Now, everyone laughs at me.

"All right, all right." I have my hands up, and I grin. "I'm not pussy-whipped. I just fucking like this woman a hell of a lot."

Dirt pins me with a look. "I think, Prez, *like* is an under-fucking-statement. Never seen you like this with a woman before. Ms. Saunders would be happy."

Everyone goes quiet at the mention of her name. Ms. Saunders is still missed by all of us.

I nod. "I'm not so fucking sure about that. Ms. Saunders was very fucking protective of her girl. I best go find her and make sure I'm not in the fucking doghouse."

CHAPTER 41

STALKER

I can still taste the blood in my mouth. If I concentrate hard enough, I can feel the blade plunging into her at the same time my cock does. That exquisite feeling of finally acting out my fantasy, and it was almost perfect. Almost.

She wasn't Kat. She was pretty, but she wasn't Kat. I had it all planned. I sat on the rooftop opposite their compound with my shotgun microphone and heard Dane ask her to join him, but she said no, said she wanted a day at home. I'd been waiting for her to be alone.

I need her to understand how much I love her. I need her to understand she can't be with a deviant, a low-life. Kat can do so much better. I'm going to ask her to marry me, and I am going to take her away from this backward little nowhere town.

Kat is meant to be with me. I'm meant to be with her. It was so much fun playing with her friend, but with Kat, it will be so much better because I love her. Getting into her house is the easy part. I was shown how to pick locks ages ago. I'm super fit, so after I was finished, I hiked into the mountains behind her house and set up a camp there. The codes for her house were fucking simple, though. Kat really should be more careful. She's kind of predictable when you get to know her. It's not the first time I've been in her home. I've even watched her sleep.

I've been waiting for her to be well again. I wanted to show her how much I love her, but then she fucked that heathen after only one day! One fucking day, and she's in his bed!

Slut. Whore. Cunt!

So, I showed her, I left her a present in her bed, and I threw all her slutty clothes on the floor. I've been waiting since then for her to be alone. Since she met him, she's spent all her time with him. But he doesn't love her, and she really doesn't love him. She loves me. I had her first, and I know she loves me.

The police are still going through her house, and those fucking bikers are everywhere. The fucking reporters aren't helping, either. But I'm patient, I can wait. Kat will be mine again.

I'm looking forward to doing all the things to Kat, I did to her friend. In a way, it's good I've had practice.

That means, next time, it will be perfect.

CHAPTER 42

KAT

I'm so totally wearing the wrong shoes for trekking through the wilderness. This is such a bad idea. I know I've done a stupid thing, but pride is a curse I was born with. I've made my way to the bridge when all the hairs stand up on the back of my neck. I can't see anyone around, and I'm suddenly reminded of what Dane said the first time I met him—there are people and things in the woods watching me. Can I feel someone watching me, or is it my overactive imagination? I'm standing perfectly still, listening, and I can't hear anything except the normal sounds of the woods, but I can't shake the feeling I'm being watched.

Thankfully, I've remembered to bring my phone with me, and I call Dane.

"Kat? Darlin', I'll be up in a minute. You couldn't wait?" Dane sounds amused, but I know he'll lose his shit when I tell him where I am.

"I'm not upstairs, I needed some fresh air… please, don't be mad. I'm at the bridge where we met…" I feel like a child admitting I've done something wrong.

"You're fucking where?" Dane roars into my ear.

I sigh. "I'm at the bridge, headed to my home. You pissed me off, but I'm kind of—"

"Kat, stay where you are, I'm on my way. Stay on the phone with me. Jesus-fucking-Christ, Kat, what were you thinking?"

I pace on the bridge, waving my hands around as I talk to him.

"Well, if you hadn't been such a dickhead to me, I wouldn't have left." Now I'm mad, and I yell into the phone.

There's movement in front of me, and I look up to see someone walking toward me from the direction of my house.

"Dane, someone is coming toward me from my house…"

"Darlin', I need you to be moving as fast as you can back toward me. I'm coming, just keep on the phone."

I can hear the concern in his voice, and now panic fills me. "Okay, I'm moving." I turn around to see how close my would-be attacker is, and from a distance, I can see it's Rebel.

"Dane, it looks like Rebel. Sorry, babe, didn't mean to rattle you, it's only Rebel." I laugh nervously, relieved it's a member of the Savage Angels.

"Kat, I need you to keep coming back toward me. Don't stop until you're by my side, we clear?" I look up at the nearing figure of Rebel and walk toward Dane.

"Kat!" It's Rebel, and he's jogging toward me. I have no idea what to do, so I quicken my pace away from him. "Kat! Wait up!" He gets closer, and looks like he has a bag over his shoulder.

I stop moving and let him catch up.

"Hey, Rebel, how's it going?" My phone is still to my ear and I can hear Dane swearing, his breath more labored.

"Kat, you shouldn't be out here alone!" Rebel looks concerned as he looks around. "You don't know who could be out here!"

At that moment, Dane comes into view, and he's followed by Dirt, Fith, and in the distance, I can see a very red-faced Bear.

Dane thunders past me and grabs Rebel by his wife-beater. "What the fuck are you doing here, Rebel!?" I've never seen him so angry. His face is a mask of fury.

Dirt and Fith move to flank Rebel, and when Bear catches up, he stands in front of me.

"What the fuck, Dane? You asked me to go and get clothes for Kat!" Rebel looks baffled, and so am I.

"You left on your bike. What the fuck are you doing coming back this way?" Dane walks him backward, and Rebel is having a tough time staying on his feet.

"The fucking reporters and cops were everywhere. I figured it would be easier to come back this way and get my bike later!" Rebel is clearly confused, and he's trying to give Dane the bag on his arm. "Look, man, it's just her fucking clothes!"

Suddenly, we all talk at once.

"Dane! What are you doing?" I'm so totally bewildered.

"How the fuck can there be reporters on the road when we have it fucking blocked off?" Dirt shouts, pointing a finger at Rebel.

"He knows the code to her house, Prez, you said it yourself." Fith looks amped, his eyes are bulging, and the tattoo on his neck looks like it's pulsing with every breath he takes.

All eyes are now on Fith. What the fuck does he mean by that? I look at Rebel, and I remember what my bedroom looked like after the last time he was sent to get me clothes. I back away from him and shake my head from side to side.

Dirt sees me backing away and says, "Kat, what

is it?"

Dane has let Rebel go, and Fith has grabbed him by the back of his jacket. "Kat? Speak to me, darlin'."

"I'd forgotten the first time you sent Rebel to get me clothes, he trashed my room, and my bed was… I thought he was a fan… I should've said something. Oh my God, did you do that to Jess?" I walk toward him, my voice rising. "How could you fucking do that to Jess?" I launch myself at him, but Dane catches me by the waist.

"Kat, calm down." Dane walks me backward and into Bear's embrace. "I need you to calm down. I need you to go back home with Bear. Understand?" His voice is so gentle, and he's got me pinned with his eyes. "Say it, darlin', say you understand." My body's trembling and I can barely move my head in understanding. "I need to hear you fucking say it, Kat. We need to have a conversation with Rebel, and for us to do that, I need to know you're fucking safe, not wandering about. You stay with Bear, no matter fucking what, you get me?" Dane has a fierce expression in his eyes, capturing my complete attention.

"I get you. I'll go back with Bear and stay at your house, but what are you going—"

"That's for another time. Right now, darlin', I need you to do this for me, yeah?" Dane kisses my forehead and gives a chin lift to Bear.

I move up the path but stop and look at Rebel

standing between Dirt and Fith. Fear has etched itself onto his face. Dane nods at me, turns around, and heads toward a retreating Rebel.

CHAPTER 43

DANE

I want to make this motherfucker bleed. I want him to feel what it's like to have your own warm blood pulse out of you and drip onto your own skin. I want to hurt him as much as he hurt Jess. Pummel him with my fists and feel his teeth loosen in his mouth. I want this motherfucker to be overcome with pain, and only when he can't handle it anymore, I'm going to put this motherfucker out of his misery.

"Dane! Man, I didn't do anything! I couldn't hurt Jess, I couldn't!" His voice is filled with desperation as he looks at all of us. Turning around in a circle, he pleads with us, "You know me, you fucking know me, man!" He's fallen to his knees on the bridge, the bridge he helped me build, the bridge we built for Ms. Saunders. He's always been a valued member of the MC. He's quiet and loyal. Could he really have done this? "Dane, check with Keg. I was with Keg when that shit with Jess went down. Just fucking check, please!"

Keg has been a member of the Savage Angels for as long as I can remember. He's beginning to look like his nickname, and I can't even tell you his real name.

I flick my eyes to Dirt. "Make the call." No one else speaks.

Dirt turns away from us, takes out his phone, and walks a couple of paces away. I look at Fith, and he has death in his eyes as he stares at Rebel. The fucker can be scary as hell.

"Thank you, Dane, thank you. I didn't do fucking anything! I went to get her clothes like you asked, but that's it! I did nothing else!" He looks between Fith and me. Fith reaches behind and pulls out a gun from the waistband of his jeans. It's a Glock, the most common handgun for civilians. Most of us have one, some of us even have a license to own them. But I don't think Fith does.

Rebel turns completely pale, and his eyes are glued to the gun.

Dirt walks over and extends a hand to Rebel. "Get up off your knees, Reb. Keg confirms it couldn't have been you who murdered Jess, and he also explained why the fucking reporters are at the house."

It takes Rebel a while to peel his eyes from the gun and to grab onto Dirt's hand.

Fith shrugs and puts it away, then he smiles at Rebel, claps him on the shoulder. "All's well that ends well, hey, Reb?" You can't help but feel like he has ice running through his veins. One minute he's fully prepared to kill you, the next he wants to be your fucking friend.

Rebel's looking at me, waiting for me to give my approval. I hold out my hand, and he looks at it. He takes a second, then he grabs it, relief flooding his features.

"I really thought you were going to end me there, Prez. I really thought it was the end." He nervously smiles at me, clearly rattled.

"We don't do anything without proof, Reb, you know that."

As I say this, I'm staring at Fith, who shrugs and smiles, but his eyes are full of darkness, and he looks away.

"Dirt, explain to me how the fucking reporters got past our roadblocks?" I'm annoyed.

"Sheriff said they had a right to be there. The brothers only let those with credentials through, the rest are still at the barricade we set up. I thought the fucking sheriff was on the same page as us over this fucking mess!" His hands are on his hips, and he looks pissed.

"It's a high-profile case. The reporters probably threatened the sheriff with legal action if they weren't allowed to get closer to the scene of the crime. The road is, after all, public property." I'm staring at Rebel when something that Kat said comes back to me. "Reb, I need the fucking truth from you now. Whatever you say, we won't hurt you. Did you do anything at Kat's house the first time I sent you there?"

Rebel's eyes widen. "No, I didn't. I got her clothes and left. I didn't do any-fucking-thing else. I swear on my cut. Nothing else." He backs away from me again.

"Relax, Reb, relax. I believe you. Brother, I'm sorry for what just happened, but we have to be careful. You fucking get that, yeah?"

"Careful? Careful is letting her wander around the fucking woods by herself? Is it?" He has a point, and I know the adrenaline is running through his veins, but I'm the president of the Savage Angels, and he'd best remember it.

"Kat was upset, and she left without my knowledge. I thought she'd gone upstairs. You need to watch your fucking tone with me, Rebel. Remember who I am and how I got to fucking be here." I'm looking down on him, and Fith and Dirt have closed ranks on him.

He's breathing heavily, trying to get it under control. "Sorry, man, sorry. I'm fucking concerned about her. Okay? I don't want her to end up like Jess."

I'm beginning to think Rebel has more than a crush on Kat, but I don't have time to deal with it right now.

"When you were at the house, did the cops have any new information? Did they tell you anything?" Dirt asks him.

He shakes his head from side to side. "No, man, so far, they've got nothing. The DNA hasn't come up in any database, but it will still be another three days, according to Billy. That is *if* he's in the system. The cops seem to think this isn't his first time doing something like this. They've got some profiler up there who thinks the guy is just getting warmed up."

I swear, turn around, and head back up the path. "Come on, let's get back, and Reb, I owe you one."

He's picked up the bag and jogs up to me. "No, Prez, you don't, you were doing right by your woman, and that's all that matters."

He's holding out the bag to me, so I take it and nod. We all walk back to my place in silence.

Whoever is behind Jess' murder, it's clear he's been in Kat's house before. Maybe he's been stalking her for a while? Maybe he's a friend or a crazed fan? All these options are running through my mind as I head back to the woman I love. Yes, love. The woman I want to spend all my days with, the woman who'll not end up in the hands of this maniac.

CHAPTER 44

STALKER

Well, well, well, wasn't that fucking interesting?

I was about to approach Kat when the biker with the shaved head came out onto the path. I liked watching that large, lumbering, idiot, Dane, do his overprotective macho bullshit with baldy. I can't believe they thought he had the balls to do something like that? Him? I mean, really? He probably can't even spell his own name. Rebel, *such* an original name.

I could tell from her movements she sensed my presence, she could feel I was close. The way she stopped on the bridge and stared straight at me, I felt we had finally connected, but then she called the Neanderthal. I thought about taking her right then and there, but then Rebel appeared. During his interrogation, I noticed he didn't mention how he'd been watching them and playing with himself by the window. Can't wait to tell Kat about it when I get her alone.

What she sees in the biker, Dane, is beyond me. I can give her the world. I can give her everything. As soon as the cops leave her home, I'm going to sneak back in. I have a secret hiding place in her house. It's not very big, but they'll never find me there. The builders put it in when they were remodeling her home. It's big enough for me to slip into and wait until she's alone. She has to come home at some point, right?

I'll wait for her, I have time.

No one is going to be looking for me. I'm not in their database because I've never been caught before.

I'm smart, I'm good-looking, and I blend in. Maybe I'll go back to my 'life' for a while, but I don't want to leave her.

I need to be close to her now. Kat Saunders, the musical has-been. The things that woman can do with her mouth. It's heaven.

Very fitting she called her first song that. When I'm finished with her, she'll be in heaven, and I'll be even more famous than I am right now. Everyone will know how much I love her. All of the others have looked like her, except for the last one.

But the last one was so good. It must have been the connection with Kat. It tipped me over the edge.

CHAPTER 45

DANE

I'm watching Kat as I sit on a chair on the front veranda. She's pacing, her band and her manager should all be here within the hour. Kat's been totally wired since she woke up. It's like she can't wait to see them, but then the next minute, she seems scared to death of them.

I know she has a lot of issues with these people, and from the little I know about them, they feel like her family. If Kat keeps pacing, though, she's going to put a hole in my veranda. She's wearing a pair of jeans, black sandals, a black t-shirt which has red swirls on the front, and the best part of it, her hair is down. I love her hair. It feels like silk, and when she gives me head, I like to wrap my fingers in it because it feels so bloody fantastic.

The reporters have been a real issue for us. We found two of them near the back of the house taking pictures. I've had to double the number of brothers looking after the house and road. I'm hoping her manager, Dave, can fix the mess this fucking murderer has created.

Kat has stopped pacing and looks at me as two limousines pull into the courtyard. She turns back around and runs toward the first limousine. It hasn't even stopped when the door flies open, and a very large black man gets out, picks her up, and throws her over his shoulder. This must be Blair.

Kat squeals like a teenager as he swings her around. I get up and slowly make my way down the stairs as both limousines come to a stop, and people emerge from them. All eyes are on Kat, and she laughs as they all gather around her.

"Hello, princess, I can see life is treating you well," says an older man who's looking at me now.

"Dave! How are you?" Kat is still draped over the big guy's shoulder as I approach them.

I walk up to Blair and hold my arms out, and he smiles and throws Kat at me. She squeals again as I catch her in my arms. Kat looks at me, smiles, and kisses my mouth as I put her on the ground.

She keeps both of my arms around her as she says, "Everyone, this is Dane. Dane, this is everyone!" It's obvious she's happy.

Keeping Kat tucked into my side, I hold out my

hand to each of them as they all introduce themselves.

"Welcome to you all," I say. "Please come in and make yourselves comfortable." They all move toward the stairs when Kat finally lets me go.

"Thank you, babe. I didn't realize how much I missed them until now. I didn't know how much I needed them until now, either, so thank you for letting them all stay here." Kat kisses me then follows them into the house.

I watch her walk away and admire her as she does, and the sick feeling I've felt in my gut since Jess was murdered grows. I hope we can survive the coming storm. I hope she and I will come out the other side unscathed and stronger.

If that fucker was after my woman, he'll have to go through my boys and me to get to her, and it's not going to happen.

CHAPTER 46

KAT

It feels like it used to when we were on tour and all living under the same roof. If only it hadn't taken a horrific death to bring us all together. I meant what I said to Dane, I've really missed them. We all sit around the dining room table, and some of the Savage Angels have joined us.

Dave gets up and looks at me. "Okay, princess, let's start from the beginning. I need to know everything that's happened if I'm going to fix this mess. The press is having a field day, and we need to get ahead of it before it turns into a disaster."

"I'd say it's already a disaster with the murder of Jess, wouldn't you?" Dane looks at Dave, and some of his boys have gathered closer to us.

"I meant no disrespect to the girl, but I need to

know everything if I'm going to spin the story, so it's good for all of us." Dave looks apologetic.

"Babe, Dave didn't mean anything by it. He's trying to protect me from the media and protect the band," I say, trying to reassure Dane.

"Protect the band? From fucking what? It's not the fucking band the fucker attacked. He attacked Jess, but we all know he wanted you." Dane's features look like they're carved from stone, and Judge and Dirt nod in agreement behind him.

"Okay, okay. I think we've gotten off on the wrong foot here. Dane, I look after The Grinders. It's my job as their manager, and right now, their lead singer is being portrayed as a lovesick slut who's under the influence of a leader of a motorcycle gang who is at war with a rival gang. They also wrote, that said gang tried to kill her to send a message." Dane looks pissed as Dave continues, "We know it's not the case, but unless I get that point made, that's what the media will keep saying. Like I said, it's my job to protect The Grinders. We're all here for you and Kat. You're family now, and I look after my family." No one says a word, so Dave continues, "It's also my job to protect the image of The Grinders, their brand. Ever since Kat's accident, sales have been pretty steady, and it helps having Blair and Jamie on TV every week. You two should've done it a while ago, by the way." Dave turns to look at Jamie.

"Dave, we wanted to do it some time ago, but you kept us on the fucking road." Jamie smiles, shaking his head.

"Well, my boy, if I'd known sales would be this good without touring, I'd have let you!" says Dave.

"As if our Mistress of the Microphone would've let us stop touring!" Truth enters the conversation.

Everyone laughs, and I look at Dane and motion for him to come with me into the living room.

The others keep talking as we leave. Judge and Dirt follow us in.

"Darlin', I don't like what he's saying about me and my MC." Dane's visibly pissed.

"Yeah, we aren't at war with anyone, haven't been for a little while, so it's all fucking bullshit." Dirt does not appear happy, either.

"Guys, that's not what he's saying. He's saying what the media is saying, and he has to get on top of this. He's good at his job, and you need to listen to him. He'll sort it all out, he always has." I grab the front of Dane's t-shirt. "Babe, it's all going to be fine. I have you protecting me physically, and I now have Dave protecting my name from the media. You're both going to do a fantastic job."

Dane smiles and nods. "Well, he has one thing right." I tilt my head to the side, and raise my eyebrows as he continues, "I do have you under my influence, and, darlin', it's where you're going to stay."

Judge laughs, Dirt shakes his head, and I can't help but laugh as well. We move back into the dining room.

"Now, boys and girls, are we all good?" I love Dave, but he needs to tone it down for the very masculine bikers in the room. They aren't used to gay men.

Judge laughs. "Yes, Dad. Now, what do you need to know about the Savage Angels MC, not a fucking biker gang?"

Maybe I'm wrong, maybe Dave doesn't need to tone it down. As I look at the bikers in the room, they are all listening to what Dave has to say.

"Kat, my princess, tell me about Jess, your impressions of her, how you met, everything." He's looking at Dane, then he says, "I'll need a lift into the sheriff's office later. It's important I get a feel on what he thinks, and I'd like to talk to you as well, Dane, and get your take on things."

"Not a problem. I'll get one of the brothers to take you in 'cause I'm not leaving Kat."

"Hmm, not willing to part with the princess? I like him, I like him a lot!" Dave turns to me with a smile on his face.

Truth stands and walks toward the kitchen. "So glad you approve of the biker, Dave. I'm sure our rock goddess is overjoyed. I need coffee."

"Since you're already up, Truth, I could use a cup, too. Anyone else want to take advantage of him?"

says Curtis.

Truth glares at Curtis when Jasmin says, "I've been trying to take advantage of him for years, so I might as well get a cup of coffee out of him."

Everyone laughs because it's no secret Jasmin has held a torch for Truth over the years. As far as I know, though, they've never gone there, just a lot of heavy flirtation.

"Okay, Jasmin, you managed to make coffee sound dirty, so I'm making my own. Anyone else?" Jamie says to Jasmin.

"Fuck, Jamie! It's coffee, nothing more. I can't help it if you've got a dirty mind." Jasmin smirks.

"Jasmin, please! We all know you meant it in a dirty way, you always do. Jamie, I'd love a cup," Blair scolds Jasmin while giving her a one-armed hug.

The banter around the table continues as the men go into the kitchen and try to find coffee and mugs. I can hear Dane trying to navigate them.

"Okay, princess, from the top!" Dave is patting a chair next to him, and I sit down, sighing a bit.

"I only met her a little while ago, here, at Dane's. She made everyone laugh. Jess had this way of lighting up a room simply by being in it. She didn't deserve to die the way she did."

"Why weren't you at home? How did she get into your house? Where were you, Kat?" Jasmin has reached out across the table to touch my hand.

"I was supposed to be there, but these guys drink a lot of coffee. I invited Jess over but then realized I didn't have any left, so I went into town and got tied up with the locals. You know what it's like sometimes."

Dave nods at me and says, "How did she get into your home? Did she have a key?"

"No, Dave, I told her where to find the spare key and gave her the code to get in. He must have been inside when she got there. I was running late. It took me two hours to get home, and, when I got there, she was…" A tear escapes my eye and rolls down my cheek.

"Okay, princess, let's not go there. Has anything else happened I should know about? Nefarious rival biker gangs? Have you been two-timing the big guy? Anything?"

"No, Dave, the only thing that's happened is someone has been inside my home before Jess's murder, messed up my clothes, and may have left me a present in my bed."

"May have? Kat, what does 'may have' mean?" Blair has walked back into the room and is looking at me questioningly.

"Dane asked one of his boys to get some clothes from my house, and when I got home the day after, my bedroom had been trashed, and my bedsheets were messed up. I thought the guy he sent, Rebel, must have been a fan." I look up as Dane and the others filter back into the room. "So, I washed the sheets and all of my clothes."

"Why didn't you say anything? Why didn't you tell Dane?" Jasmin shakes her head at me.

"Sugar, it doesn't matter. We know it wasn't Rebel. The guy must have been in the house, hiding, or turned up after Rebel left. Rebel isn't the guy." Judge is staring at Jasmin as if she's the sexiest thing he's ever seen.

"Well, hello, handsome, my name's Jasmin Trevaine, and you are?" she asks in a sexy voice.

"Sugar, my name's Judge, and I'm a huge fan." They both smile knowingly at each other.

"Ahh, hello? Other people in the room are feeling slightly awkward here. Could you two take it outside?" Truth smiles as he says this, but you can tell he's not in the mood to watch Jasmin devour yet another man.

"Took the words straight out of my mouth. Wanna go for a ride, sugar?" Judge asks and stands up.

"Hmm, a ride? What the hell? I could use the exercise, I mean the fresh air," Jasmin says, her eyes locking on Truth. She gets up from her seat and walks toward Judge. "Lead the way, handsome."

They are an unusual pair. Jasmin's only five foot four with straight, blonde hair with bangs and no tattoos. Judge is six foot four, has dark-brown hair with flecks of gray in it, has lots of tattoos, and is all muscle. He smiles at her, grabs her hand, and walks toward the front of the house.

"Judge, best keep her safe, nothing reckless, yeah?" Dane stares at them, smiles, and shakes his head.

"Now, where's the fun in that?" Jasmin asks, lifting her shoulder in a casual shrug.

"Don't worry, sugar, I'll keep you safe… but not too safe." Judge chuckles and leads her out of the house.

I look at Dane, who shrugs, still shaking his head in disbelief.

"You should be more worried about Judge than Jasmin, Dane. She's a man-eater." Truth is staring after them and then looks at Dane. "He doesn't stand a chance."

"I'm pretty sure Judge can look after himself." Dane sits down beside me. "You okay, darlin'?"

"Yes, babe, I'm good. I'm talking things through with Dave."

"Dave, do you have everything you need?" Dane has draped an arm over my shoulder and is staring at Dave intently.

"Well, one little thing, and, Dane, I need you to keep calm while I ask this. Is it possible this is a gang thing?" Dave looks uncomfortable.

"No, it fucking isn't. They would come after me or one of the brothers, not my fucking woman." You can tell by Dane's tone he's annoyed at answering this question.

"Had to ask, big guy. I'll get one of my girls to go back over Kat's scary fan mail for the last twelve months and deliver it to the sheriff." He pauses and looks at me. "I'll arrange a cleaning crew, call a press conference, and I want all of you to be there." Dave gets his phone out of his coat pocket. "And I'll also arrange protection for Kat and the rest of the band."

"No," Dane growls.

"No? What do you mean no?" Dave has his phone out and is looking at Dane quizzically.

"No to the protection. My boys and I will be looking after Kat and all of you. As far as the rest goes, you can do what you like, but you're all under my roof, and I'll take care of you."

"Kat?" Dave is looking at me.

The atmosphere in the room has gotten slightly heated. Dave is used to handling everything, and so is Dane. *Interesting.*

I wouldn't have thought of Dave as an alpha male, but I guess he has to be to handle everything he does in our industry. But this is Dane's house and his town, so we're going to have to play by his rules.

"Dave, sweetheart, Dane and his boys are perfectly able to protect us. You have to leave it to him. As for everything else, I'd appreciate it if you handled it."

"Not everything. I have a friend coming to redo Kat's security system and to see if there are any holes in it. He's the fucking best in this state, and I trust him completely," interjects Dane.

"Is that all? You know I'm her manager, and she normally looks to me to do everything."

Dave's right. I have let him organize everything in my life, except for the direction of the band. Of course, he had a say in many aspects, but we always had a clear vision as to where we wanted to go, and he let us lead the way. I wrote the lyrics and sometimes the music, but most of it was written by Truth. He often collaborated with all of us if he got stuck on something or wanted to take it in another direction.

"Dave, man, can't you see she's happy? Can't you see he's looking out for her, not for what he can get from her? It's been a while since she's had that. Fuck, it's been a while since any of us have had that." Curtis is standing in the doorway to the deck looking at Dave.

"I thought you were happy? Aren't you getting married again?" I ask Curtis as he shakes his head at me.

"No, Kat, I told her I needed to be with you, and she told me I had to choose. Wasn't a hard decision." He looks sad. "The band has always come first for me. I'd pick all of you over any of my wives any day."

"You shouldn't have to choose, Curtis. When you find the right woman, you won't have to, they'll be by your side through everything. If the woman you left behind doesn't get it, then she isn't the right fucking one, and thank the Lord you got out before you married her." Everyone nods. "But the question is, how much did it cost to get rid of this one?" Curtis looks at Dave, and I continue, "You haven't quite gotten rid of her yet, have you?"

"No, Kat, I haven't. Dave, could you handle it for me? I really don't want to see her again." Curtis looks apologetic.

"Of course, I'll handle it, it's my job." Dave looks at Dane. "Is there anything else you're going to look after for Kat? Anything I should be aware of?" Dave asks, sounding resigned.

"I know you have looked after her for a long time now, and thank you for keeping her safe, but it's my job now. No one will get near her or any of you. The only fucking thing I ask of you is, you don't go anywhere without one of my boys. My home is your home, so feel free to use it as if it were your own." Dave nods and punches numbers into his phone.

The others all look to me. "Come on, I'll show you to your rooms. You're up on the third floor."

Blair groans, and Truth slaps him on the back.

"Third floor? I don't suppose there's an elevator?" Blair isn't a gym junkie.

"Aww, honey, the exercise will do you good!

Come on!" I grab him by the arm and lead them toward the stairs.

"Kat, you know there's an elevator behind the kitchen, don't you? It's big enough to fit a bed in. Dane put it in so it would be easier to get the furniture to the upper levels. We never use it, most of us use the stairs. The only one who does use it is Bear," says Dirt, looking amused.

"Hallelujah! Praise the Lord! An elevator! Lead the way!" I don't think I've ever seen Blair this happy.

The guys turn back around and head for the kitchen.

"Hang on a minute, it's only stairs! Surely, you can walk up a few steps!" I yell after them.

"It's three stories, Kat. You can walk it if you want to, but me, I'm taking the elevator," exclaims Blair.

All I can do is laugh, but why am I surprised? Blair has never liked exercise. Truth, Jamie, and Curtis are also heading in the direction of the elevator.

"Really?"

I'm staring after them in disbelief when Truth turns back around, walks up to me, and grabs my hand. "Come on, my rock goddess. Let's take the elevator and save our energy for other things." He's waggling his eyebrows up and down in a suggestive manner.

"Now, Truth, I know you and Kat are friends, but you aren't *that* fucking friendly, and I'd appreciate it if you kept your hands off my woman." I look at Dane, and even though he's smiling, there's an edge to his voice.

"Just fucking with you, man. But it's cool, won't do it again. We good?" Truth already has a good understanding of how my man works. He puts his hands up, palms out in a defensive manner, and walks backward toward the elevator.

"We're good, brother. Just letting you know where I stand. Let's get you all upstairs. Kat and I are on the second level. There's a gym in the basement if you want to work out, and if you don't know where everything else is, feel free to explore… just not my bedroom."

Dave has joined us, and we all head for the elevator. I finally feel like I've found a home. Dane has made this possible. He has accepted my band and made me feel safe. The sooner Jess's killer is caught, the better life will be. This stalker will not take away my family or my sense of belonging.

He will not win.

CHAPTER 47

DAVE
Manager

I've been looking after Katarina Saunders since she turned twelve years old when that mother of hers brought her to me to listen to her sing. I know Kat loved her mother, but I didn't like her very much. The woman could recognize her daughter's talent, though, so at least she did right by her in that department.

When it came to organizing a contract for Kat, her mother made sure she got a cut until Kat turned twenty-one. Her portion may have only amounted to five percent, but she made millions out of her girl. Kat didn't even care, she said it was the least she could do for her mother. In fact, when Kat turned twenty-one, the contract had a clause which said the payments could continue at her discretion. I will never understand why she did it, though. Her mother only stayed with Kat until she turned sixteen and then left her to me and the big bad world.

I have always loved Kat. She's the daughter I never had. I cut her loose after her accident, and it was the hardest decision I've ever made. At first, I wanted to phone her every day, but she needed to find herself in this world without someone telling her what to do.

Now, when I look at her, I'm wondering if she traded me in for a biker. I guess only time will tell. For bikers in the middle of the country, they sure are good-looking. Dane alone could make a grown man's heart stop. He must be six foot six, built, and has those gorgeous blue eyes. I don't mind a bit of rough every now and then, but I like being the one in control, and I don't think he'd let me do that. Curtis is right, though he doesn't appear to want anything from my girl. He does seem to care about her, but I'll wait and see.

As for who would be after my girl? I have no clue. There've been lots of crazies over the years, but no one has gone this far.

My team and I have already put the wheels in motion as to how we're going to spin this fucking debacle and try to boost record sales. It is, after all, what I do.

Kat sure does like this one. You can see it in her eyes. Maybe my princess has finally found someone to love instead of her steady stream of douche canoes. I've run background checks on all of the MC members, especially after I discovered her mother had left them her transport business. Dane, the president of the Savage Angels, is fairly clean. He did do a stint in juvie in his early teens for car theft. It surprised me he even went to prison for it, seeing as it was his first offense. The judge on the case obviously wanted to make an example out of him. Being a member of the Savage Angels probably didn't help his case. Apart from that, he's kept clear of the law, but, as for doing lawful things, I'm not entirely sure. Once he took the presidency of the Savage Angels, you can see he has made a real effort to get them out of drugs, guns, and whores. Most of his moneymaking businesses are on the up-and-up, and this fucking house is amazing.

Kat has never really had very good luck with men. They've always been about how much she could help them to reach their own goals. Not sure what Dane's end game is, but there isn't much I don't know about him. I can't trust him until I fully understand his relationship with Kat's mother. No way that woman wasn't getting something out of him or his MC—she had her fingers in too many pies. I told her when Kat turned twenty-one, she had to stay away, or I'd tell Kat what she was really like. But she smiled at me and said I could try but Kat would never believe me. She knew her girl, and I didn't want to risk losing Kat, who adored her mother.

I should've gone through the will with Kat, but I didn't. After her accident, losing her voice, and the death of her mother, I couldn't do it. I should have, the business should have gone to Kat, but I couldn't help but think if her mother owned it, it couldn't be all above board, so I didn't let Kat know, and advised her legal team not to fight it. My princess was in no condition to go through her mother's will, and as usual, she left it all to me. Her mother had millions in her bank accounts, and she'd purchased land all around Tourmaline. Whatever Kat's Ma got herself into, I hope it doesn't come back to haunt my girl.

CHAPTER 48

TRUTH
Lead Guitarist

As soon as I got out of the limo, I could see the change in her. There she is, Katarina Saunders, hanging upside down over Blair's shoulder, squealing like a five-year-old, but you can tell she's finally truly happy. The only time I've seen her happy was with us, singing, and it doesn't matter if it's in front of fifty thousand people or in a studio or just the two of us messing about. She loved to sing. It concerned me she might never find happiness again. Guess, I'm wrong.

Not sure what to make of Dane, though. You can tell he cares for her because why else would he put up with all the crap which comes with being with someone like us? Unless, he's a user, but so far, he doesn't appear to be cashing in on her fame.

His house is amazing, and it would've taken a lot of money to build it. Maybe it's what he's after? More money? I'll have to sit down with Kat and try to find out if he's made any 'suggestions.'

His boys look like the kind of people we eject from our concerts if they get too rowdy. They all seem to be looking out for our princess, but you can never be too careful. I wonder if Dave has run background checks on any of them, but knowing Dave, I probably shouldn't wonder about it. He's always been a careful fucker, and he's saved my ass on more than one occasion. Fucking groupies always trying to get pregnant!

When Kat shows us to our rooms on the third floor, I was surprised to see each room has its own bathroom, and they all open up to the veranda. Pretty swish for a biker boy. Dane has to be into something illegal to afford all this.

I can't believe someone got murdered because of Kat. I'm standing on the veranda looking out at the view when Kat joins me.

"I'm sorry Jasmin left with Judge, Truth. Are you okay?" she asks quietly. Ahh, my long-running flirtation with Jasmin, and that's what she thinks I'm worried about.

"My gorgeous rocker, don't worry yourself. He's not the first she has whisked away in front of me, and I very much doubt he'll be the last." I smile and wink at her.

"Well, Truth, what's got you looking so concerned?"

I look at her and laugh. "You're joking, aren't you?" Kat looks confused. "My lovely songstress, I'm thinking about that poor girl who got killed and what it has to do with you."

"Of course, of course, sorry. I've got so much on my mind, and I'm so glad you could all come. I've missed you."

I engulf her in a hug. Kat gives great hugs if she loves you. She holds on tight, and it's for longer than normal, but over the years, I've grown to love them. I'm not a touchy-feely guy, except for when I'm with my rock princess.

"Truth, do you know of anyone who would do this? Are there any crazy fans who stand out? I've been wracking my brain, but the only ones I can think of have always been harmless."

I let go of her and look into her eyes. "Dave asked all of us to go over the freaky fan mail, but no one seemed that disturbed. I'm not sure, but I think it's the same for the others. Could this be a home-grown from Tourmaline who thinks they have a relationship with you?"

"Fuck if I know. Nothing comes to mind. Nothing! I feel like I'm letting everyone down by not having a clue about who this fucker is. All I know is if I'd been home, Jess would still be alive."

"Now, now, my sultry singer, had you been home, I suspect you'd both be dead. What do the police have to say? Do they have any leads?" I ask.

She balances on one foot, and it's funny to watch. Kat always does this when she gets nervous.

"I haven't spoken to them since I gave my statement. Dane told me there hasn't been a murder in Tourmaline for a while, so although it's possible, I don't think this is someone from town."

"Okay, well, Dave is going into town to talk to the police, and I guess we all need to be available for his press conference. No one is going to hurt you, Kat, no one. Your biker boy certainly has enough security." I laugh. "Did you see Dave's face when he said no? Thought his head would explode on the spot! No one has said no to Dave in a really long time. Thank God, your biker boy can back up his claim regarding our security. Dave would have a meltdown if anything happened to any of us, which reminds me, how is it you didn't have any security at the house? Did Dave let them go?"

Kat looks down when she says, "I let them go. There didn't seem to be a reason to keep them. I mean, the press settled down, the fans stopped trying to get in, and I live on the side of a fucking mountain. It's not exactly easy to get into my home, what with the high-tech gates and the security system. I thought it was safe."

"My rebellious rocker, you should've been safe.

It isn't an accusation, I simply wondered why you didn't have a bodyguard. None of this is your fault." I really need to lighten the mood. "This house is magnificent, but it must have cost plenty of coin to build it. Your boy related to a fairy godmother? Or a rich rocker?"

Kat laughs. "Subtle, Truth, really subtle. He hasn't asked me for a dime, not for anything. As for this house, I haven't asked him how he could afford to build it. Just like he hasn't asked me how many people I've fucked."

"Didn't mean to cross a line, my regal rocker. I'm just curious."

"You know what they say about curiosity, don't you, Truth?"

"Yes, my love, I do." I pause for dramatic effect. "They fucked the cat."

"Yeah, baby, they sure did."

We're both laughing as Curtis walks out onto the veranda to join us.

CHAPTER 49

CURTIS
Bass Guitarist

She looks good, and her scar has healed well. I've been listening to Kat and Truth talk. Truth may be a dramatic motherfucker, but he cares about Kat. She's right, he's oh-so-subtle asking about Dane and his finances.

"Curtis! My favorite bass guitarist, all settled in?" Truth loves to play the drama queen.

"Yes, Truth, all settled in. Nice digs, Kat. Your man's got taste."

Kat nods, and Truth says, "Well, my beautiful band members, I'm off to get some exercise. After all, you can't keep looking this good without a little pain and torment."

"Keep telling yourself that, Truth, maybe one day

it'll be true." I like him, but he's always been a cocky fucker.

"Why, Curtis, are you saying it's not true when the Truth is right in front of you?" He laughs as he walks away from us. I look at Kat, who smiles and shakes her head, resigned to Truth's antics.

"Keep going, Truth, keep going," I say to his retreating form, then I look at Kat. "So, you wanna see my room?"

She nods and walks toward my door, saying, "Bet you say that to all the girls."

"No, only the ones I'm trying to get into my room…" She stops and looks at me, so I wink and say, "And only the ones who say yes."

"Hmm… Curtis, you're a naughty boy." Kat walks in and sits on my bed.

"I could be, but that man of yours would probably kill me and bury me in a shallow grave." I smile at her. "Moving on to a more serious note, how are you doing?"

Kat flops back on the bed and stares at the ceiling. "I'm okay… a bit frazzled. I'm so glad you're all here." She sits up on one elbow to look at me. "I appreciate you being here, and I'm sorry about your fiancée."

I laugh, but there's no humor in it. "You saved me from another horrendous mistake. Christ, I can pick 'em, can't I?"

"Well, love, I didn't even meet this one! How

about next time you don't ask anyone to marry you until she's met the entire band at least twice?" Kat moves to a sitting position and continues, "And we should all approve of her."

"Deal, Kat. Deal."

Her head is tilted to the side, exposing her long neck. Kat's studying me. "You cut your hair... why?"

"I only cut off six inches, but I've been thinking about cutting it all off, anyway. I'm sick of plaits and ponytails. Too much maintenance." Today, my hair is in a plait, but a few strands have escaped and are loose around my face. Where Truth is all dark with tattoos, I'm the opposite, and I like to think of myself as the light to Truth's darkness.

"Curtis, if you cut off your hair, hundreds, no, millions of girls are going to cry themselves to sleep." Kat's making fun of me now, and this is the woman I know and love.

"Very funny, Kat. You should take your act on the road."

"Oh, Curtis, always so serious! Wanna help me get dinner ready?" She gets up off the bed and heads for the door. On the road, Kat and I were always the ones making sure the band and even some of the crew members got something to eat. We learned to cook good, easy meals which didn't take a lot of time to prepare.

"Yeah, but first, tell me something. This guy, is he good to you? Are you happy?" Kat stops and turns around.

"He's better than good to me, and I've never been happier even though I can't sing anymore. You know I'm so sorry for having the accident, and I'm sorry it finished the band. Well, finished what we had."

"Babe, it didn't finish the band, we just needed to go in different directions. I never blamed you, Kat. Shit happens. Now, lead the way back to the kitchen."

Kat looks a little sad, and I understand why, but what she doesn't know is, I had arranged a sabbatical. At the time, I wasn't sure if I even wanted to come back. I know I should tell her, and one day I will. I was sick of constantly being on the road or in a studio. This last year has been really good. I needed to recharge my batteries, but Kat has never had an off button. She's always been moving forward.

I wonder if this new biker boyfriend has experienced the Kat who can't sit still. The one who has to be recording or singing or practicing or doing interviews or something. I bet she's been on her best behavior, and he hasn't even got a peek of the real her. It'll be interesting to see how he'll react when he sees Kat is our leader and how she bosses us around. I wonder if she manages to be the same with him? The only person who Kat doesn't order around is Dave. They have more like a father/daughter relationship, and she always looks to him for guidance.

As we walk toward the stairs, I pull her hair, and she gives me the finger.

Yeah, Dane ain't seen nothin' yet.

CHAPTER 50

JAMIE
Drummer

I'm in the basement lifting weights. It's a very well-equipped room, and I'm glad to be alone. It gives me a chance to gather my thoughts. We've all been through the files, we've all received some pretty crazy fan mail, but a murderer? None of us have had something like that to worry about before. To think someone would think they love us enough to kill us, is unbelievable. It's even more frightening they would kill an innocent bystander.

I joined the band after their original drummer, Mick Tap, died. Can you believe it wasn't a stage name? Said he was born to play the drums because he liked to 'tap' all day long. He was an average drummer, though. He had the potential to be a good one if he'd stopped doing the drugs, alcohol, and general partying. Me, on the other hand? I'm excellent. I was voted best drummer in the world by an MTV poll. I'm twice, no three times the drummer Mick was. I don't do drugs or alcohol even though it's easy to get caught up in the bullshit in our industry. I'm a part of that world, but it isn't my whole world, you know? You have to have outside interests, or this life will suck you dry.

Kat is a surprise. You can see she's happy, and I'm glad to see it. I didn't think she'd survive without her voice, but she has. All Kat ever did was work. She's driven, and without her, we wouldn't be the band we are today. I know she can be replaced as a singer, but Kat's the heart and soul of this band.

My mind is mulling over everything that has happened this last year. I'm lifting weights, totally lost in my thoughts when Truth says, "Jamie, man, you really shouldn't be pressing that amount of weight without a spotter."

He moves into my line of sight and stands above me.

"I'm good, man, I'm good," I answer.

"Yeah, you'll be real good when you drop it on your neck. We've already replaced our drummer once. We don't want or need to do it again."

He always reminds me I'm a replacement. I know he and Mick were tight, but, fuck me, it's been ten years. Ten years of me trying to live up to a ghost. I sit up with my back to Truth.

"Why the fuck do you do that?"

"Do what, try to save your life?" he jokes.

I get up and turn to face him, "You always compare me to Mick, and let's face it, he wasn't half the drummer I am. It's been ten years, Truth, time to get the fuck over it!"

"Whoa, Jamie, you doing steroids, man? What the fuck are you on about?" Truth might pretend to be a drama queen, but we've trained together, and I know he's not to be messed with.

"I know you miss Mick, man, and I get it, but seriously, do you have to remind me every fucking day we're together?"

"Calm the fuck down. Jamie, man, I didn't mean anything by it. You're right, you are a better drummer than Mick ever was. I'm sorry if I said anything to make you feel less than a part of this family. We chose you because of what happened to Mick, but before that, we all knew Mick had to go. His addiction was starting to affect the band, but he did it for us when he overdosed. I do miss him, but Jamie, oh master of the drums, you're worth a hundred Micks."

"Oh, master of the drums? Really?" I'm amazed Truth has admitted this.

"Fuck, yeah, man. The way you play the kit?" He raises his arms and swings them down as though he's playing the drums. "I mean, damn!"

"Thanks, Truth, I appreciate it. Sorry if I'm a dick, just got a lot going on, yeah?"

Truth studies me as though he's seeing me for the first time.

"It's all good. Being back with Kat makes us all a little crazy, especially with a murdering asshole on the loose," says Truth.

"She seems happy with the biker. Think he's a good guy?"

Truth shrugs, walks around the bench, and sits down.

"Who the fuck knows? You're right, she's happy, and I'm glad to see it. I was worried she'd never get to that place again. Time will tell if he's a good guy and not just some user who wants something out of her."

I nod at him and extend my hand. Truth looks at it and slowly puts his hand in mine.

"We good?" I ask him.

"Oh, maniac of the drums, we're beyond good, man. We're fucking sublime."

We both laugh as Dane walks in.

CHAPTER 51

DANE

"Hey, are you all settled in?" I ask.

Jamie and Truth are shaking hands and laughing as I walk into the room to check up on them. It's a fairly large space. It is something I had to have in any home that I built—a place to work out all my frustrations and keep my body in top condition.

Truth gets up from the bench. "Yeah, Dane, we're good. How are you coping with having a house full of moody musicians?"

Jamie laughs and nods at me. "You ever had a house full of creative types, Dane? It goes from normal to crazy in the blink of an eye."

"Try looking after an MC. It's full of egos and aggression. Creative types or musicians should be a walk in the park. Besides, even though Kat can be a handful, she can be reasoned with."

They laugh again, and Jamie walks toward me and claps me on the shoulder. "Well, thanks for letting us stay here. We'll try to be on our best behavior. Your gym is cool, man, thanks for letting me use it." I nod at him as he walks out of the gym.

"Are you able to use all the machines, or do you need any help?"

Truth stares at me as he changes into a black tracksuit.

"I'm good." I can tell he wants to ask me something, so I make it easy on him.

"You know, Kat thinks of you as her family, and seeing as I'm with her now, I guess we're all one big happy-fucking-family. If you've got anything to say, feel free to say it, my man."

Truth grins at me and sits back down on the bench. "I appreciate everything you've done for Kat, and, I guess, for us, but I need to ask you a few questions."

"I said feel free to say it." I grin at him and lean against the wall.

"Kat hasn't had a lot of luck with men. She doesn't normally pick good ones. Kat tends to attract the wrong types, types who only want something from her or want to use her to get what they want, and then sell it to the highest bidder."

"Truth, is there a question in there 'cause I didn't fucking hear one?" I get he's looking out for Kat, but

I don't appreciate being lumped in with a bunch of losers I'm nothing like.

"Do you have an angle? Are you after something? Is she only a fuck, or is she more? I guess what I want to know is, what are your intentions?"

I laugh. "What are my intentions?" He looks a little contrite. "Truth, Kat didn't pick me, I chose her. I literally picked her up and carried her to my home. I've been watching her for a while. Her ma was my friend, and me and the boys owed her a debt which most of us now feel belongs to Kat. If I tried to screw her over, I'd probably have a group of pissed-off brothers who would kick my ass. I don't want anything from Kat, except Kat." I push off the wall and look at him.

"Good. She deserves some good in her life. So, badass biker, I need to exercise, then eat. Thank you for not taking my questions the wrong way. Kat means a lot to me."

"All good, Truth. She means a lot to me as well. But if you ever call me a badass biker again, I might have to kick your ass." We both laugh, and he moves to the treadmill. I nod at him and walk out of the gym.

It feels strange having all of these people in my home. Sometimes, a few of the boys will crash out here, but I've never had this many people in my home all at once. It takes a bit of getting used to. I'm only getting used to having Kat in my life, and now, it's Kat and a bunch of people I don't know.

Her manager, Dave, is a piece of work. One minute, he's nice as pie, but when I challenge him on anything, he turns into a huge-fucking-asshole.

As I wander down the hallway and head up the stairs, I try to decide the best way to handle all of them. When I said running an MC isn't an easy thing, I wasn't exaggerating. This should be a walk in the park as long as I can keep everyone happy.

I make it to the first floor, and I can hear Kat laugh in the kitchen. As I move through the door, I find her and Curtis with my fridge open, talking about what to feed all of us.

"Come on, there can't be that many people to feed, Kat. There're six of us, and how many bikers?"

"Well, if you include everyone who's in the house right now as well as the bikers, it makes fifteen," I answer, beating Kat to it. They both turn around and look at me. Kat's face lights up, and she quickly moves toward me and throws her arms around my neck.

"Fifteen? Really, there are nine of the brothers here?" She looks so happy, better than yesterday, that's for sure.

"Yeah, darlin', I have three of them out front, three out back, two in the driveway. And then there's me." I like her arms around me, but, fuck, I like her legs around me more.

My vixen leans in and says in a low voice, "I can't

wait to be alone with you. I can't wait to show you how thankful I am you have my band in your home. You know, I can be very..." she gets up on tiptoes, so I lean down, and she puts her mouth near my ear, whispering, "... thankful."

My dick gets hard, instantly becoming an ache as it presses against my jeans. I want her now, not later. I've forgotten we have an audience until Curtis says, "Get a room, you two, sheesh! But not until we've fed the masses, Kat."

She laughs and pushes away from me. I immediately feel her absence. I want her to be back in my arms, but I know she has work to do.

"Aww, Curtis, I wouldn't ditch you. Come on, let's get back to it. I think your idea of a stir-fry is the best and easiest. We can cook it in batches and feed everyone fairly quickly if we're both cooking. Sound good?"

And just like that, she's commandeered my kitchen and left me wanting her more. It's going to be a long evening.

CHAPTER 52

BLAIR
Musical Genius

I'm sitting on the back deck looking through the window and at the scene with Dane, Kat, and Curtis. I can't hear what's going on, but I can see they all look happy. I'm on the phone with the producers of *Rock Star*. They aren't pleased Jamie and I took off, so I'm trying to explain we won't be gone for more than a few days, and we'll be back in time for the shooting of the next live episode.

They aren't easy to appease, and I'm trying to keep them happy. "It'll all be fine. I'm bringing all of The Grinders back with me. The audience and the fans will love it!" I have no idea why I said that. I haven't even discussed this with the band yet.

How the fuck do I get them to do this?

The producers are extremely delighted now, and I promise them we'll all be in the studio in four days. Which means I have two-and-a-half days to convince everyone it's a good idea.

The hardest one to convince will be Kat, or maybe even Curtis. He hates being in the limelight unless he's on a stage, but he'd do anything for Kat. Which means I'll have to convince Kat it's a good idea.

How the hell am I going to do that?

My phone rings again, and it's a number I don't recognize, so it's probably the press. I turn it off and put it in my pocket. I'm taking in the sun, and there are two of the MC standing nearby. One of them has a wicked mustache, and he's looking at me now with disbelief.

"Just wondering there, big fella, how do you intend to get our prez to agree to lettin' his woman go off to record an episode of that show? In case you haven't noticed, he's a tad protective of her." His voice is rough, and he sounds annoyed.

"My man, first I have to convince the band, then I'll deal with your prez." He nods and goes to walk away. "I'm Blair, by the way."

I hold out my hand to him, and he looks at it for a minute, then shakes it. "Yeah, I know."

"I didn't catch your name?" I ask inquisitively.

"That's 'cause I didn't give it." He lets go of my hand and frowns at me.

"Okay, brother, only trying to be friendly," I say in a placating manner.

"I'm not your brother." He walks away from me, and I'm a little confused by the hostility. I guess he's not the friendly type.

"Don't mind Keg, he's got enough friends and doesn't want or need anymore," I hear a voice say. "I'm Bear, Road Captain of the Savage Angels MC." This guy is huge, and he has the longest beard I think I've ever seen. The other guy, Keg, looks tiny next to him. I shake Bear's hand. "But he does have a point, our prez will not want Kat out of his sight." Then he laughs. "You haven't got a hope in hell."

"I can be very persuasive when I want to be, my brother. The way I see it, if I can convince Kat, it's all cool."

"Convince me of what?"

Crap, Kat walks toward me, Dane right beside her.

"Kat, honey, I need a favor."

She hugs me. "Anything for you, you know that!"

"Jamie and I need to get back to the studio in four days, and I kind of promised the producer that The Grinders would be there."

Kat frowns at me and shakes her head, but before she can answer, Dane responds, "Kat goes fucking nowhere without me."

We both stare at him.

"Babe, I'm not going," Kat says, her eyes blazing.

"You should go. I know why you don't want to, but I think it will be good for you. Darlin', you've been hiding for way too fucking long." Dane turns to Kat and puts his arm around her.

"Dane, what would be the point of going?" Kat leans into him, looking unsure.

"Darlin', you like being in the spotlight, you thrive in it. You won't have to sing, just be there, wave, talk, shake hands. Be you, it's fucking enough."

Christ, of course, she doesn't want to come, she can't sing. Kat stands between us, her eyes connecting with Dane's. The Kat I know and love is fearless, but I can understand her hesitation. I still marvel at the incredible woman she is. On the outside, she seems happy, but I know she misses singing.

"Kat, honey, you won't have to sing. We won't be performing. All we'll have to do is wave and talk. Please, Kat, I need you," I plead with her.

Kat's the heart and soul of the band. She always has been. I realize I'm asking a lot of her. After the interview with Liz Hayes, she retreated to these mountains. She went from wild child to recluse.

"You shouldn't have promised we'd all be there, Blair. Can't you do it without me?" Kat asks.

"No, Kat, I promised The Grinders, and that means you, too." She looks up at Dane, and he nods his head at her.

After a few seconds, she squares her shoulders. "Okay, Blair, okay, but you fucking owe me! They better not ask me to sing! You better make sure it's what you said, waving and talking! Do you get me? And I can't do it without Dane being there, so you make sure everyone knows he's with me!"

That's my girl, full of fire and self-determination.

"Okay, honey, I owe you. Now, we need to talk to Dave and make sure it's all good. He doesn't like it much when we arrange things without his approval."

"Yeah, you got that right, but I'm not going to be the one to tell him. That's all on you."

Kat looks smug as she says this, and I wince. We both know how Dave can be, and we didn't get to be a number one band without him, so I'll need to tell him and soon.

CHAPTER 53

JASMIN TREVAINE
Keyboardist

We've been riding for over two hours, and I've had my lady bits pressed up against this man, Judge, the entire time. I was horny before I got on the back of his bike, but now it feels almost painful. I know I pissed Truth off by going with this bad boy, but we both know he's never going to fuck me.

I've been feeling this guy up for the entire ride, and I mean everywhere. He's all lanky muscle, and he feels good to touch. I was hoping to be fucked by now, though. Don't get me wrong, I love being on the back of a motorcycle, but two hours of sexual frustration is scandalous.

Finally, he pulls over. We're way up in the mountains, and in front of me is a run-down shack. He stops the bike, and I hop off, and damn, both my legs are sore. I bend over, trying to straighten all the kinks out when he walks up behind me and grabs my hips.

"Sugar, after all the things you put me through on my bike, we're going to fuck like rabbits all night long. My dick is trying to make its way out of my jeans all on its own, but I'd really like it, sugar, if you helped with that."

His voice is like honey, and it sort of rolls over you. I think if he kept talking to me, I'd do anything. "First, I need to see what the accommodations look like because, if I don't like what I see, we're fucking on your bike, bad boy. Second, I can't stay overnight, I'll need to get back to the band."

Judge chuckles and says, "Accommodations? Well, come this way, sugar, you should never judge a book by its cover, just like me. I think you'll be pleasantly surprised. And if you can't stay, we'll have to make this one hell of an afternoon, now won't we?" I grab his hand, and we walk toward the shack. He grabs the key from above the door, and we go inside.

He's right, it's nothing like it looks from the outside. It's well lived-in, and everything's all in one big room—a bed, a beautiful fireplace, a kitchen, and a bathtub over in the corner at the back of the shack. It's cozy, decorated in shades of red, and above the fireplace is the Savage Angels' emblem. There's no television, though, and as I look around the room. I wonder if there's even electricity because, if not, it would mean no hot water.

"So, sugar, what do you think?"

"It's really nice, but where's the toilet, and is there any hot water?"

Judge roars with laughter. "The toilet is through the back door. Go out back, turn immediately right, then open the door, and there it is." He looks at me as he undoes his belt, walking backward.

"Uh, Judge? You didn't say anything about hot water?"

He stops what he's doing and laughs again, "All right, sugar, I'll fire up the wood-burning stove. It'll heat the water for the shower or bath. By the time I'm finished with you, it will be nice and hot."

Judge walks out the back door, and I follow him. There's a small shelter with wood stacked up inside about thirty feet from the door, and to my right is the door to the toilet. I open it and am pleasantly surprised—it's all white and very clean. I go in and quickly use the facilities. There's a mirror above the sink, and I look at myself, shuddering. I look like I've been dragged through a hedge backward! I'm a mess. I try to untangle all the knots by using my fingers, but it's not really doing very much.

"Ah, well, Jas, you didn't come here for a beauty competition. You, my darling, came here to get fucked, so we better go find the fucker." I open the door and find Judge waiting on the other side.

"You often talk to yourself, sugar?" Judge looks amused as if I'm the funniest person on the planet.

"Yes, I do. Do you happen to have a brush?"

He bursts out laughing again, and his eyes look good when he laughs. They sparkle.

"Yes, I do." Judge mimics me, then he grabs my hand and leads me back inside.

He motions for me to sit on the bed, and walks to one of the side tables, opens it, and produces a brush. He positions himself on the bed with his back to the wall and proceeds to place all of the pillows behind him. When he seems satisfied, he pats the spot between his legs, and I move to sit between them.

"Ever had your hair brushed by a man, sugar?" Judge is slowly brushing out the knots in my hair.

"Yes, I have but not in a long time."

Judge stops what he's doing, and he says, "Ever had your hair brushed by a man in a cabin far away from civilization?"

I laugh. "Well, come to think of it, no, I haven't."

"Ahh, well, you're in for a treat, sugar. Now relax, and let Judge do all the work."

"Okay, but there better be sex later. I'm horny as hell."

The sound of his laughter reverberates through me, sending a delicious shiver down my spine, spreading into my limbs and my core. He sweeps the hair off the back of my neck and lays kisses across my skin.

"How do you like to be fucked? Any preferences, sugar?"

"As long as I get to Nirvana, you can fuck me any way you like. Oh, but getting head? I really like head," I purr at him.

"Nirvana?" he says questioningly.

"Yes, Nirvana, I want to come, I want to feel that exquisite sensation of nearly being in heaven or Nirvana. I want you to take me there. After having my lady bits pressed up against you for hours, I want to come, and I want to ride your face."

Judge laughs, drops the brush, and grabs my breast. "Your lady bits pressed up against me?" He chuckles. "Fuck, I love a dirty mouth. Does your dirty mouth like to give head as well?"

"Baby, I'll suck you all night long if you get me to Nirvana. Fuck, I'll let you do anything, but you have to get me there first."

"You like kink, sugar?" His voice has gone rough as he lets his hands explore my body.

"Kink? Depends on how far you want to go. I like to use my hands, though. It's not fun for me unless I can use my hands. I don't mind being tied up occasionally, just not every time."

"Okay, so we'll keep your hands available. Anything else you don't like?"

I'm wondering how far I'm willing to let this man take me. After all, we've only just met.

"No anal on the first date, no videotaping, no photos. Pain is something I have to work up to. If you don't get me all hot and horny and begging for it, you can't hurt me. I have to be in the zone."

Judge stops what he's doing, and I look up at him. The only word I can use to describe him is hungry. I've never seen a man look at me like that before.

"I won't hurt you, sugar, I'm not into pain. I don't do videos or take photos because I don't need them. I have a great imagination." Judge taps the side of his head.

"So, what are you into, what gets you off?"

A slow smile spreads across his face, and his hands resume their travels over my body. I have too many clothes on, and I'm undoing the buttons of my shirt.

Judge grabs both my hands and says, "No, sugar, I get to do that. It's like unwrapping a present that's only for me." He pauses then continues, "I want you to lick me."

"You want me to lick you? Honey, that's not kink, that's vanilla."

I giggle, and I reach up to touch his face, then I move one of his hands toward my mouth and suck his fingers, one by one. When I get to his thumb, I bite it a little, then continue to suck it.

"I don't think you understand me, sugar. I like to have my balls, my cock, and just about everywhere... licked."

"Oh, honey, I understand, but no play for you until I get to Nirvana. Do you have any honey, cream, or something sweet I can lick off you? Let's get messy!" I say excitedly.

Judge chuckles and moves me away from him as he gets off the bed.

"I'm sure to have honey in the pantry. Can I pour it on you, sugar?"

"Baby, you can insert it, fuck me with it, or eat it off me, but can we get to the fucking?"

"Insert you with it? Hmm." His eyes are full of passion and playfulness. "Do you like Geisha balls? I could cover them in honey and lick you clean."

"Geisha balls? What are they?" Judge smiles and moves to the bedside table and pulls out two little gold balls joined together with a chain. He places them in my palm, and I can see they both have another ball inside of them, moving around.

"They move when they're inside you and stimulate your beautiful cunt. You'll love it."

"Cunt? Not sure if I like that word, even if you did say beautiful."

Judge opens a cupboard in the pantry and holds up the honey jar, then he opens it and drops the Geisha balls into it.

"Take off your jeans, sugar, so I can get to your cunt. I want to put them inside you and bring you to Nirvana."

"Okay, cunt it is." I jump up and shimmy out of

my jeans as quickly as I can. Judge laughs, and I stop and look at him. "What?"

"Sugar, I can tell you're excited, but I think we need to get your boots off first."

I look down, and, sure enough, my boots are still on my feet. I decide it's time someone takes control.

"On your knees, boy, take off my boots, and be quick about it," I say to him.

"Your wish is my command." Judge is chuckling as he gets into position and removes my boots, then he reaches up and pulls my jeans and panties off in one go.

"Take off my shirt and bra and suck my nipples," I order him as I spread my legs and move closer to him.

"Fuck, I love a woman who knows what she wants. Talk dirty to me, sugar, and you'll be my perfect lay." Judge runs his hands along my thighs, just brushing my pussy, then undoes my shirt.

"Judge, hurry the fuck up. I want your mouth on me. I want you to pour honey on my breasts, and then I want you to lick it off. You had better be good at sucking my nipples."

Finally, I'm naked, and he dips his fingers into the honey and smears it down my chest, my belly, then he pushes me, so I'm flat on the bed with my legs dangling over the edge.

"Spread your legs for me, sugar, so I can put these…" Judge pauses, dangling the Geisha balls over me as honey drips from them onto my body, "... in your cunt."

I spread my legs further apart and bend my knees up to my sides, grabbing them with my hands.

"My cunt is ready for you, Judge, so are you ready to let me ride your face?" I pant, excitement building inside of me.

"Patience, sugar, you said you wanted me to suck your nipples, and I'm going to do just that. You can ride my face later."

He pushes them inside me one at a time, and there's a feeling of fullness. Then he lowers himself onto me and draws a nipple in between his teeth and sucks. His hand rolls my other nipple, and electricity spreads through me.

"Do you like it, sugar?" Judge asks as his tongue licks my nipple.

"Fuck, yes! I want more, give me more!" I pant, arching up into his body.

He chuckles and continues to work my nipples, then his hand is working between my legs, and he hits my sweet spot.

"I want to ride your face. I want you to give me head now!"

Judge stops what he's doing and gets up off me.

"No! Why'd you stop?! I didn't say stop!" My body is screaming for release, and I've had enough of waiting around.

"Relax, sugar, I want to enjoy you, and I want to do it naked." Judge sits back on the bed and takes off his boots.

It feels like he's taking his time, so I masturbate, but he grabs my hands, and I shout, "Judge!"

"No, sugar, I want to be the one to get you to Nirvana."

I look at him. He's tanned and well-built but not in a massive way. His penis is really wide, not huge in length, but I wouldn't say it's small, either. Judge kneels next to the bed, grabs my ankles, and pulls me toward him.

He sucks, bites, and licks the inside of my thigh, and I squirm because I want him to suck, bite, and lick my slit.

"I want to ride your face, Judge, put your mouth and tongue in my cunt now," I demand in a breathy tone.

His tongue licks my slit, and I feel my vagina clench in anticipation. He puts both hands under my ass, and inserts his tongue into my pussy. The sensation of the Geisha balls and his mouth on me are more than I can stand as my orgasm quickly builds. Grabbing the back of his head, I grind into his face.

"Yes, let me fuck your face." I hold him in position, and as he sucks on my clit, I finally find my Nirvana. "Judge! That's it, baby!" I scream and let him go.

"Sugar, you taste better than honey, and I fucking love a woman who knows what she likes and is experienced in bed."

I laugh and say, "Baby, wipe your face, you're covered in me and honey."

Instead of doing what he's told, he licks my body and slowly makes his way to my mouth.

"Sugar, I do believe it's my turn."

"You're my new favorite fuck, babe. Move your way up, sit on my face, and I'll suck and lick all you want."

He leans down to kiss me, and it suddenly dawns on me, we haven't done that yet. His tongue slips into my mouth, and I suck on it before letting my tongue dance with his. This man knows what he's doing, he feels amazing, and I'm getting lost in his kiss. My hands explore his body, and he rolls us, so I'm on top before pushing me down his body.

"You don't want to ride my face?" I ask him.

"Not this time, sugar, I want to be in the same position you were. I want you to bring me to Nirvana."

There's honey everywhere. It's even in my hair, and it's really sticky, but the taste of it mixed with his sweat is incredible. I lick his very well-defined abs when he grabs a fistful of my hair and says, "Sugar, as much as I appreciate you taking your time, I'm fucking wound up and ready to go, so let's speed this up a little."

I look him in the eyes, and Judge smiles. "You want me to suck your balls or your cock? How wound up are you?"

"I want you to lick my balls and my cock, and I want you to suck on them. If it's okay with you, I'll use my hand, and when I'm about to blow, I want your dirty little mouth on my cock."

I smile, put my hand between my legs and smear honey all over his cock and balls. "Just to make sure you taste as good as me, babe."

"Whatever works for you," Judge groans.

He pushes me down. I love my hair being pulled. I lick the tip of his cock on my way down to his balls. The noises he makes are nothing short of animalistic, I like it when my men make noise. Nothing worse than a lay who's quiet. Judge has one hand around his cock, moving it up and down at a punishing speed, and the other is entangled in my hair, pulling and pushing me around. I'm down there for a while, so I ride my hand, enjoying myself.

All of a sudden, he yanks me up by the hair and says, "Change of plans, sugar."

Judge reaches under my arms and pulls me up his torso so I'm straddling him. The honey is sticky and I burst out laughing, wondering what the hell I look like, my hair must be all kinds of messed up. Judge grins as his hand moves from my hip to my vagina and he pulls out the Geisha balls. I gasp at the loss and then moan as he impales me on his cock, moving me backward and forward. I'm rocking my hips as fast as I can, but I sense I'm not going fast enough.

"Need to change positions, sugar, you up for it?" Judge growls at me.

"Baby, I'm up for anything," I purr.

"Get on your hands and knees on the edge of the bed." I get off him and position myself. "Spread your legs wider for me, sweet."

I do as I'm told, and as soon as I get myself spread as far as I can go, he thrusts inside me. This position works wonders for my G-spot, and he hits it with every thrust. Judge pounds inside, getting rougher, and his nails are biting into my hips. I can feel myself on the verge of another orgasm.

"Use your hand, sugar. Let's get to Nirvana together."

I drop down onto my elbows and push my ass up higher, rubbing my clit. And then it hits me, and I let out a loud moan.

"That's it, sugar, come for me." I can feel him pounding me even faster, and I feel like I'm about to be split in two when he thrusts in as far as he can go, making a growling noise. "So fucking tight! Fuck me, sugar, so fucking good!"

Judge stays impaled inside of me while his breathing evens out and my aftershocks slowly subside, then he pulls out of me, slaps my ass, and flops on the bed. I slowly crawl forward and lay down beside him.

"Did I hurt you, sugar? I like a little of the rough, hard, and fast."

I laugh. "I told you if you got me to Nirvana, you could do what you liked with me, but next time we have to cut your nails because they hurt."

Judge laughs, and I watch his chest go up and down. My hand reaches out, and I stroke it.

"Time for a bath, sugar. I'll need to strip the bed, too, can't have the creepy-crawlies making a nest where I like to sleep."

"Cool, go run me a bath, and I'll strip the bed. Do you have anything to drink? Coke, lemonade, anything fizzy?"

"Ah, sugar, the only fizzy thing I have is beer." Judge chuckles.

"Beer it is! Now get your ass to the fridge and run me a bath!"

"Sugar, there isn't a fridge. I do have a cooler I use, but as I haven't been up here in a while, my beers are bound to be warm. Is that okay?" Judge asks questioningly.

"Fuck, warm beer? Hmm… well, beggars can't be choosers. I guess I'll have to slum it."

Judge gets up and walks toward the kitchen, chuckling to himself. "Slum it? Fuck, sugar, I think you've been slumming it from the moment you took my hand."

After I strip the bed, he gets me a beer. Seeing as

it's warm, I don't drink all of it. The bath is to die for and big enough for two. We stay in the tub until the water gets cold, then he towels me off, and we get dressed. The day is nearly over by the time we leave the shack. Night is creeping its way into the world.

It's a nice way to spend the afternoon and blow off some steam. Judge isn't a complicated man. He has his club, his motorcycle, and the shack. I'm not looking for something permanent, and he's been a nice diversion. Kat has to be my main priority right now. I need to make sure she's in the right frame of mind, make sure she's safe, and I have to protect the band. It's been good having time off from everything because I needed the time away from them. They are family, and like all families, we have our problems. I'm giving myself another six months, and then it's back in the studio.

As a group, we haven't discussed who, if anyone, will replace Kat, but I want to start recording before another year rolls by. The public can be fickle, and I don't want to be replaced by some ridiculous boy band where all the members were handpicked to be together by some fancy record label, only to churn out teeny bopper bullshit I wouldn't wipe my ass with.

I'm kind of glad Judge took me out for a ride to the middle of nowhere. The ride back will give me time to process all the shit that's going through my brain.

CHAPTER 54

DANE

Dinner with Kat and her band is a new experience. Jasmin and Judge get back from their ride as we sit down to eat. It's interesting seeing Judge with a woman. He's usually a love-'em-and- leave-'em kind of guy.

I can't be certain, but I think he went back to her room after we parted ways and went to bed. No one told Dave about the impending trip, which, to tell the truth, surprised me as they are probably going to be advertising it on television. It isn't my place to say anything, so I kept quiet. Now, I'm waiting for Kat to get out of the shower.

I'm hard just thinking about her. I grab my shaft and stroke it, and with my other hand, I play with my balls. I've closed my eyes, my thoughts consumed with Kat, and like a dream, I feel her hands on me, then I feel her tongue on my balls. Kat slowly takes one of my balls into her mouth and sucks then licks.

I grab her hair and drag her up to my shaft, saying, "Open your mouth, darlin', I have something for you."

Before she can say anything, I force my dick into her mouth. I move her head up and down, slowly at first and then more quickly. Her tongue is working me like a virtuoso, and I can feel it building. I fuck her mouth hard and fast. Kat moans, and it goes straight through to my dick, but I don't want to come in her mouth. I yank her off my cock, jackknife up, flip her over, and ram into her. She's so tight and wet. I keep a hold of her hair, giving me the control I need. My grip keeps her head up and her ass raised against me. I can feel myself on the brink of an explosion, so I pull out slightly and then thrust back into her, hard. She's warm and feels like velvet caressing my dick. The sensation sends me over the edge, and I orgasm.

It's never felt so good.

This woman gets better the more I know her, but as I'm coming down from my high, I realize she hasn't had any fun. I pull out of her and roll her onto her back. Latching onto one of her nipples, I suck it until it pebbles under my tongue. Kat arches off the bed and makes the most fucking unbelievable noise. I use my finger and find her sweet spot. She rides my hand, pulling her bottom lip into her mouth, stifling a moan. I kiss down her belly, and now it's her turn. Kat pushes my head down between her legs, and I suck her clit. She rides my face, pulling my hair, and I put my fingers back inside her as I work her with my tongue. The taste of our juices mixing is fucking unbelievable.

"Dane, please don't stop, please, baby!" I can tell she's close, and then she spreads her legs even further apart and moans. Kat's fingers twist in the sheets, and she pants. "That's it, baby, that's it, baby, that's it, baby!" She comes on my face, but I keep working her until she grips my hair in her hands and yanks my face up. "No more, baby, please, no more!"

I move up her body, grab the sheet, and wipe my face with it, but she soon grabs the top of my head and pulls me by the hair to her. Kat's kissing me and grinding into me.

She's fucking insatiable.

"Do you like the way you taste, baby? Does it turn you on?" I growl at her, and she laughs.

"Fuck, yes, I do! Your taste is mingled in there as well. I fucking love it."

"Thank fuck for that. I love the taste of you, too, darlin'." I roll off her and land on my back. Kat sits up and straddles me.

"Don't tell me you're finished, babe. I'm going to

go get cleaned up, so I'm ready for round two." Kat smiles at me, slides off, and goes into the bathroom.

I smile at the ceiling and then hear the shower. Kat's the only woman I've fucked in this house, and I intend to fuck her in every room. I get an idea and slowly get up and walk into the bathroom. She's bent over washing her legs, and I'm instantly hard, again.

I walk up behind her and say, "Stay in this position but spread your legs for me, darlin'. I want to fuck you again, but I need you to do exactly as I say, or you don't get to have any fun."

Kat moves slightly forward, spreads her legs further apart, and puts her palms flat on the tiles. She keeps silent, but I can hear her breathing has picked up. Fuck, she's getting turned on by my commands.

"Good girl, now did you clean your pussy for me? Pass me the soap." Kat stands up. "Did I say you could fucking stand up?" I slap her on the ass, she gasps, immediately bends over again, only moving her arm to grab the soap, and she passes it to me. "That's my darlin'. Now I need to check if you're clean." I put my hand under the water and lather up the soap. I slowly wash her back and move my hands down her ass. When she pushes it up against me, I slap it again. "Now, what did I tell you? Stay. Still." She's making little noises, and I can tell she's turned on. I put my fingers inside her, and she arches her back, needing more. I twist her hair around my fist and lift her head so she's still slightly bent over. "Tell me what you want me to do. Tell me how you want me to fuck you," I whisper in her ear.

"I want to sit on the vanity. I want to face you when you fuck me." Kat sounds all breathy, and as I remove my hand from her cunt, she cries out in protest. I push her toward the vanity. The shower is still running, and the steam is filling up the room.

I use her hair to turn her around. "Get your ass up on the vanity, darlin', cause my woman wants to be fucked while facing me." Kat uses her arms and gets herself up on the vanity as I drop to my knees in front of her. I look up and say, "No touching, or I'll stop, and I'll fuck you from behind, and you won't get to finish."

I move into her as she braces herself by holding onto the top of the vanity. Fuck, the smell of her drives me crazy as I lick her slit.

"Spread your legs wider, darlin', I want your pussy wide open for me." She does as she's told, and I suck on her clit. When she's wet enough, I put my thumb to my fingers and push them inside her and slowly work my hand in, then I close my fingers into a fist and go back to working her clit with my mouth. Kat moans loudly, and her orgasm hits. I can feel her cunt pulsing around my fist as she screams my name, and she's crying. I know I have pushed my woman to her limits. When the spasms stop, I slowly draw out my hand and stand up, gathering her in my arms.

Kissing her tears away, I say, "I'm not finished yet, darlin', I still have to have my fun. Put your feet up on the vanity." She looks spent, but she does as she's told, and as soon as her feet are up, I push and pound into her as hard and fast as I can.

The orgasm hits me quickly, and she cries out when I plant myself in as far as I can go. She sags up against me, and I quickly pull out, and I carry her back into the shower. Very slowly, I lather her entire body. I rinse her off, give myself a very quick once-over, then grab a towel and wipe my woman down and do the same to myself. Picking her up, I carry her into the bedroom, lay her on the bed, cover her, and walk around to the other side, where I slide in. As soon as I'm settled, she moves into me, draping a leg over mine and placing her head on my shoulder.

"You okay, darlin'?" I'm nervous I may have pushed her too far.

"Never been better but so tired… I can't keep my eyes open." Kat's tone tells me she's sleepy.

"I didn't hurt you?"

"Hurt me? Hell, no! It was a first for me, baby, but it was un-fucking-believable!"

I chuckle. "Good, we'll do it again another time."

"Yes, please, when I'm well rested and can keep up with you. You wiped me out."

"It can be very…. intense. Go to sleep, darlin', go to sleep."

We lie there in the dark, and I can feel her breathing get heavier, then I feel her fall asleep, and I follow not five minutes later.

CHAPTER 55

DAVE

Over dinner, everyone is surprisingly quiet. I've been managing these guys for too long not to know something is afoot. Whatever it is, it must be a big deal. Blair barely speaks throughout the entire night, and Kat teases him relentlessly, which means it has something to do with him and probably the television show he and Jamie are tied into.

I'm exhausted.

After making sure the band is all settled in, I ask Dane for a ride into town in the morning.

Then as I lay my head on the pillow, I wonder and not for the first time, why I don't retire and let someone else look after the bands. It's a full-time job keeping up with their love lives let alone trying to organize tours or get them into a studio.

Maybe it's a younger man's game?

Slowly I drift off, wondering what the hell Blair has done now.

Surprisingly, the next morning, he sends two of his boys in an incredibly large SUV to collect me. They aren't talkative, which turns out to be a good thing as I spend most of the time on my phone arranging for the press to be notified that The Grinders are in town, and I was asked to go to the sheriff's office to give a statement. This isn't true, of course, but they don't need to know that. The story is less than forty-eight hours old, so the sooner we get ahead of it and spin it to our advantage, the better. Whoever let the truth get in the way of a good story should be shot.

Tourmaline is bigger than I thought, but it's still rudimentary. Lots of mom-and-pop businesses, which is cool, but they don't have a huge variety.

Pulling into the café, which looks like something from the stone age, I ask for a soy mocha decaf, but I end up with a skinny cappuccino. It's good. I'm trying to cut back on the caffeine, but I do enjoy the hit.

When I'm finished my morning coffee, I walk the

short distance to the sheriff's office. I'm surprised to see how many of the press are in town as I battle my way through them. It's a pity Kat can't sing anymore. I'd be making millions off them right now. Well, I am, but I could always make more.

Two deputies come out and escort me inside. I'm brushing myself off when a deep voice garners my attention. He's not talking to me, instead he's addressing the deputies who helped me.

"Tell them to move on," he orders.

"I did, Sheriff, but they won't leave."

He lets out a sigh his gaze goes from the throng outside and eventually lands on me. He's tall, lanky and all Latino hotness. My gaydar isn't going off so unfortunately, he's straight.

He quirks an eyebrow at me, and says, "Sheriff Carlos Morales, and you are?"

"Dave Lawrence, Manager of The Grinders. Nice to meet you, Sheriff Morales, or should I call you Carlos?" I said this in my most professional voice with a hint of 'you may fuck me' as I extend my hand.

He grips mine firmly, giving me a brief shake. "Sheriff Morales is fine. What can I do for you, Mr. Lawrence?" He's making it very clear he doesn't swing my way, but he can't stop me from looking.

"Please, call me Dave. Is there somewhere more private we could talk, Sheriff?"

He motions for me to follow him, and we walk

toward an office at the back of the bullpen.

"This is much better!" I clap my hands and turn around in the tiny space that's obviously his office. Mine is much bigger than his. I look at the walls and see a picture of an older man holding up a fish— he's either the sheriff's father or a close family member as the resemblance is striking. "Oh, do you fish, Sheriff? I haven't done that since I was a boy!"

"Is there something I can do for you, Mr. Lawrence?" The sheriff asks, all cold and to the point.

"May I sit, Sheriff?"

"Of course, Mr. Lawrence, but can we get to the point and quickly, please? I have an FBI profiler coming in here today. An FBI profiler, I might add, who has no right even to be here, but because the victim was murdered in the home of a famous person, they got sent, and they don't want to be here anymore than I want them here. But we all have our jobs to do, so what's yours?" Sheriff Morales looks more than mildly annoyed and slightly tired. Being the sheriff in a small, quiet town, probably doesn't prepare you for the world press to be at your door.

"Sheriff Morales, my job is to ensure my girl, Kat, is looked after and her band, The Grinders, aren't dragged into anything which would portray them in an unsavory light."

"Unsavory light? I don't follow you, Mr. Lawrence."

He has nice eyes, but there's an edge to them. I'm trying to figure him out, get a feel for the man. Hopefully, he'll see things in a way which could benefit all of us if I can spin this correctly.

"Sheriff, The Grinders are an international brand. It's my job to always be on the lookout for them and to help them in any situation that may arise. The death of this young girl is horrible but—"

"Murder." The sheriff's voice is hard and cold.

"Yes, of course, murder." He's looking at me as if we're already done. Who would've thought a small-town sheriff could put me on the back foot? "It's horrible, but I need to make evident to the press, and, hopefully, you, to see this from a different light. I can't have there being any hint that any of The Grinders would've been caught up in this. If I do my job properly and get the press on our side, it will make your and my job a hell of a lot easier."

Sheriff Morales takes in a big sigh and rubs the back of his neck. "How are you going to help me?"

"I'll handle the press for you, and even after we've gone, I'll leave an associate here to handle any lingering journalists or fame mongers for say, a month?" I pull my phone out and start to flip through my contacts to see who would be best to handle things after I've left.

"Fame mongers?" I look up, and the sheriff is staring at me.

"Sorry, Sheriff, just trying to find out who'd be a good fit for you, but yes, fame mongers. Normally, they come fairly quickly and lie to the press, so they get their fifteen minutes of fame, but the smart ones stay awhile, get the lay of the land, and know enough of the truth to be believable. These ones will try to befriend you or a member of your team, or they may already be living here and want to be famous or want a payday."

"Fucking great." Again, he sighs, but now he's rubbing between his eyes, he flops down in his chair. "This town, Tourmaline, is a nice little town, Mr. Lawrence. The last murder we had here was five years ago, and it was before my time. I came here from a bigger city, one that had more crime, more murders, more rapes, more everything. I figured the only thing I needed to worry about coming here were the Savage Angels, and, truthfully, even before I got here, they were beginning to go straight. I keep an eye on them, and I've weeded out most of the cops on the take. They don't bring their illegal activities into this town, and I'm pretty sure Dane Reynolds, their president, will break this chapter away from the others to keep it clean. I might have it all wrong, but I've been studying them for a while, and that's what I think he'll eventually do."

"Let me help you, Sheriff. Let me call a press conference. The only thing I need from you is information, and you tell me what you want the press to know or what you think they need to know, and I'll do it."

"What I think they need to know?"

"Yes, Sheriff, I can report you're very close to making an arrest, or you at least have someone under suspicion, or I can give them the facts as they are now. It's completely up to you, Sheriff. Utilize me. I can handle the press better than most, certainly better than any person you have in Tourmaline. I'm good at my job, Sheriff, and if I'm not, I'll get someone who's better."

"I haven't made any kind of statement to the press yet, so what do you need?" the sheriff asks me.

"Can you tell me about the murder?"

He stares at me, weighing me up while rocking in his chair. I need to seal this deal.

"Just the facts, Sheriff, the girl's name, who she is, where it was done. Not specifics, nothing to jeopardize the case. Allow me to help you by helping me."

"Mr. Lawrence, Dave, if you screw me over on this, I'll find a way to make you pay. Do you understand?"

"Absolutely, Sheriff. Absolutely."

He explains what happened to the girl, Jess, and

how they still haven't managed to get in touch with her parents. I go outside, make a statement to the press, but don't release her name.

When I'm done, I ring a publicist I know and ask if they would come out and look after everything, especially the press.

All that was hours ago. Now, I'm standing in a towel in my room, in Kat's new boyfriend's house, sipping a scotch. I've got the television on, but I'm not really watching it until I see an ad for *Rock Star* stating The Grinders are going to be on their live show Saturday night.

Fucking Blair!

So that's why Kat was teasing him over dinner. They all fucking knew, and no one said anything to me! Fucking typical!

I guess I'm going to have to give them all a talking-to in the morning. But right now, I'm unbelievably tired. I traveled nonstop to get here as soon as I heard the first news report. I was already on my way when Truth called me. Then one of my assistants called me.

I look after my bands, all of them, but The Grinders, and especially Kat, are family.

CHAPTER 56

KAT

It's early in the morning, no one is up yet, and Dane has his face, or more importantly, his mouth between my legs. He's put a finger inside me, and I have my hands in his hair, keeping his head in position. I fucking love oral sex, both giving and receiving.

It's a lovely way to wake up. A girl could get used to it. I'm grinding into his mouth, and I am chasing that special feeling, the feeling which will put me over the edge. I've almost caught it, it's teasing me. Dane sucks on my clit, and that's it, I've found it. I'm riding the wave as it crashes into me.

Fucking perfect.

"Stop, baby." I let his head up, and he smirks at me.

"Good mornin', darlin'." He's on his knees between my legs, and he's got a hard-on.

"You want a blow job?"

Again, he smiles.

"No, babe, want to fuck you missionary style." He spreads my legs further, pushing inside me, and lays down on top of me.

"Babe, I can't breathe, you need to—"

"Relax, Kat." Dane pushes up from me and links his fingers with mine, then he starts to move. He's huge, his dick fills me, and it feels amazing. As he pumps into me, I move with him. Dane smiles at me and increases his speed.

"Can I get you there again, darlin'?"

"Babe, it's all good for this to be about you." I spread my legs further and pull my knees up toward my side.

"Darlin', not the way I work, not with you, so use your hand."

Dane slides out of me and flips me over. I move into a kneeling position, and he rams back inside me.

"Use your hand, come with me at the same time. Do it for me, darlin'."

I'm rubbing my clit, and I spread my legs further apart. My ass is up in the air, and he's pulling me harder and harder against him. The feeling is barely there on the surface, I can feel it. Dane moves faster, he must be close.

"Darlin', tell me you're almost there, I can't hold out for much longer," he groans.

"So close, baby, so close."

"That's not good enough. Come for me, Kat, do it now."

His voice is commanding, and he stops pumping into me and slaps me hard across my ass. The orgasm hits me like a tidal wave, and I can feel him moving faster, vigorous thrusts as he powers into me over and over again. The virile sound which escapes from deep within his chest sends raging heat through my limbs. Dane rams into me one last time and stops.

"Now, that's a good fucking way to say good morning, darlin'." He pulls out of me, and I push up to my knees. Dane wraps me in his arms and he rubs my nipple, which pebbles under his touch. "Fuck, I love this body. I love the way you respond to me, darlin'."

"Babe, you need to stop unless you're ready to go again, or I can ride your face."

Dane laughs. "Do you think you could get there again? You can use me if you want, you know. I have no fucking problem with that."

"Stop, stop, stop, it's too early, and I've already come twice. I think I can handle not being satisfied a third time before breakfast.

Dane laughs. "Come shower with me?"

"As long as it's only a shower."

I slowly get off the bed.

"Now, darlin', I didn't say it would only be a shower."

Dane grabs my hand, and we head into the bathroom. I think I'm going to like this shower.

CHAPTER 57

DANE

I'm toweling off as I watch Kat do the same. We have a lot to discuss, and I'm not one to drag things out.

"Kat, we need to talk about the gig."

"Babe, what's there to talk about? I'll go, make an appearance, and then we'll come home. You're coming with me, right?" Kat's looking through drawers trying to decide which underwear goes best with her outfit. I didn't even know women do this, but it's fucking hot.

"Yes, I'm coming, but I have a lot of work to do here. It's not fucking easy for me to leave."

Kat's putting on her underwear and tries to walk toward me at the same time. "Tell me what you need. Tell me how I can help." I stand there with only a towel on me, and when she makes it to me, she puts her hands on my chest. "I'd do anything for you, Dane. You only have to ask."

No woman has ever said that to me before. None of them have ever cared enough.

"I need to make sure the garage is running properly and the freight company has all the orders filled and can get on the road."

"Okay, what can I do?" Kat has her head tilted to the side and is chewing her bottom lip.

I bend down and kiss her. "Could you pack for me? Could you make sure the house is cleaned and in order? It would mean a lot if you did this for me."

"That's it? Pack and clean the house? Fuck, baby, I can do that! I'll get the boys to help, maybe even Jasmin if she's up to it."

I chuckle. "Is it me, or were she and Judge really quiet over dinner last night?"

"Yeah, she doesn't really do relationships. She's kind of a loner. Always has been."

"Hmm… well, so is Judge. Never seen him fuck a woman more than once. Okay, I have to go into town and sort out the garage and the depot. You don't leave this house without me." I pause and look at her. "Are we clear about that?"

"Yes, He-Who-Must-Be-Obeyed, we're clear about that!" Kat pokes her tongue out at me and goes to walk away, so I hook her around the waist, and she yells, "Dane!"

"Darlin', I'll not have you hurt, and the fucker who killed Jess may be long gone, but I will not take that fucking chance. I'll not risk you. Are we clear?"

"Yes, babe, we're clear. Dane..." she pauses then asks tentatively, "... have you spoken to Luke?"

When he was first told about Jess, he shut down completely. Now, he's angry and looking for trouble. I've assigned Keg to him to be his unofficial keeper, just in case he provokes the wrong person or persons. As president of an MC, you have to look after everyone, and it's not always easy. Luke will be patched into the club, he's proven himself, but everyone has to do their time as a prospect, and he's no different. Within the MC, there are those who need us because they have no family of their own, and these usually make good members as they are often the most loyal. Luke didn't have any family, and as far as the sheriff can find, neither did Jess. It's probably why they gravitated toward each other.

I hope Luke can see his way past this. I've seen how men react when they've had too much ugly in their lives and how it can twist them. He's a good man, and my hope is he'll make his way through this mess with help from the club.

"Luke is doing as well as can be expected. The MC looks after its own, and he'll be fine, eventually."

Kat nods and walks back into the bathroom. I finish getting dressed and head downstairs to the kitchen to grab a coffee and a quick breakfast. I have a lot to do today and not a lot of time to do it in.

My home phone rings as I'm drinking my coffee, and I answer it. "Hello?"

"Hey, Prez, it's Jonas. You got a minute, or are you too busy fucking a rock star to talk to me?"

"Jonas! Man, it's good to hear your voice. And the rock star is off-limits, by the way." I laugh. It's been too long since Jonas checked in.

"Off-limits? Well, that's a new one! I'm nearly done down here, Prez, so do you want me to come home and help with your situation, or is everything cool?"

Not having the VP and my closest friend around for almost a year hasn't been easy, so I'm relieved to hear him asking to come home.

"Jonas, I have to leave town with Kat, Ms. Saunders' daughter. I won't be gone for long, but I'd feel more comfortable if you were fucking home, brother."

"I know she's Ms. Saunders' kid." Jonas pauses and then continues, "I need to come home… if you'll have me."

He sounds conflicted, but why? He's my VP, there's no way I wouldn't want him to be here.

"Jonas, this is your home, man. Why wouldn't we want you here?" I'm greeted with silence on the other end. "Ray wasn't your fault, brother. No one blames you. Come home, I miss you, and so does the club. Fuck, I sound like a chick! Let me rephrase that, get your fucking ass home, I need you to look after shit and stuff!"

I can hear laughter on the other end. "Aw, Prez, if I'd known how you felt, I'd never have left you. Seriously, though, I'd be honored to come home and look after shit and stuff."

Jonas is still laughing when I say, "Very-fucking-funny! Jonas, can you be here by tomorrow, and can you look after the depot and the garage?"

"Glad you said I could come home, Prez, because I'm already at the compound. I've been to the garage, had a look to see what work we've got lined up. Seriously, we're fixing old man Turner's car again? He didn't fucking pay last time!"

Now it's my turn to laugh. "Yeah, brother, I know, but he's old, and he has helped the club out on a few other issues, which I won't get into over the phone. I'll come to you, be there in thirty. Oh, and you can buy the beer."

"You were always a stingy motherfucker. I'll see you in thirty." Jonas laughs as he hangs up, and I chuckle.

I put bread in the toaster and am staring out my kitchen window drinking coffee when Dave comes into the kitchen.

"Good morning, Dane. Black t-shirts really suit you, they show off your... physique."

I like Dave, especially now I know he's gay and more like a father figure to Kat, but I don't like him that much.

"It's a tee, Dave, I've got a few of the fuckers. What's the plan for you today?"

Dave takes the hint and becomes the professional manager, fixing himself a cup of coffee.

"I have, of course, hired a private jet to take us to the studio. It would've been nice if someone had told me about it before it got arranged. I'm assuming you and your boys will provide security to the jet?" I nod and butter my toast. "Good, then all that needs to be arranged are the hotel and added security for the studio. How many boys are you bringing with you?" Dave sounds resigned.

"Sorry, Dave, wasn't my story to tell. I'll be going, of course, and Judge and Dirt. They're good men, loyal. They know how to handle themselves."

"How on earth do you come up with these names, and why don't you have a nickname? Something strong and primal. Like… Conan?"

I laugh at this peculiar man who has no idea how my club or I work.

"Dave, my name is Dane Reynolds, and my nickname is Prez, as in president. Some of us earn our names, and some fall into them. Judge, for instance, is Jeremiah Judge. As for Dirt, you try to tease or fuck with him, and he'll use his fists on you. He prefers his fists, and there are none better in a fight."

"That doesn't explain his name, though."

"I'll give you a hint, then, you'll be spitting your teeth in the…"

"Dirt! Oh my! Does he do that often?" Dave looks excited. I wouldn't have thought he'd like us, thought he'd find us a little too rough for him, but maybe I'm wrong?

"When he was younger, yes, but now, not so much. Everyone knows not to fuck with him."

"Ahh… I see. Well, I'll be sure not to make that mistake." Dave chuckles to himself and looks down at his phone, completely absorbed.

"I'm outta here, going into town. You need anything?"

I'm heading for the door when he says, "Dane, please wait. There's something I need to discuss with you."

I stop, turn around and say, "Dave, I have a lot to do today, so can we do this later?"

"Unfortunately, no. I need to ask you about how you would like me to handle the press. As of tonight, you'll be in the public eye, and the public loves The Grinders."

He looks totally serious, the phone in his hand forgotten.

"Dave, it's your territory. I know nothing of your world. Here in Tourmaline, I call the shots, but in rock-star land, I guess I'm fucking clueless."

Dave nods. "I'll need to release some information about you to the press, but most of all, they'll want pictures. Can I book you and Kat in for a shoot?"

"A shoot?"

Is he fucking serious?

"Yes, Dane, a photoshoot. We'll need photos of you and Kat together, they'll eat it up. Do you have a favorite charity? We could maybe sell the photos to a magazine and make some money for it."

"Fuck, really? All right, if I have to do this, then I want the money to go to the local high school here in Tourmaline. They need new equipment for everything from the musical department to the basketball team."

I place my hands on my hips, my thumbs sliding into the belt loops as I stare at Dave.

"Okay, local high school, it is! We'll say the Savage Angels donated the money. Are there other places in Tourmaline that need help?"

"Doc Jordan in town could probably use some money for his health clinic. I know he does work with some of the hill folk, and I'm pretty sure he funds most of it himself."

As I give Dave all this information, he uses his stylus on his phone to, I assume, write everything down.

"Dave, I don't want Tourmaline turned into a circus. Whatever you do, I don't fucking want that."

"No, Dane, I'm here to see it doesn't happen. Hell,

if it did, your Sheriff Morales would hang me by my balls in the town square."

I laugh at him and say, "He can be a tough bastard. We done? I've got shit to do."

Dave nods. "See you later. I'll handle everything."

He winks at me and goes back to his phone. I'm headed for the front door when Kat appears at the bottom of the stairs.

"You're still here, baby?" she asks me, looking surprised.

"Darlin', I'll never leave without giving you a kiss." I embrace her, and she feels so good. She's smaller than me, so it's easy to hold her, and she fits me perfectly, her softness against my hardness. I kiss her neck and slowly make my way to her mouth. By the time I get to her lips, she's making noises and grinding into me. "Darlin', I have to go."

"Okay, baby. Go, I'll be here when you get back."

Kat grins at me with a fuck-me tilt to it as she runs her hands up and down my chest.

"You make it hard to leave. I'll be in Tourmaline for most of the day, so if you need anything, you call me, yeah?"

"Yes, babe. I'll call savage, and I will miss you."

I lightly kiss her on the lips, then she makes her way to the kitchen. I watch her walk away from me, and I feel a sense of loss. I'll miss her too. The realization this woman is mine washes over me, and for the first time in my life, I find myself belonging to a woman. I'm hers. We are one, and I'll protect her. We'll get the motherfucker who's trying to hurt my woman.

The courtyard in front of my house is one of the best features of my home. It allows for cars to circle past the stairs or drive straight into the garage, which is where I'm headed. My Harley is waiting for me, and it's been too long since I've ridden her.

As I get on, Dirt approaches me, "Prez, you going into town?"

"Yes, Jonas called, he's back. We've got some shit to sort through before we leave. You cool to come to LA, brother?"

"I'm not a fan of flying. I'd rather fucking ride, or, fuck it, walk! But I go where you go. I'd make a lousy Sergeant-at-Arms if anything fucking happened to you."

"I know you always have my back, brother. Are you coming into town with me?" I ask.

Dirt nods and walks toward his ride. "Yes, Prez, I'm coming with you. It'll be good to see the VP. The fucker's been gone too long."

We both ride out into the courtyard, then down the drive, and we hit the road. I nod and do a two-finger wave at some of my boys. When we hit the barricade, they make sure to let us pass, and move the reporters out of the way.

Tourmaline has some of the most beautiful roads you'll ever ride. There are lots of curves and gorgeous scenery. Unfortunately, the road into town isn't long enough to work out my frustrations, and all too soon, we're at the compound. I'm surprised to find more reporters at the front gates. I'd have thought the brothers would've made them leave by now.

The gate opens, and the reporters swarm around me, and I shout, "You all need to back the fuck up, or someone's going to get hurt."

They move back slightly, but it's enough to get me through. Dirt is right behind, swearing at them.

I hear Jonas yell, "Shut the fucking gates, and if any of them are left in here, I get to play with them, so can we try and make sure it's female this time? The men scream too fucking much!"

The reporters fight amongst themselves to get onto the sidewalk as a police cruiser pulls up. I get off my bike and walk over to Jonas.

"The men scream too fucking much? What the fuck are you up to, VP?" I laugh but stop when I hear a scream coming from inside the compound, and I stalk toward it when Jonas gets in front of me.

"It's not what you think, Prez. Calm down!"

"Jonas, what the fuck?"

Another scream pierces the air, and the deputy in the cruiser is out with his hand on his gun and runs for the door to the clubhouse, going inside. Dirt is hot on his heels.

"Dane, it's all good, I promise, but we need to get

inside before the deputy there bites off more than he can fucking chew!"

Fucking Jonas! Always the prankster. This can't be good, though, and the reporters out front are snapping away.

As I get to the doors, I can hear laughter coming from the other side. I open them to see the deputy doubled over in laughter, and Keg slaps him on the back as he does the same. Dirt is standing with his hands on his hips, smiling, but he's not happy.

"What the fuck?" My voice is raised and commands the attention of everyone in the room. They all stop what they are doing, except the deputy, who can't stop laughing.

Jonas gets in front of me. "Prez, let me show you, it's okay! Reb! Reb! Come here!"

Rebel walks out from the back, and Jonas says, "Do it, Reb, do it!"

Rebel screams, and all the boys laugh. I look at Jonas quizzically when he says, "We don't have anyone in here, Prez, but none of us can scream like Reb. We've been taking turns, and he's the best!" I'm not amused, and by the look on my face, everyone is well aware of it.

"This isn't going to fucking help the image of this fucking MC. Did any of you think of that? Did any of you use your fucking brains? There are reporters out there from all over the fucking globe! They'll be saying we're torturing one of their own, and this will not reflect very well on my fucking woman!" I roar at the lot of them.

Jonas laughs. "Fuck me, this will not reflect well on your woman! When the fuck did you get pussy-whipped?"

Some of my boys laugh, but a glance from me silences them. I can't believe even the deputy thinks this is funny. Dirt has a scowl on his face, knowing it's wrong to challenge me so openly.

"Deputy, you need to inspect the clubhouse to prove we don't have a reporter held hostage in any of the rooms. If you wouldn't mind doing it quickly, I'd appreciate it."

"Dane, I mean, Mr. Reynolds, I think we've all had enough of the reporters. One of them even followed me home and harassed my wife. Said he was trying to get the inside story. He scared her half to death. I'll have a look around, but, truthfully, if you do have someone tied up in here, I think they're getting what they deserve. Of course, I'd have to take them with me."

"See, Prez, we aren't the only ones who've had enough of them." Jonas looks at me with defiance in his eyes.

"I want complete fucking silence until the deputy has cleared our house. Is that fucking understood?"

I stand in the middle of the room with my hands on my hips. I stare at the floor, waiting for the deputy to go through our house, my house. No one talks or moves, the air is thick, and my rage is pouring out of me in waves.

"Mr. Reynolds, your clubhouse is clear of hostages. It was interesting to meet you, sir, and on behalf of the parents of the Tourmaline Tigers, I'd like to personally thank you for your donation to the team. Without it, our boys would be hitting the courts naked."

He walks toward me and holds out his hand. I tower over this man and have no idea who he is. I stare at his hand for a second, then grip it in a handshake. He smiles and walks out the door.

Jonas clears his throat, and I look at him. "Don't mistake my love for you, brother, as a fucking invitation for you to talk down to me in front of my own fucking men or outsiders. This is my club, and if you ever talk about me or my woman like that again, I'll beat you until your teeth fall all over this floor." I move right into his face and maintain eye contact. "Are. We. Clear?"

Jonas is the same height as me—six foot six.

His eyes don't waver from mine when I hear Keg say, "Prez, we meant no disrespect, we thought it was funny. We caught one of the reporters on this side of the fence, and we took him out the back way and had Rebel leave him on the outskirts of town. When Rebel came back, he told us how the guy was screaming to be let go. I asked how loud he screamed, and then all the reporters who were inside the compound began moving back. It was a joke, Prez. A stupid joke."

Dirt has moved to flank me. He's a loyal MC member.

Jonas and I haven't broken eye contact. He finally concedes with his focus on the ground and steps away from me.

"It's good to see you, Prez, I meant no offense." Jonas backs down, and it's what I needed him to do.

Walking away from him, I take a seat at the bar. "I believe, VP, you owe me a beer, and seeing as I'm a stingy motherfucker, you're buying."

The atmosphere in the room changes completely. Keg laughs and walks over to Jonas and punches him lightly on the arm. Dirt looks at him, nods, and moves toward a stool.

"Yeah, VP, I believe you owe us all a beer. It should be on you, you've been away too long!" Keg breaks the awkward silence in the room with his outburst, and the guys laugh, still a bit nervous, but they all make their way to the bar. Everyone wants a free beer.

"Yes, I've been away too long." There's something in his eyes I can't read, and he avoids my gaze. "And you're all a bunch of stingy motherfuckers!" Jonas laughs and makes his way behind the bar, getting us all beers.

CHAPTER 58

DAVE

All I can say is thank the gods of money we can afford to fly in a private jet. Kat spent most of the time playing guitar, sitting on the floor between Dane's legs with the guys sitting around just chilling. Jasmin and Judge disappeared down the back of the plane for the entire flight. I spent the flight glued to my phone and laptop with one of my assistants trying to help. Her name is Veronica, she's new, but learning quickly. I like her, she's ambitious, and she's already informed me she wants to look after one of my bands on her own. I've never had an assistant be so upfront with me. Let's hope she can handle the pressure of looking after a group of prima donnas. I'm lucky, The Grinders have always been professional.

Apart from Curtis, who gets married at the drop of a hat, The Grinders are a dream. I'm thinking of giving Veronica one of the up-and-coming bands to see how she does. Normally, I wait until my assistants have been with me for a while before they get promoted, but I like her attitude, and I think she'll leave me if I don't give her a push up the ladder.

I'm about to ask her to double-check the photographer when I realize she's staring at Dirt, who's pacing up and down the aisle at the front of the jet.

"Veronica?"

"Yes, boss?"

"You see, a problem in this industry, you fix it before it becomes a media sensation."

Veronica looks at me, leaves her chair, and makes her way to Dirt. He's an attractive-looking man in a rough kind of way. The scar which runs from his temple into his hair makes him more interesting. If he cut his hair a little, he'd be sort of handsome. Whatever she's saying to him makes him laugh, and he looks at her as if he'd like to eat her for lunch.

I'm going through the newsfeed on my laptop when I come across a story about the Savage Angels torturing a member of the press.

"What the fuck?" All eyes come to me, and I read out loud, "Headline, *The Savage Angels Tortured*

Reporter. Does someone want to explain this to me?"

I can feel all the blood rushing to my face. I have a photoshoot lined up with Kat and Dane, I have reporters lined up, fuck me, I have been spinning the MC, so they look like a group of boy scouts, and now they do this?

"Dave, man, it's not what it looks like." Dane is looking at Dirt as he shakes his head.

"I've been working my ass off trying to make the public think you lot are a good match for my Grinders, and you go and do this? I don't care if it's not what it looks like. What I care about is, you didn't tell me about it, meaning I can't fix it before it hits the fucking mass media!"

Dane stands up, and the plane suddenly doesn't feel big enough.

"Kat, what is the golden rule with the press?" I'm so angry, I stand as well. Dane may be taller and bulkier than me, but this is a complete fuck-up.

Kat puts the guitar down and stares between Dane and me. "Public perception is the most important thing, and Dave can spin anything. But Dave, they didn't know, and Dane, you didn't really torture a reporter, did you?"

"No, Kat, I didn't torture a reporter, and neither did my MC."

I'll give it to him, he has a commanding voice. Judge has come out from the back of the plane, and

Dirt has stopped talking to Veronica. Both bikers stare at their president.

"Okay, perfect. Thank you for clearing it up for me. Now, how the fuck did they come up with that? Did they make it up?" Sarcasm drips off my words, and my voice rises.

"Dave, I'm sure you can fix this. You can fix anything," Truth says.

"Yes, Truth, I'll try to fix this, but if I'd known about it before we got in the air, it would've made my job a whole lot easier!"

Dane stares at me. "You have a point. It's not like I was trying to keep it from you. It was a practical joke gone wrong. I reprimanded my boys, but I didn't think to tell you. We aren't from your world, Dave. We didn't set out to hide this from you. For that, I apologize." I'm impressed he's taken responsibility for this fuck-up, and before I can respond, he continues. "As for trying to spin us to the press? I don't give a fuck. Kat and I are a partnership now. She's the public image, and I realize, as her partner, I'll have to be in the limelight from time to time, but I don't live in it. She does."

Dane moves toward me and stares down at me. Inwardly, I cringe, but outwardly, I square my shoulders and try to look taller. I glance at Kat, and she's looking at him with utter devotion.

Well, well, well. Dane Reynolds has tamed the wild child. The only thing I want is for her to be happy, and it would seem this man does that.

"Veronica!" I lock eyes with Dane as I ask her, "Can you fix this?"

"I agree with you, boss, it would've been easier if we had been told about it right after it happened. Public perception is the most important thing, and Dave can spin anything. If you give this to me, I promise I'll make it smell like roses."

This assistant is going to go far. She just backed me up, and she's telling them she can fix it.

"Well, Dane, it appears we can fix this. I can appreciate you haven't lived in our world, but now you do. I'm here to help you, and I'm here to protect The Grinders. You're now part of our world. If you're truly committed to Kat, you need to let me know when things happen. At the end of the day, I work for The Grinders, and I have responsibilities for you as well."

Dane looks at me and bursts out laughing. He turns to look at his boys, and they do as well. Kat joins them, and eventually, we're all laughing, and I have no idea why.

"You're responsible for me as well?" Dane asks. He doubles over with laughter. "Dave, man, good-fucking-luck with that! I'm the president of an MC, and we aren't a church choir!"

I smile at him and silently admit to myself he's right, but out loud, I say, "You would be surprised what a good public relations person can do."

Veronica gets on the phone and moves to sit by herself at the front of the jet. Dirt watches her like a hawk. Judge and Jasmin have disappeared into the depths of the plane again, and the rest of them laugh at something Blair has said.

Me?

I watch all of them and work my ass off on my phone to make sure everything runs smoothly at the live recording of the show tonight.

CHAPTER 59

KAT

We arrive in LA and are greeted by one of the producers of *Rock Star*.

"Welcome! Welcome, all of you! My name is Gordon, and I'm here to help in any way I can." He smiles at us and ushers us into a limousine. "I'm also here to run an idea past you."

As soon as we all pile into the limousine, Truth plants his ass in the seat and says, "Ahh… here it comes, the offer, and, Gordon, it had better be good!"

I have no idea what Truth is talking about, and confusion must be written across my face.

Dane grabs my hand and asks, "What is going on?"

I shrug. "Offer?"

"Now, Kat, I mentioned to the executives, you only wanted to smile and wave at the public," says Blair.

Then Gordon intervenes, "We couldn't possibly have The Grinders make their first public appearance in over twelve months and not have them perform, it would be scandalous!"

"What the fuck, Blair!" I yell at him.

"Kat, calm down. I thought we could do one of our numbers where you play lead guitar and Truth sings. You, technically, wouldn't be performing. I mean, you would be, but not singing…" Blair's voice trails off.

"We agreed when I said yes to this that I would not be performing, technically or not." I pin Blair with my gaze.

"Oh, Kat, darling! Your public is awaiting you! You don't want to upset them, do you?" replies Gordon.

I look at Gordon. "Not one more word from you, or I'm on the first plane home," I hiss at him.

Dane puts his arm around me and pulls me closer. Gordon looks at Blair pleadingly, and Truth grins like a lunatic. We drive in silence for a while.

Finally, I say, "What do you all want to do?"

And I look at each of my bandmates.

"Kat, my groovy guitarist, I'm all for performing. It's been way too long since we've done it together. You play a mean guitar, not as good as me, but it's hard to beat perfection." Truth thinks a lot of himself, always has.

"Pfft, Truth, really?" Jasmin waves a hand in his face. "It's just one gig, Kat. I say yes, but it's up to you. If you don't want to do it, I'm cool with that, too."

Curtis says, "I agree with Jasmin."

"I second that," says Jamie.

"Kat, the decision is yours." Blair looks at the floor of the limousine.

I look at Dane. "What do you think?"

"I think you should do it. If only to see if you still want to do it." Dane puts my hand to his mouth and gives it a quick kiss.

I look at Blair. "You know how I said you owe me for coming here?" He nods. "Well, Blair, now you owe me double."

A smile spreads across his face, and he looks like he's about to say something, but Gordon beats him to it. "Marvelous! Now, we need to get you to the studio for rehearsals, and I have you two gorgeous ladies booked in for spray tans, costume, and makeup!" he says, flamboyantly waving his hands in the air.

"I'm sorry, you already have us booked in for all of that?" I sound surprised.

"Well, Blair said he could talk you into anything! And honey, we're all so thankful he did!" Gordon claps his hands and looks so pleased with himself as Blair tries to make his big hulking frame sink deeper into the seat.

"I know, I know, I owe you triple." Blair looks guilty, but a grin soon spreads across his face. "Did you really think we'd come all the way here and not perform?"

"Yes, Blair, she did because you fucking told her it's all she'd have to do," Dane answers for me. "In the future, if you have other plans for Kat, I suggest you let her know in fucking advance."

Blair nods furiously as he takes in Dane's frosty glare. I can't help it, but laughter bubbles up out of me. Soon everyone laughing.

"So, Blair, have you picked a number for us?" I ask through my laughter.

"We thought we'd do a song off the 'Placebo' album. I sang a fair bit on that one," Truth blurts out.

"So, you knew, too!" I shriek at him.

"Well, my gorgeous groover, of course, I knew! Blair didn't want to offend me by taking away my axe, so he had to let me in on it."

"Blair didn't want to offend you?" I say in a high-pitched tone.

The Grinders, Dave, Veronica, and I all burst out laughing, with Gordon and the Savage Angels staring at us like we're mad.

I look up at Dane. "Creative and musical-fucking-types? Give me my MC any day."

Jamie points at Dane, laughs harder, and shakes his head in the affirmative. A smile works its way across Dane's features, and he pulls me closer to him and kisses the top of my head.

When we arrive at the studio, they split us up so Jasmin and I could go for our spray tans. Dane and his boys headed for some peace and quiet, and the rest of the band rehearse.

The day really goes quickly, and now the big moment is almost upon us. They've just finished putting my hair up in a ponytail and have given me very dramatic makeup. With the fake tan, my hair looks lighter, and I definitely look healthy. The wardrobe people were trying to find an outfit which will cover my scar, but I told them not to bother. I'm clad in silver and six-inch platform heels. When the lights hit me, I sparkle. My dress has a plunging neckline, and they've dressed Jasmin in a similar outfit, except hers is gold. Neither of us can afford to fall over as the dresses are so short, we'll be flashing the nation.

I'm nervous as hell. Dane stands behind me, running his hands up and down my arms to calm me. I can hear the audience screaming my name. A technician comes up and makes sure my mic is working, and he smiles at me, giving me the thumbs-up. Then the crowd goes wild, and it's our cue to get our asses on stage. I walk out first, with Jasmin and Truth close behind.

I'm strutting out to the stage, waving and shaking hands as I go, and the others are doing the same. Blair and Jamie are waiting for us on the stage. Tonight, we're doing a number with Truth singing and me on lead guitar. It's not something we've done in a while, and rehearsals this afternoon were a bit shaky, but I know, with the energy of the crowd, we're going to own it.

Blair lets loose on his sax, and, one by one, we all slowly join in. It's one of those numbers which builds into a kick-ass rock song. We all play for the audience, and we're having a good time. Glancing up from my guitar, I notice Dane has moved to the edge of the stage. I give him a quick chin lift and walk his way. His smile is enough to make me forget why I was so nervous in the first place. I rake my gaze over him and take in his choice of clothing—faded jeans hugging him in all the right places, a black shirt, and a black jacket with his boots. He looks utterly hot and desirable.

When the song finishes, I put the guitar around me and throw my arms around him, kissing him passionately. The audience goes wild. I pull back from his sensual mouth and smirk. I give him another kiss and walk back to my band. I grab Truth's hand and hold it over our heads, and the audience goes wild. The host, Simon Craft, can't get the audience to calm down, so they go to an unscheduled commercial break.

The cameras are on us, and Simon is asking us how we feel about being back together. I let everyone do the talking and smile and nod and really don't say anything.

Then, Simon asks me directly, "So, Kat, is that gorgeous hunk of man the nefarious Dane Reynolds we've all heard so much about?"

"Nefarious? He is my gorgeous hunk of man, Dane Reynolds, but he's not nefarious." I chuckle.

Again, the crowd goes wild, and when Simon finally gets them under control, he asks, "Well, he certainly looks the part. Hmm… true love?"

When he asks me this, I can feel my face flush. This isn't something Dane and I have even talked about. I really don't want to have this conversation on live television, but I needn't have worried because Blair cuts in and saves me.

"Aww, hell, Simon, The Grinders do a live performance, our first in over a year, and all you're interested in is Kat's love life? She's happy, she looks freaking fantastic, wouldn't the audience agree?" The audience goes ballistic, and we're forced to go to another commercial break.

When we come back, all of us are sitting behind the judges' desk. We're waiting for the bands and singers to come out one by one to perform. I'm really excited as I've never been involved in a show like this before.

The first band comes out, and they have a few problems, but overall, they aren't bad. I listen to the other judges' comments. There are five of them—Blair, Jamie, Susan from the rock band, Evening Fell, Travis, a country music legend, and Celeste, who's one of the best female recording artists out there today.

Celeste's comments are a bit caustic, and although the band that performed had a few problems, it isn't something that time and practice can't fix. When it's my turn to speak, I tell them practice makes perfect, and their lead singer asks to come and shake my hand. I get up and walk onto the stage and hug him. Then, the rest of the band lines up for one. Simon goes to another commercial break as the crowd gets louder.

I'm having a fantastic time. Dane is sitting behind me, the audience loves us, and performing went off without a hitch. Somehow, I knew it would because we've always been better live than at rehearsals. It must be the energy of the crowd, and we feed off of it.

Up next is a male singer who oozes sex appeal and is singing the rock song, 'Are You Gonna Be My

Girl' by Jet. He's put a new spin on it, and he's working the stage. Both the audience and I like it. His name is Dan Kelly. He has curly blond hair, blue eyes, and a wicked smile. He's also only nineteen years old, and I think to myself that he'll be a rock god with time and age.

Dan is obviously a crowd favorite, and when he finishes, many of the women throw flowers, underwear, and small stuffed animals at him. I'm with the crowd, he was good, and I stand up and clap. He looks at me, winks, and bows, which sends the crowd into a frenzy. Laughing, I sit back down, grinning at his boldness.

Celeste is the first one to speak. "So, Dan, how do you think it went?"

"Yeah, I thought it went well. Both the crowd and Kat seemed to like it." He smirks.

Celeste leans forward and looks at me, then stares back at Dan. "So, in the first verse, when you sang the wrong words, you thought it was good?"

I'm confused, he didn't sing the wrong words. Before I realize what I'm doing, I lean forward, stare at Celeste, and I say, "Ah, babe, don't know what version of the song you were taught, but he didn't sing the wrong words. He nailed the verse."

The audience and fellow judges have all gone quiet, and Dan shuffles from foot to foot on the stage. All eyes are on me, and Celeste has a small, amused smile on her face.

"Well, *babe*, perhaps, at the end of the show, you can go back and listen to the recording, and you'll hear, *babe*, that he did, indeed, get it wrong."

I can't believe she's being such a bitch.

"Okay, Celeste, even though he didn't get the words wrong, let's say, for argument's sake, he did. He freaking nailed the melody." I stop looking at Celeste and give Dan all my attention. "It isn't a technically difficult song, but I liked what you did with it, especially at the end. You really built it. Your voice is sublime. Take care of it because it's your future."

"Thank you, thank you, Kat. I really appreciate your words of encouragement."

He looks so impressed with himself, but then Celeste chimes in, "If you want to survive in this industry, I suggest you listen to someone who's still in it. Learn the words and don't mess with good songs if you don't have the talent." Her voice drips with contempt.

My mouth is hanging open, and I look up at Dan, who looks shattered.

What a bitch!

I turn to him again. "Dan, you did a fantastic job. If you don't win this competition, you come find me, and I'll produce you." The audience goes wild, so I stand and try to get them to quiet down. Then I say, "I still have strings to pull in this industry, and I'm far from done with it. I may not sing anymore, but, sister..." I look back at Celeste and say, "... you can kiss my ass."

Celeste's face goes red, and I sit back down, smiling at her as I do. Simon walks on stage and tells the audience and the folks at home that we're going on a commercial break. As soon as the cameras are off, Celeste gets up and storms out of the studio.

Truth looks at me and says, "Never a dull moment, my goddess of the silver tongue."

"Very funny, Truth. Fuck, Blair, Jamie, I'm sorry if I caused a problem." Blair bursts into laughter, and Jamie has a hand over his mouth to stifle his.

"Ahh, Kat, cameras are still filming, they're streaming it live on the internet, too." Blair points at a camera. I look at it and shrug.

"Sorry, America, I didn't know. I'll be sure to watch my language from here on out." I nod at the camera and cast a glance at Dane. He's laughing.

He gets up, swivels my chair around, and positions himself between my legs. Dane whispers in my ear, "Fucking little upstart got what she deserved. You wanna blow this joint, you say the word, darlin'."

I kiss him, and without even thinking about it, I say, "And that's why I love you."

He goes rigid in my embrace and looks down at my face.

Oh. My. God. What have I said?

"You love me?" He's gone all serious, no humor in his voice.

I'm dumbfounded. I stare at him and find, I can't speak.

"Kat, did you just say you love me?" His tone is demanding.

My head has a mind of its own, and I nod. A smile quickly spreads across his face, and he grips the sides of mine with his hands and kisses me. This isn't a peck on the cheek, this is a tongue-dueling, core-clenching epic kiss. The world around me fades away until he abruptly pulls away from me, leaving me feeling devastated. I want more, so much more. Then I realize where I am and the whole of America is watching me. I quickly spin back around and face the stage, and I can feel my blush creep its way up my face. Blair, the motherfucker, is laughing.

Celeste rejoins us on the judging panel and tries to pretend for the rest of the evening that I don't exist.

CHAPTER 60

KAT

At the end of the show, I feel exhilarated. It's exciting to be around up-and-coming musicians and singers. The only downside to the whole evening is having Dane sit behind me, not knowing if he feels the same way. I could feel his eyes boring into my back for the rest of the show. The only time I forgot he was there was when an artist was performing.

    We all head to a party at a club downtown called the Music Room. There will be people from the industry there that I haven't seen in ages, as well as the contestants from the show, the judges, and everyone involved with the production. I love a party, but I'm anxious to find out how Dane is feeling. He holds my hand in the back of the limousine, absently rubbing the pad of his thumb over my knuckles. Dane is physically next to me, but he's miles away. He stares out the window, and in the glass, I see a look I can't quite read.

"Kat, my rock rebel, I love how you put that fucking little upstart, Celeste, in her place. I wanted to slap her into next week." Everyone laughs at Truth's statement.

"She's a bit of a bitch. Why is she so mean to the contestants? Surely, your job is to encourage or to tell them how to improve? Not tear them down."

I'm staring at Blair.

"You obviously haven't watched any of the shows, Kat. She's been a pain in all our sides since day one." Blair really doesn't sound like he likes her very much.

Jamie laughs as he says, "It could have something to do with who she's dating at the moment."

A few of my bandmates look at me knowingly, but I'm clueless.

"Okay, I'll bite, who's she dating?" I ask, looking around at them.

Dave looks at me and says, "Gareth Goodman, action superhero!"

Dane stiffens next to me. "And what would that have to do with Kat?"

We've never had a conversation about my previous lovers, and I don't want to have it right now while everyone I know is listening in.

I stare at Dane, about to say that I think we should have a chat in private when Jasmin opens her mouth. "Kat and Gareth were a thing. Didn't you ever see them on TV? Their arguments were legendary. Kat, the two of you went out for over a year, yeah?"

I want to punch Jasmin for even mentioning Gareth's name, but more so, I want to shrink down into the seat and disappear. The atmosphere in the limousine goes frosty.

My torment isn't over as Truth joins in the conversation, "That's why, my sexy songstress, she was such a bitch to you. I'm guessing she and Gareth aren't as solid as she's trying to make the world think they are."

"Yeah, I was watching him at the studio, and his eyes never left you, Kat," Jamie says.

I can't believe I didn't even see Gareth at the show.

"He was there? How come I didn't see him?" I ask Dave.

"Well, princess, it could have something to do with the big hunk of a man sitting next to you. You only had eyes for him all night. Everyone could see it."

Thank you, Dave, for trying to save me from a very unhappy Dane.

The minute we arrive at the Music Room, I want to leave. Dane opens the door and stalks away. I have no idea how he's feeling or the thoughts running through his head. I feel a surge of panic rise in my chest as I see him so far away from me, both physically and emotionally. Judge and Dirt are in another limousine which has just arrived, and they join their president on the sidewalk, keeping away from the rest of us.

As we get out of the limousine, the paparazzi go crazy, and we're quickly surrounded by fans and flashing cameras.

I'm hustled into the club by Dave, who has a protective arm around me.

"Dave, is Dane with us? Is he in here with us? Did he get in?!" I sound frantic. I really need to talk to him.

"Be calm, Kat, be calm. I'll go check. Get yourself a drink and try to relax. The man cares for you, everyone can see it."

He's trying to put me at ease, but until I'm close to Dane again and able to see his face, I'm going to be a wreck.

Standing at the bar, not really wanting a drink when I hear a familiar voice say, "As I live and breathe if it isn't Kat Saunders, destroyer of Ferraris and men's hearts."

Fuck me, it's Gareth Goodman. The sight of him makes my stomach turn, and I have a sudden impulse to bolt, but I fight it. Running away will only empower him. Asshole. I plaster a fake smile on my lips. There's no denying the fact that he's a good-looking man, but he's a user. All he wants is to get on top of the show business ladder, and he'll use every person he can if he thinks they can further his career.

"Hello, Gareth, how are you?" I don't want to be talking to this man, especially with Dane about to enter the room.

"I'm good. My new movie is doing well, breaking box office records. Thank you for the new Ferrari, by the way. I was told I couldn't have it for another six months, but I guess the amazing Kat Saunders and The Grinders can get anything they want." His voice exudes sarcasm, and I'm not sure what to say.

Celeste inadvertently saves me by grabbing onto Gareth's arm. "Gareth, sweetheart, I've been looking for you everywhere!"

"Well, you found me!" Gareth sounds annoyed and unhooks her from his arm.

"Gareth?" Poor Celeste looks confused.

"Yes, Celeste?" She stares from me to him, confusion still crossing her features, and Gareth continues. "Can you not see the adults are talking, and I'll talk to you later." Then he turns his back on her and stares at me.

"Fuck you, Gareth!" Celeste hisses and storms away.

"Sorry you had to see that. It's been coming for a while, but she wouldn't take the hint. She's a little... slow."

This man is such a cocksucker. He smirks at me, and I shift from foot to foot as unease settles in my gut.

"Now, Kat, I think you owe me an explanation. You did, after all, destroy my car and then left me without so much as a goodbye."

"Gareth, now isn't the time. I'm truly sorry I ended it the way I did, but you were fucking one of my backup singers." A glass of bubbles is placed in front of me, and I take a sip of it and pray someone will come save me. "I'm sorry I wrecked your car, but as you said, we got you a new and improved one."

"Yeah, and all it cost was your voice and your career."

With that comment, he has completely gutted me. I stand there in shock. I stare right through him as though I've never seen him before. Gareth stares back at me with contempt. His eyes convey pure venom. He's calculated and waiting to strike again. I can't believe I cared for him at one point in my life.

"I have to go."

I can feel the surge of tears well up in my eyes and a lump in my throat. I try to move past him, but he grabs my arm, stopping me.

"Now, Kat, I'm sorry, that was uncalled for. I shouldn't have said that, it was cruel. I miss you. We never really got to say goodbye, and I'd really like to explain about the backup singer. You hurt me, baby, when you cut me out of your life."

It feels like all the air has been sucked from the room, and I feel as if I could pass out. He continues to wear a smile, but it doesn't quite reach his eyes.

"Gareth, I'm sorry, but I'm with someone else now, and he'll not like me talking to you."

"Kat, please... could we go somewhere a little more private and talk about this? It won't take long, I promise."

I don't want another public outburst from this man. I want to be done with him, so I slowly nod my head, and he leads me toward the back of the club.

CHAPTER 61

DANE

Fucking security won't let me through and into the club. I'm nose to nose with one of their security guards, he's a big motherfucker, but I've had enough. Dirt and Judge stand behind me, and I know if I start something, they'll finish it.

"Sir, I need you to step back. If you *are* with The Grinders party, I'm sure someone will be out to notify us soon."

I look at his name badge, and it says 'Spike.' Well, Spike is about to get his teeth smashed through the back of his head.

"Prez, you need to back down. The poor bastard's simply doing his fucking job." Dirt has his hand on my shoulder, and as much as I know he's right, I want to get inside to my woman.

A flash goes off in my face, and a reporter yells out, "Dane! Look this way!"

"What the fuck?" I'm dumbfounded he even knows my name.

"Dane! Over here!" another one shouts.

I take a step back from Spike, turn and walk to the sidewalk. More flashes go off as questions are being yelled at me.

"You okay, Prez?" Dirt is on one side of me, and I have Judge on the other.

"Just been a long fucking night. I want to find Kat and get the fuck out." I rub my hand over my face, sighing.

Judge says, "Prez, I could take that motherfucking bouncer on if you like?"

I laugh and look at him.

"Judge, if I have ever doubted your loyalty, I apologize. 'Cause, brother, the guy has an extra fifty pounds on you. You really think you could take him?"

"Aww, Prez, you know what they say, the bigger they are, the harder they fall."

He grins at me, and we all turn around and look at Spike, who's smart enough not to engage us. Through the crowd, Dave emerges, and I hope he's looking for us. When he sees me, he makes a beeline for me.

"I'm so sorry, Dane. It's always a little crazy when we're out in public. Please follow me, and I'll get you into the club."

He looks a little frazzled.

"It's cool, Dave, I've reached my limit tonight. The boys and I have had enough. All we want is a meal, something to drink, and then sleep in that order. Can you help us out?"

I know I sound angry, but I need to talk to Kat. She told me she loves me, and I need to tell her I feel the same. I want to get her alone, so we can talk about us and our future. I hope she wants to settle down in Tourmaline. This city, with its invasive paparazzi, isn't somewhere I could live.

"Yes, there's a full buffet for us inside. Truth is probably demolishing it as we speak. We only need The Grinders to make an appearance, shake some hands, be seen, and then we're done. One hour, two tops."

Fuck, two more hours of this crap? Maybe I can get Kat alone inside.

"Dave, where's Kat?"

"She's at the bar, my friend." He steps next to me and makes a sweeping gesture with his arm. "Shall we?"

We all head for the entrance. As Judge walks up, he stops at Spike, smiles at him, and then he laughs and walks straight into the club. I look at Spike, and even though he looks pissed, he maintains his professionalism and does nothing. Dave stares at me quizzically but says nothing. He shakes his head and moves forward. Dirt, as expected, is right by my side.

"Dane, what's going on? You've been fucking uptight since we pulled up. The limo had barely stopped, and you were out and stalking away from it. You and Kat okay?" Dirt asks me.

He's my Sergeant-at-Arms, and I know in a fight or negotiation situation, he'll always have my back.

"You saw that, did you?" Dirt nods. "Did you know Kat dated a guy named Gareth something-or-other?"

"Gareth Goodman. He's an action movie star. A group of us went to see his latest movie, it was okay." Dirt moves us into the club. "They dated for a while. I saw them in the papers and stuff, but, man, the way she looks at you? That woman has got it bad!" He grins, and I nod at him.

"Yeah, I know, and we both know I'm not a fucking angel. I never thought about her being with anyone else."

Dirt looks at me with his eyebrows raised, a look of disbelief over his features. "Brother, she's fucking famous. Her sex life is plastered in every magazine from here to Timbuktu." He grabs my arm and stops me, his voice serious. "But, brother, she looks at you like she can't fucking breathe without you. It's rare to find a woman who's so devoted."

"I know you're right. I don't want someone else

thinking they can take or touch what is fucking mine, that's all. Apparently, he was at the studio and couldn't take his eyes off her."

"Did she speak to him?" Dirt asks.

"No, she didn't even fucking know he was there."

Dirt grins at me as we head toward the bar. "Well, then, I don't think you've got a problem."

I know he's right. My woman is loyal, and she told me she loves me. I have nothing to fear, but the feeling in my gut has returned.

I can't see Kat anywhere. Truth is surrounded by some young female fans. Blair and Jamie look like they are doing an interview over in the corner. Dave is with his assistant, Veronica, and Judge has found Jasmin and have seated themselves at the end of the bar.

The place is packed, and apart from the people from the show, there are fans everywhere. I take two steps, and an arm snakes around my waist while a hand grabs my crotch. Now, I like my women to know what they are doing in the bedroom, but I don't like overly sexual displays in public.

"Dane, you're Dane, right?"

It's Celeste, and she tries to kiss me. I move my head away from her, grab her by the shoulders, and push her back.

"Step the fuck back. What the fuck do you think you're doing?" I tower over this woman, and I've raised my voice. The immediate crowd parts and goes quiet.

"Oh, you don't know? I thought you might be up for a little payback sex?" Celeste tries to move into me, so I hold her in her place.

I look at Dirt and order, "Find Kat, now."

My Sergeant-at-Arms nods and goes in search of my woman.

"Celeste, I have had a long fucking day. What the fuck are you talking about?" My tone and body language finally get through the head of this pretentious little girl.

Suddenly, her face dissolves into tears, and she sags into me. I don't want this fucking conniving female anywhere near me.

"He said he loved me!" Celeste says through hiccups and wailing noises.

"Celeste, clue me in here, babe. I have no fucking idea why you're telling me this."

"Gareth, he left with Kat!" Again, more hiccupping as she goes on. "He's always talking about her! He even told me I'm a younger, hotter version of her!"

This chick is hot, but she's not in Kat's league. Kat is five foot four, curvy, with long, gorgeous brown hair and the most amazing green eyes you've ever seen. Celeste may be the same height as Kat, but she's one of those pencil-thin women, and her hair isn't anywhere near as long, and it also looks lank and in lack of luster. I've listened to her sing, and even her voice isn't as good as Kat's used to be.

"What the fuck do you mean, she left with him?" I growl at her, causing her to step back.

"She came in, they spoke at the bar, then he…" Celeste cries again.

"Then he fucking what, Celeste?" I grab her by the shoulders and shake her roughly.

"He fucking left with her!" Celeste screams this. The entire club goes silent, and everybody stares at us.

Celeste is reduced to a sobbing mess. I let her go and look for my boys. Judge is by my side, and I can see Dirt striding toward me with a scowl on his face.

"Sugar, you need to get your-fucking-self under control. You're a public figure, and you don't want to be portrayed as a doormat to the fucking nation." Judge has put his arm around Celeste and speaks in a soft voice. She nods, takes a couple of deep breaths, and he passes her off to Jasmin.

"What can I do?" Judge is all business.

"I want my woman found. No fucking way she left with anyone, let alone some old boyfriend without telling me."

Dirt arrives, and he mutters, "The fucking security Dave hired is as fucking useless as tits on a fucking bull!"

"Tell me," I growl at him.

The feeling in my gut worsens, and I feel like it

will eat me alive.

"According to the security guards, Kat met Gareth at the bar, then went to a room in the back, so they left them alone. When they went back later, both of them were gone. They're fucking assuming she left with him out the back-fucking-door!" Dirt's eyes bulge, and his voice has gone steely.

"Thoughts?" I can sense my rage build, threatening to overcome me.

Judge says, "No fucking way our girl left with this guy without telling someone."

"Agreed. After the incident at your house, Prez, she hasn't gone anywhere without telling someone first. No way she fucking stopped doing that just 'cause we're in LA," says Dirt as he scans the room.

Dave appears in front of me. "You're creating a stir, what's up?"

"Kat has left with Gareth Goodman, and your security didn't stop her," I growl at him.

Dave looks shocked. "I can see you're upset, and I know our girl does indeed like you, but Dane, they do have a history."

My rage pours out of me, and I wrap a hand around Dave's throat, pushing him backward.

"My woman wouldn't leave with some wannabe actor. Now, I know you think you fucking know her, but I'm telling you, she'd not have done this."

I loosen the hold on Dave's throat while Dirt and Judge flank me.

"Dave, think about it. There's no way Kat would've fucking left with this guy with all the shit that surrounds her," Dirt's voice is hard.

"Can you remove your hand from my throat?" Dave's voice is all raspy.

"Where would he fucking take her?"

My patience is wearing very thin, and if someone doesn't give me some answers soon, I'll fucking explode.

"Dane! Man, what's the problem?" Truth has disentangled himself from his harem and joined us.

"Kat supposedly fucking left with Gareth Goodman. But no one saw her leave."

I stare at Truth, who looks from me to Dave. "Dave, did she tell you she was leaving?"

"No, but it's Gareth. They had a thing. You know how she can be!" He looks frazzled and waves his hands around as he moves away from me.

"No, Dave, I don't think you do. Think about how she's been the last few days. She loves Dane. There's no way our goddess of rock would've left with him willingly." Truth looks at me, then back at Dave. "Can't you see she loves him?" Dave shakes his head at Truth. "Dave, she's not the same woman she used to be. The accident made her take stock of her life. She's finally found someone she can be herself with. He's only known her as Kat 'cause Dave, the rock singer is dead."

"No, she can still perform, you saw that tonight.

You all rocked it." Dave sighs and rakes a hand through his hair and rubs his neck. "But you're right, she has outgrown Gareth. It's not out of character for her to leave a party. How many times has she done that?"

"Dave, use your head. Didn't she ask you to go back outside and get Dane? Do you think she'd leave with that moron?"

Truth looks to Dave, but I've reached my boiling point.

"Enough!" I roar at all of them. "Can someone tell me where the fuck my woman is?"

Jasmin pushes her way through the crowd and says, "Dane, Celeste said she eavesdropped on a phone conversation Gareth had this morning, making sure his boat is ready for a sea voyage. Do we think he could've taken Kat to his boat?"

I turn, striding out the door with Dirt and Judge hot on my heels when I hear, "Yo! Dane! I've got wheels, and I know where to go!" It's Truth, and he's pointing at the limousine. "I've got a berth near Gareth's at the marina!"

I stop and look at Dirt and Judge.

"Do we have any other way of getting there?" I growl.

"Prez, we could find a cab, but, honestly, the limo will probably be easier."

Judge nods in agreement with Dirt.

"The limo and Truth it fucking is, then." I stride toward it.

Truth waits inside. "Welcome! Let's go find our girl!"

I growl at Truth and say, "I don't have a good feeling about this. Why would Kat leave the fucking club without telling anyone? Is she even with this Gareth? I can't believe the fucking security guards left her alone!" My voice is raised, and I sound more than angry.

I'm consumed with the idea if we get this wrong, and she's not there, what do we fucking do, then? Where do we even look?

"Prez, I might know a guy who could maybe hack her phone and find her, but it'll cost some dough. He doesn't come cheap."

I look at Judge and say, "Whatever it fucking takes, just get it done."

Truth has made himself a drink and stares at me. "It's about thirty to forty minutes to the marina. How long has she been missing?"

"Can't be more than twenty minutes."

"I think it's more like fifteen, Prez," Dirt says.

I nod and stare at the floor, listening as Judge makes his calls. If Kat has decided to leave with this guy without telling anyone, I'm going to lose my fucking mind, but if he's forced her to leave, I'm not sure what I'll do.

One minute, I'm thinking about planning a future

with this woman, and the next I'm praying she's all right.

"Dane?" I look up at Judge. "He's found her, and we're headed in the right direction. Her phone is on the Santa Monica freeway."

"Why'd you say it like that?" I don't understand why he has worded it that way.

"My friend said he wants you to know he's tracing her phone, but she may not have it on her."

Truth laughs. "You ever met any female who isn't attached to their phone? The dress she's wearing is tiny. You all saw where she was keeping her phone, didn't you?"

We stare at him, and no one says a word for a few seconds. Then he shakes his head and says, "Under her armpit, on the left side, there's a small pouch sewn into the dress with room enough for a mobile phone. Trust me, she's got it!" Truth looks so smug.

I'm relieved, but I can't understand why she hasn't tried to make contact if she has her phone. I'm lost in my own thoughts as we head for the marina.

CHAPTER 62

KAT

I'm being carried, and I'm cold.

I open my eyes and say, "Dane, baby, I'm cold."

"Dane! The fucking Neanderthal isn't here. Oh, no, baby, your dream man is here."

Then it all comes flooding back to me. We were in the club and had moved to a private room in the back. I sat on the couch, and Gareth sat right next to me, so I moved a little away from him, and he grabbed my hand.

"I've really missed you, baby." My eyes flared as I tried to pull my hand out of his. "I know you're with a new man now, but I needed you to know that."

"Gareth, I'm feeling really uncomfortable now,

and I think I'm—"

He leaned right into me. "Tell me, Kat, why are you with this guy? He's nothing but a criminal! He can't even protect you! That girl got killed in your home, and where was he?"

My mouth was hanging open, and I stared at him, unable to speak.

"What, Kat? You've got nothing to say to defend him? He can't mean that much to you!" His eyes were wild, and I'd never seen him look so unhinged.

"Gareth, I'm sorry for how things ended between us, but the night I had my accident, I was trying to end it. On some level, you have to know that. As for Dane, I don't want to discuss him with you. Now, I need to go back to the party and find him."

I tried to stand up, but he pulled me back on to the couch.

"What the fuck, Gareth?" I yell at him.

"There you are, there's my girl. Trying to be something you're not, aren't you, Kat? We both know this new person you're trying to become isn't really you. You're a dirty-talking, common little slut, and I've missed you!"

"Because I swore at you it makes me a dirty-talking, common little slut? Are you fucking kidding me? I have no idea what I ever saw in you! Now, this time I'm leaving!"

He got right up in my face and laughed. I tried to push past him, but he's stronger than me, and I wasn't making a lot of progress.

"Gareth! Let. Me. Up." My voice was steady and even. I was staring him in the eyes when he leaned in to kiss me.

"Are you out of your fucking mind? Do you know who I'm with now? Get off me, Gareth!"

"You know you want it! Come on, for old times' sake! They say it's like riding a bicycle, you never forget." He ran a finger down my cheek. "And I've never forgotten you, Kat."

"Yes, I'm sure. Did you tell yourself that when you were fucking one of my backup singers? Jesus, Gareth, we were over the minute you did that. I don't do cheaters. You knew it. I told you when we first met! You stay loyal to me, and I'll stay loyal to you. You broke my trust, I never strayed."

He nodded frantically, all the while looking like a deranged man. "You're right, and I am sorry. You've punished me enough, baby, I'm ready to come back to you."

"You're ready to come back to me? Gareth, I'm with someone else!"

His whole face went dark, and he snarled at me. "He can't protect you. He doesn't love you. He's a thug."

Then he paced around the room. "Me? I'm handsome. I'm famous. I can protect you. I know what you like in bed, and I'm really the perfect man for you." Gareth stopped and stared at me. *"Can't you see that, Kat?"*

I looked back at him, fear slowly creeping up my spine. He's clearly not his normal self.

"Gareth, you need to let me get off this couch and leave this room."

"Now, you sound scared. Am I scaring you, Kat? Do you think this is how the girl in your house felt? If you'd been with me, it would never have happened to her."

"Because you would've protected me? Right? Please let me leave, Gareth, I won't tell anyone about this if you'll let me leave."

Then he laughed, high-pitched, and sounding like a maniac. I slowly stood and edged toward the door.

"Do you think that's what Jess said?" he continued, giggling.

But how did he know Jess's name?

"Gareth, how do you know Jess's name?"

He stopped pacing and only moved his eyes to me. "It was on the news." A smile crept onto his face, making my skin crawl.

"Are you sure?" I knew he was lying.

He walked up to me and rubbed my arms, saying, "Yes, baby, yes. Let's get you back to the party. Your fans will be missing you."

I nodded and turned around. I didn't even make

it two steps before I felt a sharp pain in my neck, and then everything went black.

Now, here I am in Gareth's arms, and he's carrying me.

"Why are you carrying me, Gareth, and where are we?"

"I wasn't sure how much to give you, baby. Give too much, and you might not wake up, give too little, and you're awake now. I really wanted you to wake up tomorrow when we were out in the ocean somewhere, away from all this or with me inside you. Now, I know you like that."

I feel myself go completely still, then fight-or-flight kicks in, and I thrash around. Gareth drops me, and I fall on my ass and onto a wooden platform.

"Kat, baby! What are you doing? We're at the marina, no one knows where we are, and, honey, this time of night, there aren't too many people about."

Gareth crouches down in front of me, a sadistic smile on his face.

"How could you? You drugged me? You killed

Jess? Why, Gareth, why?" I feel all woozy from the injection, and I can't get my legs to work the way they should. I feel really sleepy.

"Come on, baby, let's get you up." Gareth grabs both my hands and helps me to my feet, and then he throws me over his shoulder.

"This is better, anyway. Anyone who sees us will assume you've had too much to drink, just like old times."

I hit his back with my fists, but he laughs. "Kat, Kat, Kat, don't be so eager, we're almost there. You always liked my boat, didn't you, Kat?"

Gareth walks up the gangplank and onto his yacht, the Endless Summer. We get into the cabin, and he throws me down on the bed.

"Now, baby, I have to go cast off. Be back in a minute." Gareth leans over me and kisses me, and I have to suppress gagging from the feel of his mouth on mine.

"Why?" I whisper at him.

"Why? Because I love you, that's why." He smiles at me.

"But Jess, Gareth, how could you do that to Jess?"

Gareth frowns at me and says, "I told you because I love you."

He gets up and moves topside of the boat. I roll onto my side and slowly sit up. I have to get off this boat. Gareth is right, I did like his boat. It was the only place we could truly be alone. It was hard for the paparazzi to follow us if we were in the middle of the ocean, and they didn't know where. I liked the solitude, and the boat is big enough if I wanted to get away from Gareth for a little while, I could.

I slowly get to my feet and take a few steps toward the front of the boat. There's a hatch at the bow, and if I can get through it, I have a chance to escape. I open all the doors as I go, to make it look as though I could've gone to another part of the boat and hidden. I crawl up onto the bed and look out through the hatch. I can't see him, but it's dark outside. As quietly as I can, I open it and wait to see if he comes. When he doesn't, I push it open and crawl out. Silently, I crawl along the deck when pain races across my scalp as I'm pulled up by my hair.

"Where are you going, Kat?" asks Gareth, sounding pissed.

"Fuck you!" I scream this as loud as I can, hoping someone will hear it. He clamps his hand on my mouth, so I try to bite him.

"Now, Kat, that's not very nice." Gareth sounds strangely happy. He spins me around and punches me in the stomach. I'm winded and hit the deck on my hands and knees. He puts one arm around my back and the other under my knees, stands, and takes me back below deck. "Baby, I'm going to have to tie you up now. Can't have you trying that again! Although, if you want to bite me, I'm okay with that." Gareth smiles at me and throws me back on the bed. He's already got some rope. "Roll over."

"Fuck you!" I yell at him.

Before I can do anything, he backhands me across the face and flips me over, then ties my hands together.

"I don't want to mark your face, babe, prefer to keep it pristine, but if you don't do as you're told, I have no problem helping you come to the right decision." Gareth flips me back over and kisses me on the lips. I can taste blood in my mouth, and the spot where he kisses me hurts. As I open my mouth to tell him, he can go fuck himself, he pushes a cloth inside. "Time to go! You excited? I've plotted the whole cruise. You and me for at least six months! We have enough provisions to last us at least that long, maybe even longer if we're careful. I can't wait, baby." I shake my head back and forth, and then he laughs. "You should see your face! We'll be fine! Just like old times!" He's completely lost his mind. Gareth grabs me under my arm and moves me toward the deck. "This time I'm taking you with me." He winks and adds, "It's safer this way." We get to the deck, and Gareth starts the boat. I try to kick him, but he pushes me into a seat. "Time for an adventure!"

I take in my surroundings as I try to decide what to do when I hear, "If you've hurt her, even a little bit, I'll kill you."

Gareth gets up and pulls me to his front. "Well, if

it isn't the Neanderthal. You can't have her, she's mine." Then I feel something cold and sharp against my throat. "Get off my boat, and I won't kill her right now."

Dane looks me in the eyes, and I've never seen him look so dark. It's as if the blue has been replaced with black.

His voice is surprisingly gentle when he says, "It's going to be okay, darlin', I promise."

My heart feels like it will burst from my chest. I'm so happy to see Dane, I burst into tears.

"See, she doesn't want you here! You've upset her!" Gareth screams at Dane, spittle flying through the air.

Dane takes a step toward us, and Gareth pushes the knife into my neck. I can feel it pierce my skin.

"Get back! She's mine!"

I can hear from the tone of Gareth's voice, he's becoming more unstable with every word he spewing.

"Darlin', all you've got to do is call savage, and I'll be there."

Dane nods at me once, and then I hear from below us on the dock, "Yo, my beautiful biker babe, over here!" Gareth relaxes his hold on me to look over his shoulder, and I drop to my knees. Dane moves in as I do and punches Gareth in the face. Gareth drops the knife, and a fight between them ensues. It's not much of a fight, though, as Dane has

Gareth by the front of his shirt and punches him over and over again.

Dirt is on his knees in front of me and pulls the cloth from my mouth. "You're safe now, Kat. Let's get you to your feet."

Dirt helps me stand, then turns me around and cuts the rope binding my wrists. I can hear the sounds of bones breaking and flesh being pummeled.

"Dane, honey, you need to stop," my voice comes out in a whisper, but as soon as I say his name, Dane stops his brutal assault. He lets Gareth fall to the deck, and he turns and engulfs me in his arms. "You remembered what I said the day Jess got killed about me calling out savage, you remembered." Tears course down my cheeks, and Dane kisses them all away, his bloody hands capturing my face.

"Of course, I remembered, darlin', I'm glad you let yourself fall. I needed you to get away from the knife before I did anything." Dane sounds so relieved as his hands roam my body, looking for more damage. "Did he hurt you? Darlin', do I need to take you to a doctor? Christ, darlin', if he's hurt you, I'll kill him."

I'm trembling uncontrollably now. Dane picks me up and takes me off the boat. He moves us farther down the dock, where he puts me on my feet but keeps me tucked into his side.

Truth comes up to us. "My delightful diva, so glad

you're okay! The big guy here is quite a handful when he thinks you're in danger."

Truth tries to embrace me, but Dane doesn't let me go, so he ends up hugging us both.

A whistle pierces the air, and we all look up. "Prez, what do you want to do with him?" It's Judge. Both he and Dirt peer down at us from the boat.

"Truth, will you look after Kat for me?" He nods, and Dane releases me. "I'll be right back."

With that, he goes back onto the boat, and I'm left with Truth on the dock.

CHAPTER 63

DANE

I can feel myself relax now I know Kat's safe. If he'd gotten away, I might have lost her for good. As I get onto the deck, Dirt and Judge are putting Gareth into a chair, but he's still unconscious. At the sight of him, my rage builds again.

"What do you want to do with him, Prez?" Dirt asks me as he looks at Gareth with death in his eyes.

"We've drawn too much attention to ourselves to dispose of him," states Judge. "There were too many people in the club tonight, someone would tell. I think we're going to have to hand him over to the police."

Both of my men laugh, and then I do too. Roughly, I grab Gareth by one arm, Judge takes the other, and we head for the dock.

"Or, you know, Prez, we could let the fucker fall into the water, accidents do happen…" Dirt is deadly serious, but I know if we let that happen, there will be questions to answer, and neither the club nor I need that kind of heat.

As we get to the dock, Kat moves toward us, and I ask her, "Hey darlin', did you call the police?"

"Yes, Truth did, with my phone, which was in my dress the whole fucking time! I forgot it was there!" She looks annoyed with herself, and she's so fucking cute, except for her bottom lip, which is swelling.

"Darlin', if you hadn't had the phone on you, we may not have found you."

Suddenly, Gareth pushes Judge away and plunges a knife into my side. I lock eyes with him, but there's no humanity lurking there, only the eyes of a mad man. Kat screams, and I barely register the sound as Gareth pulls the knife from my flesh, and the pain makes my blood boil. My rage overcomes everything as he tries to stab me again. I twist his hand around, and the pain in my side is barely noticeable now as I thrust the knife into his stomach and drag it upward, slicing through him. Gareth's eyes widen with terror, and I snarl into his face, hoping the life force will drain from his body. Dirt pushes his way between us, and I let go of the knife with a growl at this foul excuse for a human being. Gareth falls to the ground, a broken, bloody mess.

When Dirt ascertains he isn't getting back up, he immediately assesses my damage. "How bad, Dane?" I look over his shoulder at a fast-approaching Kat. "Prez, how bad?"

"He got me in the side, but it's only a flesh wound."

Then my woman is on me. "Dane! No, no, no, no, no!" Kat pushes up my shirt, trying to see how badly I'm cut.

"Darlin', I'm okay. It's not too bad." I grab her hands and kiss both of them.

"You need an ambulance. We need to get you an ambulance!"

"Darlin'?"

"Truth, call an ambulance, now!" I can hear her level of terror grow with each second, and I know I have to do something to calm her down.

"Katarina Saunders, I love you."

Kat freezes, terror on her face is slowly replaced with a slow smile as she gazes up at me, my wound temporarily forgotten.

"You love me?" she breathes out.

I can hear Judge laugh, and Dirt mumbles something about leaving us alone.

"Yes, Kat, from the first time I saw you in the woods all those months ago. I'm sorry I didn't say it earlier. I should have."

Kat's mouth hangs slightly open as her hands

slowly travel up my torso to my face.

"Well, you've silenced my pretty princess, how did you do—" and then Truth is out cold on the docks.

Kat doesn't break eye contact with me when she says, "Truth doesn't like blood, never has. He normally always faints."

I laugh, as do Judge and Dirt. She tucks herself into my good side and moves me toward the end of the dock.

"Kat, do you remember I got stabbed?"

She looks at me and says, "You're right! Hang on!" Kat disentangles herself from me and says to Judge, "You'll take care of Truth?"

"Yeah, sugar, we'll take care of Truth." He chuckles and shakes his head.

She gives him the biggest smile and then tucks herself back into my side.

"Ahh, Kat? What are you doing?" As she attempts, again, to move me toward the end of the dock.

"Getting you closer to the ambulance for when it gets here." Kat sounds so determined, and I know she's worried about me, but I can't contain my laugher. "Don't laugh, you might rupture something! Can you hear the sirens? I can't hear any sirens!"

"Darlin', you're talking like a crazy person. You know that, right?" I chuckle.

"You told me you love me, and I don't want anything to jeopardize it, Dane Reynolds! Now lean on me and get your ass to the end of the dock!"

"Lean on you? I'm over a foot taller than you! How am I—"

"Zip it! Let's keep your big, bulky body moving and no backchat! Do. You. Get. Me?" Kat yells at me, love and concern washing over her beautiful features.

I smile and nod. We make our way to the end of the dock together. I had no idea she could be so bossy, but I like it.

I wonder if she'll ever be this dominant in the bedroom. I can't wait to find out.

CHAPTER 64

KAT

The police did a very thorough investigation in LA. I think it's mostly because of who Dane is. Dave said it was a good thing because then, at least no one could say my fame and fortune helped a known MC member exploit the system. Dane wouldn't have had it any other way.

It was really interesting watching him interact with the police in LA. Some of them didn't hold their contempt back, but he was respectful and helpful at all times. I wonder if it was for my benefit.

I wouldn't be surprised if Gareth ended up in a psychiatric hospital. Dane kept me away from him after the incident at the marina. I really didn't want to see him, anyway, so I was grateful.

Dane spent a week in the hospital and another

week answering all the questions from the police. We've been home for a month, and It's been a wonderful month. Dane has let me boss him around, but I can tell he's had enough.

Jonas has arranged for me to go shopping today so he and Dane can go for a ride. Jonas doesn't know I know. Men, they can be pretty dumb sometimes.

Dane pulls me out of my thoughts. "Darlin', you going out?" he asks, almost sounding disappointed.

"Honey, if you want, I can stay home and look after you some more?" I ask, trying hard not to laugh as a look of panic crosses his features.

"No, no, no!" Dane quickly answers, "You need to go into town and do some shopping. It will do you good to get away from me for a while." Dane smiles, and I nearly laugh.

"Well, if you're sure?" I grab my bag. "Don't do anything too stressful! I need you fit and healthy, baby, especially if we're going to let me be in charge tonight."

Dane's smile goes all sexy. "Darlin', in the bedroom, you can be in charge of anything you fucking like. So, take your time in town, maybe get something sexy? Don't hurry, I'll be here when you get back."

I smile at him and throw my arms around his neck. "I might be a few hours then, you sure you'll be all right?"

His hands are on my ass. "A few hours? I'll be

fine. I'll watch TV or something." A smile creeps onto his handsome face.

"I have my phone, and if you need anything, you call me, yeah?" I give him a quick kiss on the lips and turn to move out of his embrace.

"Kat, darlin', I love you and thank you for taking care of me this past month. I've never had a female put me first, even my own mother. You mean the world to me." All the breath goes out of me as he continues. "I put you first, above everything, the Savage Angels, this house, this town. As long as it's you and me together, it's all I fucking want."

"Dane, I'd never ask you to put me before the MC. They are your family. I'll never ask you to choose 'cause, baby, you always make me feel like I'm the only one in the room." I kiss his lips lightly. "I love you, and together is all I want, too."

He leans down and kisses me. It's not a quick kiss, and it leaves me breathless. I know I have to leave as Jonas is on the way, so I break away, wink at him, grab my keys, and head for the front door.

Dane has shared very little about his family. I know his mother died and his father is sick, but Dane doesn't want to see him. From what I can gather, his father disowned him when he was in his teens, and his mother didn't do anything. I get the impression his father was abusive. He also has a much younger sister. It explains why the MC is so important to him and why he loves me the way he does. I'm sure, in time, he'll share more with me.

As I hit the veranda, Judge appears. Dane still won't let me go out alone. I'm used to bodyguards, so it doesn't bother me.

"Hey, sugar, how long do we have to be gone for?" Judge smiles as we both know what's planned for today.

"Do you think three or four hours to do the Gorge properly and get back?" I ask.

"Hmm… let's give him four. We could do a movie or long lunch or go to Pearl County?" Judge has become a loyal friend. He still sees Jasmin whenever she's in town, and sometimes he goes to see her. I'm surprised it works, but I think the distance between them helps. I get the impression from both of them, it's a casual thing, but to me, it doesn't look casual. From what the guys say about Judge, he doesn't do relationships, and I know Jasmin doesn't either. Maybe this is their version of a relationship. Time will tell.

"Let's stick to local. I don't really want to leave Tourmaline. Maybe see a movie if we have time, and we're definitely doing lunch!" I smile and throw the car keys at him.

Judge catches them and dramatically bows, waving his arms toward the car. "Your chariot awaits!"

CHAPTER 65

JONAS
Vice President of Savage Angels MC

It's been six weeks since the incident in LA, and Dane's wound was probably almost gone after the first week, at a stretch two. His woman hasn't let him lift a finger, and it's been funny to see such a big man get bossed around by such a small woman. I've had enough of looking after all the club's business, the garage, the depot, and the MC. I'm breaking him out from his lovely prison today. I've gotten to know Kat Saunders a little since they got back, and I can tell she's fiercely protective of him, but he's got to get back to work. I'm not stupid enough to tell her this, though. I've arranged for her to get taken into town for some grocery shopping, and I had Rebel get Dane's bike ready for a ride. I think it's time we hit the Gorge. It's a good ride, and he can blow out some cobwebs. I like being VP, but I have no desire to take over from Dane just yet.

He had to spend a week in LA, first in the hospital, then another week filling out police reports and doing interviews. I was amazed at how Kat's manager, Dave, controlled the press and the story.

Dave made it sound like a fucking love story. The broken singer, who falls for the knight in shining armor, who, in turn, saves her from the evil ex-boyfriend. When they compared Gareth Goodman's DNA to the national database, they found out he'd attacked several women. Poor Jess was the only one he killed. The police think if Kat had been at home that day, it would most definitely have been her, he'd have murdered.

He survived the knife attack and is still in the hospital. They say it will be another few months before his case goes to trial. Until then, he'll be in a prison hospital, waiting. The studios all distanced themselves from him, but his latest movie broke all box office records before he was arrested, and after his arrest, it went completely crazy.

I'm amazed the public wants to see and understand him. Gareth is a sick fucker who didn't like being dumped by a beautiful woman. Apparently, Kat tipped him over the edge to murder. The attacks on the other women showed how he had progressively gotten more brutal. All they had to do to provoke him was turn him down for a date or simply give him the brush-off. He thought he was God's gift to the female race. Gareth is smart, though, he'd stalk them and wear disguises or masks to conceal his identity.

When I pull into Dane's circular driveway, I rev my Harley to let him know I'm here. I dismount, take the steps two at a time, and find Dane walking out the front door, grin firmly in place.

I call out, "Hey, hey, Prez! Where are you off to?"

"Oh, Jonas, thank God it's you. Did you arrange for Kat to go shopping? 'Cause if you did, I owe you a fucking solid, man!"

"Had enough of Madam President, Prez?" I tease him.

"Really-fucking-funny! Kat won't let me do anything, and if I spend another day in this house cooped up without a fucking thing to do, I might fucking kill someone!"

I laugh. "I had Rebel get your bike ready. Wanna hit the Gorge?"

"Fuck, yes!" He claps me on the shoulder and practically skips across the courtyard.

"Do you want me to call her, tell her where you are?" I try to make it sound like an innocent question, but I can't help it, I laugh.

"Everyone's a fucking comedian! Let's go!"

"Wait, Prez, there's something I wanted to ask

you about. A guy came into the garage yesterday, an Italian, and he started asking questions about Ms. Saunders and the depot. I followed him and saw he went back to the motel where he got a visitor."

"A visitor? Well, who the fuck was it?" Dane starts his ride, a smile spreading across his face as he listens to the sound of the engine.

"Emily."

The smile freezes in place, he looks into my eyes, and then he kills the engine.

"What the fuck is my sister doing in town? And what the fuck is she doing with an Italian who's asking questions about Ms. Saunders?"

I shrug. "Guess we'll find out soon enough."

EPILOGUE

DANE

I'm cornering a bend, and I glance over. Kat is right beside me on her Harley Davidson Sportster 883, with a huge grin on her face. She's trying to beat me into town. My woman loves to go fast, and she loves to win. I let her win once, and she gave me grief for a week. Kat also withheld her body from me. I'll never do it again.

We're about to hit the outskirts of town when I hear a siren. I look over my shoulder, and sure enough, there are lights flashing and a cruiser.

Fuck!

We pull over, I get off my bike, and rip the helmet from my head. I look at Kat, and she's laughing as she sits astride her bike.

Sheriff Morales emerges from his vehicle. He

shakes his head as he walks toward us.

"Dane." Carlos does a chin lift at me. "Kat, do you know how fast you were going?" At least he's smiling.

"Sorry, Sheriff, I was trying to beat Dane! How fast were we going?" Kat's grinning at him, and she's just admitted we were racing.

Fuck.

"You were going twenty miles per hour over the speed limit. Speed limits are there for a reason."

Carlos is trying to sound like he's chastising us, but he grins at Kat. Her personality is infectious.

I clear my throat to get his attention. "Sorry, Sheriff. If you'll just write us up, we'll be on our way."

Seeing as Kat has admitted we were racing, I see no point in trying to talk him out of it.

"Aww, really? Carlos, are you really going to write us up? Come on! We promise not to do it again!" Kat pleads with him.

"Now, Kat, we both know it's not true. But I left my ticket book in the car, and I was hoping to persuade you to come to the town meeting on Friday night. If you come, I could look the other way, and I'll buy you dinner," Carlos says, flashing her a smile.

Before Kat can respond, I say, "Now, Sheriff, that would be a dinner for three, right?"

I can't believe this fucker asked my woman out

with me standing right next to her. Lawman or not, I'll take his head off if he thinks he can get away with that.

"Dane, Carlos is only trying to negotiate with us, and he knows we're a package deal. Right, Carlos?" Kat says, trying to placate me with a big smile.

"Of course, I do. But Dane, to be honest, I didn't think you'd be interested in a town meeting."

He stares at me, and we both know he's right, but my woman goes nowhere without me or one of my boys.

"Sheriff, if I get a meeting and a dinner to get out of a ticket, who am I to complain?" I chuckle.

We both look at Kat, and the Sheriff has his eyebrows raised in question.

"All right, all right! But so you both know, I was going anyway! I have a meeting planned with Justice before it." Kat looks so smug.

Kat had a sit-down with Justice Leaverton, and it turns out Ms. Saunders had a business deal with him, which obviously didn't go through when she died. Kat went with her lawyers and worked out a better deal and got into partnership with him. I don't trust Leaverton, but I trust my woman. She's smart, she sees through people, and she's good for me.

"It's a date, then! I'll save you both a seat." Carlos winks at Kat, then his expression becomes serious. "Stick to the speed limits, you're both role models in the community now, so act like it." He winks at Kat and goes back to his car.

I place a hand on Kat's bike and do a chin lift to the sheriff as he passes us, then I look at Kat, who is still grinning.

"You know I'd have beaten you, don't you?"

"Well, darlin', we'll never know now, so we'll declare it a draw. What would you like in payment?" I smile at her.

"Hang on, if it's a draw, don't we both get something?" Kat asks.

"That sounds fair, but you go first."

"I want you to be home by six o'clock every night, so we can eat together."

She has her hands on her hips, and she looks so damned cute astride her bike.

"Okay, darlin', I can do that." I chuckle at her.

"Now, babe, what do you want?"

I look at my feet, I'm nervous. I raise my eyes to her. "Katarina Saunders, I want to spend the rest of my days with you and only you. Will you marry me?"

Her mouth drops open, then she says, "Marry you?"

I nod at her.

"Dane, we haven't talked about it. We haven't even moved in together properly." Kat looks shocked.

Kat spends most of her time at my home. She's

been converting part of her house into a recording studio so she can produce up-and-coming artists. After she did *Rock Star*, one of the contestants who didn't win, Dan Kelly, sought her out as she promised him a recording deal. My woman finally found her door, and like everything she does, she excels at it.

Our eyes are locked as I say, "Is that a no, darlin'?"

I shuffle my feet, waiting anxiously for her answer. Kat stares at me for a long time, and I'm beginning to think she doesn't want to, but a smile slowly creeps onto her face.

"Dane Reynolds, I love you." Kat pauses dramatically and says, "Yes! Yes! Yes!"

I stalk to her and wrap her in my arms.

"You had me worried there for a minute, darlin'."

"Sorry, babe, it shocked me. But I know I'm safe with you, and I know you'll always protect me. I love you, Dane."

I kiss her, my tongue invading her mouth, and my hand travels over her body, settling on her breast. She moans into my mouth, and I feel her hand on my crotch. My cock is straining against my jeans. I move my hand to her crotch, and she grinds against it.

I stop my kiss but continue my assault on her pussy and look her in the eyes.

"All I want is you and me forever."

"Baby, all I want is that, too… and can we please go to the clubhouse and fuck?" I roar with laughter and move away from her.

"Whoever gets there first is in charge in the bedroom!" Kat starts her bike and is gone in a cloud of smoke.

So much for being role models.

TO BE CONTINUED

Kathleen Kelly

If you liked this story,
you can continue with book 2:

The Savage Angels MC Series
Motorcycle Club Romance
Savage Stalker Book 1
Savage Fire Book 2
Savage Town Book 3
Savage Lover Book 4
Savage Sacrifice Book 5
Savage Rebel (Novella) Book 6
Savage Lies Book 7
Savage Life Book 8
Savage Christmas (Novella) Book 9

The MacKenny Brothers Series
An MC/Band of Brothers Romance
Spark Book 1
Spark of Vengeance Book 2
Spark of Hope Book 3
Spark of Deception Book 4
Spark of Time Book 5
Spark of Redemption Book 6

Tackling Romance Series
A Sports Romance
Tackling Love Book 1
Tackling Life Book 2

Standalones
Wraith
Cardinal: The Affinity Chronicles Book One
Crude Possession: Crude Souls MC
Snake's Revenge: Gritty Devils MC

ACKNOWLEDGMENTS

This is my first one of these, so, if I miss you, please know it's not that you aren't important to me, it's that I have a really bad memory. So, please forgive me...
P.S. If you really know me you, KNOW how bad my memory is!

To my SL – thank you baby. Thank you for putting up with a dirty house and coming home most days to someone who hasn't had a shower yet or who even knows what time it is. Thank you for always answering my endless phone calls when you are at work. You are my world xx

To my family and you know who you are – I LOVE YOU, unconditionally. I know my endless questions and rambling must drive you crazy but you love me anyway…right?

My beta readers, Christina & Brandi, thank you so much for all your help. Savage Stalker wouldn't have made it without you both. I appreciate you taking the time out of your normal lives to give me feedback and help with the plot. I value you both xx

To the Bloggers and everyone who signed up for the Release Day Blitz – THANK YOU! Actually, that doesn't seem like enough. Without you all sharing and pimping me out I doubt if anyone would even know about Savage Stalker. So from the bottom of my heart thank you!

To my Street Team, we really need a name, yeah? When we hit 50, I'll run a competition and let one of you pick it. Amy, Kathy, Christina, Brandi, Debb, Jolanda, Yvette, Maddie, Ann, Lisa, Francesca, Janja, Cindy, Jennifer, Melanie, Marie, Dannielle, Caroline, Shawna, Brookland Paradise, Jeanette, Lauren, Debra, Michellean, Sherry, Jacqueline, Courtney, Hannah, Peta, Tania & Jess – Thank you all for helping me. It means more than you know xx

To My Readers,
Thank you for buying my book. I am amazed that you would do me the honor. I hope you've enjoyed reading Savage Stalker. I hope you are hanging for the next instalment!

Please contact me and let me know if you loved Dane & Kat as much as I do. If you did, could you PLEASE leave a review for Savage Stalker on the site you purchased it from? Reviews help other readers decide whether to purchase a book, which in turn will help me continue down this path.

Thank you xx

CONNECT WITH ME ONLINE

Check these links for more books from
Author Kathleen Kelly

READER GROUP
Want access to fun, prizes and sneak peeks?
Join my Facebook Reader Group.
https://bit.ly/32X17pv

NEWSLETTER
Want to see what's next?
Sign up for my Newsletter.
https://www.subscribepage.com/kathleenkellyauthor

BOOKBUB
Connect with me on Bookbub.
https://www.bookbub.com/authors/kathleen-kelly

Kathleen Kelly

GOODREADS
Add my books to your TBR list
on my Goodreads profile.
http://bit.ly/1xsOGxk

AMAZON
Buy my books from my Amazon profile.
https://amzn.to/2JCUT6q

WEBSITE
https://kathleenkellyauthor.com/

TWITTER
https://twitter.com/kkellyauthor

INSTAGRAM
https://instagram.com/kathleenkellyauthor

EMAIL
kathleenkellyauthor@gmail.com

FACEBOOK
https://bit.ly/36jlaQV

ABOUT THE AUTHOR

Kathleen Kelly was born in Penrith, NSW, Australia. When she was four, her family moved to Brisbane, QLD, Australia. Although born in NSW, she considers herself a QUEENSLANDER!

She married her childhood sweetheart, and they live in Toowoomba.

Kathleen enjoys writing contemporary romance novels with a little bit of steam. She draws her inspiration from family, friends, and the people around her. She can often be found in cafes writing and observing the locals.

If you have any questions about her novels or would like to ask Kathleen a question, she can be contacted via e-mail:
kathleenkellyauthor@gmail.com

or she can be found on Facebook. She loves to be contacted by those who love her books.

Printed in Great Britain
by Amazon